The Man Who Met

TARZAN®

Apologia Pro Vita Tarzani Simiarum

Tarzan, a superman unlike the one of which Nietzsche dreamed, was born on the west coast of Equatorial Africa.

He was the most beautiful, but at the same time undeniably masculine, man that I've ever seen. I was silenced by the exceedingly charismatic force which he radiated even when he was quiet. Perhaps tigerish would be a better term. Something burns brightly inside him.

I got the feeling that I was in the presence of an immortal, though I knew that he could bleed and die even as I. that he was eighty years old then but looked only about thirty-five seemed unbelievable now that I am no longer in his presence. Of course, he did not produce any proof that he was born in 1888, and I didn't ask him for it. It is possible, I suppose, that I was the victim of a hoax. All I can say is that anyone who met him would not believe that he was anything other than what he claimed.

Burroughs, who based his early novels of Tarzan on incomplete and sometimes inaccurate data, described the "mangani" as great apes and was thereafter stuck with that term. Not that he minded. He was writing novels, and the facts did not always have to be adhered to. Indeed, as I will be demonstrating more than once, he sometimes went out of his way to make sure that the reader thought that his Tarzan books were entirely fictional.

—Extracts from Philip José Farmer's introductions to *Tarzan Alive*

The Man Who Met

Philip José Farmer

Meteor House

Meteor House

ISBN 978-1-945427-23-7
First Trade Paperback Edition

This book is dedicated to Philip José Farmer—
the questioner of mysteries, the discoverer of the truth,
the chronicler of a legend.

And in memory of Rias Nuninga, collector extraordinaire
and diligent cataloger, whose International Bibliography
of Farmer's works is a joy and a boon to fans and scholars alike.

Meteor House would like to thank the following people who helped this book mature from a germ of an idea into the completed item you are about to read: Robert R. Barrett, Charles Berlin, Christopher Paul Carey, Michael Croteau, Win Scott Eckert, Henry G. Franke III, Keith Howell, John Solie, Paul Spiteri, James Sullos, Bjo Trimble, Cathy Wilbanks, and, of course, Philip José Farmer.

TABLE OF CONTENTS

WELCOME, MEET THE
LORD OF THE JUNGLE

PAUL SPITERI

How do you choose a piece of art to illustrate a book like this? What would set the right tone? What image would impart the feeling of a meeting; a connection from the page to the reader? It's no exaggeration that hundreds of images were viewed and discarded before alighting on the one which magnificently adorns the book in hand. Two lords of the jungle engage directly with you, holding your gaze, promising to tell you all if you have the will for it. It's a wonderful image rendered in an array of colors that enhance the feeling of secrets to be shared.

The painting, rendered in acrylic, was originally commissioned by The Thought Factory in 1978 (although the copyright sits with ERB Inc.). At the time, the Thought Factory were selling great posters such as Rocky, Batman, Thor, and Wonder Woman and they wanted to add Tarzan to their portfolio. Famed artist John Solie was hired to paint this iconic hero. With a career that includes over 200 film posters and over 200 book covers, Solie was the perfect choice.

Here's what John Solie had to say when asked to write something for this book.

> When I was a child I rarely got a report card that didn't include a note from the teacher that said, "John tends to daydream." It was a severe criticism and resulted in rather bad

grades. I now think of it as a compliment as it contributes to almost everything I draw or paint.

Tarzan was one of my favorite stories when I was young and still is, so when I was asked to do this painting it was pure pleasure.

Tarzan was, of course, a hero to me, but at an early age a circus came to town and had in a large cage a gorilla. I must have been about five years old at the time and as I stood outside the cage Gargantua turned and looked right at me. Whether my heart actually stopped, I don't know, but to this day I can recall the powerful feeling, and when I look at the Tarzan poster I still feel the pleasure of the experience.

John Solie was a pleasure to work with when compiling this book. He paints and writes every day, a commitment to his craft that has spanned many decades. A true gentleman and a wonderful raconteur, Mr. Solie is brimming with tales of his work and travels and is a delight to listen to.

On behalf of all those involved in crafting this book, not least the subject himself, let me warmly welcome you. As with most anthologies it has been an exhilarating, if daunting, task to choose the right entries and build the right structure for this volume. I hope you enjoy this enthralling collection that celebrates Farmer's lifelong interest in, and love of, Burroughs' most famous protagonist.

THE PROFESSIONAL TARZAN FAN

HENRY G. FRANKE III

No other professional writer can claim such a close and sustained association with Edgar Rice Burroughs and his creation, Tarzan of the Apes, as could Philip José Farmer. Farmer presented his thoughtful analyses of Burroughs' Tarzan mythos in fanzine articles, presentations at fan conventions, and extensive correspondence. He skillfully brought together his ideas and research in *Tarzan Alive*, his 1972 biography of the ape-man. This groundbreaking work influenced generations of fans and professionals, and helped to expand the genre of metafiction that continues to endure. Farmer's fascination with Tarzan and the "Tarzan theme" of the feral man did not end here. He penned novels that examined Burroughs' basic premise from different perspectives and added new dimensions to the original mythos. Ultimately, Farmer realized his lifelong desire to write an authorized Tarzan story with 1999's *The Dark Heart of Time* (now officially part of Burroughs canon, the novel was reissued in 2018 by Meteor House as *Tarzan and the Dark Heart of Time*.)

Farmer interwove his fan interests and professional endeavors related to Tarzan over a span of decades, with the late 1960s through the 1970s as his most prolific period. With the general public's rediscovery of ERB in the early 1960s, nearly all of his oeuvre was published in great numbers thanks to two major paperback booms in the United States in a ten-year period. This fostered the heyday of academic examinations and critical reviews of ERB and his work. Burroughs fanzines flourished with the surge in fans, while the growing demand for Burroughs' type of fiction led to both the reprinting of nearly forgotten writers, like Robert E. Howard, and the publication of new work in genres that had all but disappeared. Readers' appetites were so great that publishers even sold nonfiction works about Burroughs and his stories. This was the right time for Farmer to emerge as the leading professional Tarzan fan.

Farmer's love for the Tarzan character, which began when he was a child, progressed to mature assessments of ERB's framework for Tarzan's Africa. Farmer's approach was to treat the character as real and Burroughs' stories as fictionalized accounts of actual events in the life of the ape-man. His aim was to establish a more grounded foundation for the Tarzan mythos. A restless and imaginative polymath who studied anthropology, linguistics, genealogy, history, and much more, Farmer applied all of this knowledge in his examination. Like most professional science fiction writers of his generation, Farmer was comfortable interacting with fans, appearing at conventions, and simply being a fan himself. This gave him sounding boards for his ideas, with the opportunity for critical discussions through articles, speeches, letter columns, and private correspondence.

The annual meeting of The Burroughs Bibliophiles—the primary organization devoted to Burroughs and his work—is named the Dum-Dum after the gatherings of the Great Apes in the Tarzan novels. Recognized as both an influential fan and a talented professional writer, Farmer was the guest of honor and banquet speaker at the 1970 Dum-Dum held in Detroit, Michigan, on 5 September, hosted by the Detroit Triple Fan Fair Convention. The text of his speech, "The Arms of Tarzan," was printed in the *Burroughs Bulletin* #22 (Summer 1971, original series), edited by Vern Coriell.

By the time of the 1970 Dum-Dum, Farmer had already written a number of stories inspired by Tarzan, featuring characters that were clearly stand-ins for the ape-man. Notable was the start of a story cycle, "Secrets of the Nine," with protagonists Lord Grandrith (a veiled Lord Greystoke/Tarzan) and Doc Caliban (representing Doc Savage) as half-brothers who are involved with an ancient cabal that rules the world behind the scenes. *A Feast Unknown* was published in 1969, while *Lord of the Trees* and *The Mad Goblin* appeared together in a "two-in-one" format in 1970. These novels highlighted Farmer's penchant to cross over characters drawn from different parts of pop culture and to explore themes using seminal storylines. The novel *Lord Tyger*, also released in 1970, presented another version of a feral man, this one a man-made experiment in raising a human in the wild.

But the author was just hitting his stride as a leading scholar in ERB fandom, and one who could reach a significantly larger audience because he was a professional writer at his peak, able to write full-time beginning in 1969. By the time he was invited back just three years later by the Bibliophiles as the guest speaker at the 1973 Dum-Dum in Toronto, Canada, on 1 September, Farmer had changed the "intellectual landscape" of Burroughs fandom. Arguably he had taken over the mantle of senior commentator from Richard A. Lupoff, author of 1965's *Edgar Rice Burroughs: Master of Adventure*, the first comprehensive critical review of ERB's body of work. Farmer had studied Burroughs' Tarzan mythos in great detail, and more of his articles and letters presenting various concepts appeared in fanzines in 1971 and 1972. As a highlight, Farmer took on perhaps the most significant conundrum in ERB's Tarzan timeline—the inconsistencies in the birthdates of Tarzan and his son. The earlier Tarzan novels established the age of Lord Greystoke's son Jack such that he would have been a child during World War I. Then suddenly Jack, who had acquired the ape-name of Korak the Killer when he grew up on his own in the jungles of Africa, makes an appearance as a combat veteran of the Great War. In "A Reply to 'The Red Herring,'" published in D. Peter Ogden's *Erbania* #28 (December 1971), Farmer proposed that Korak was adopted. With his article "The Great Korak-Time Discrepancy," which appeared in issue #57 (dated April 1972) of Caz Cazedessus' Hugo Award-winning fanzine, *ERBdom*, Farmer suggested that Jack was Bulldog Drummond's younger brother, John, adopted by Tarzan and Jane.

The pivotal event in Farmer's personal and professional relationship with the ape-man was the publication of *Tarzan Alive: A Definitive Biography of Lord Greystoke* in hardcover by Doubleday & Company in 1972. This seminal work synthesized Farmer's many ideas into a cohesive whole. The presentation as a biography was convincing enough that some libraries even shelved their copies in the nonfiction section. Farmer created a complex framework around a consistent chronology, genealogy, and prehistory. *Tarzan Alive* was a springboard for Farmer's Wold Newton Family, where he linked fictional characters in an intricate multi-century lineage. This extended family tree became the foundation for a significant part of Farmer's fiction, while his reconstructed Tarzan mythos was the basis for new stories. His chronology inspired, if not directly influenced, many a Tarzan chronologist. This book also cross-pollinated fans of Burroughs and of Farmer; many a follower of ERB discovered Farmer, while a number of Farmer enthusiasts gained an appreciation of Burroughs.

Tarzan Alive confirmed Farmer's fascination with Tarzan, as he admitted that the time to research and write the book was well beyond that to pen a novel, which meant a real sacrifice in income. Farmer's enthusiasm did not end with the publication of the biography, nor were his notions limited just to this book. He wrote a complementary article, "Tarzan Lives," for the April 1972 issue of the mainstream magazine *Esquire*. Subtitled "An Exclusive Interview of the Eighth Duke of Greystoke," this was clearly not a satirical, humorous, or tongue-in-cheek fluff piece. Whatever the reason *Esquire* published "Tarzan Lives" for its audience, Farmer wanted readers to take the content of his piece seriously. The art by Jean-Paul Goude, presenting a suave Lord Greystoke seated in a drawing room, instead of a nearly naked ape-man, supported the author's aim.

Farmer wasted no time creating new fiction building on the ideas in *Tarzan Alive*. First was the novel *Time's Last Gift*, also published in 1972. The mysterious protagonist, calling himself John Gribardsun, time-travels back to Africa in 12,000 B.C. The story not only intimated that he is actually Tarzan, but that he becomes a deity to the inhabitants of the ancient empire of Khokarsa, the cradle of ERB's lost city of Opar.

More articles by Farmer continued to appear in the fanzines. "The Lord Mountford Mystery," describing how the stories of Tarzan and H. Rider Haggard's Allan Quatermain crossed, was published in *ERB-dom* #65 (December 1972). "From ERB to Ygg (Part 1," printed in *Erbivore* #6-7 (August 1973), presented a genealogy of Burroughs himself that led back to the Norse god Ygg. *Erbivore* editor

Philip Currie lamented that the planned Part 2 was never written. In "A Language for Opar," appearing in *ERB-dom* #75 (February 1974), Farmer explained how Tarzan and the present inhabitants of Opar could share a common language.

When the author spoke at the 1973 Dum-Dum banquet, he announced that he had received approval to write a cycle of novels featuring "ancient Opar" and the Khokarsan empire as described in *Tarzan Alive*. He had planned for up to ten books in the series, but only completed two—*Hadon of Ancient Opar* (April 1974) and *Flight to Opar* (June 1976)—before his writing career took a turn to more lucrative projects. New tales of Khokarsa have recently been published, based on material that Farmer had developed for the series. Farmer said that he got the idea for the series from an extensive article about the history of the city of Opar by fans John Harwood and Frank J. Brueckel. Ironically, this article would not see publication until 1999; Farmer would play a role in that, as will be explained later.

During his presentation, Farmer declared that a major indicator of "the true importance [of an author] in the field of literature was if the writer generated a tremendous amount of work past his own work." That is, he or she inspires others directly or indirectly in the stories that they create. Most classical writers, such as Melville and Hemingway, "would probably have given their souls" to create the character of Tarzan or Sherlock Holmes. Burroughs was no less of a writer in his own right, even though his aim was entertainment. (Farmer saw the worth in all literature and all writers. He was comfortable, for example, comparing ERB and James Joyce in terms of their strengths and weaknesses.)

In a letter posted in the March 1971 issue of the *Riverside Quarterly*, Farmer responded to author James Blish's "remark about the attention paid to ERB in RQ being a waste of critical effort . . . So I can't see why Blish should be against us ERB-fans having fun when we don't object to his joys in working out the four-dimensional crossword puzzles of *Finnegans Wake*. If his main objection is that there isn't much ore to be mined in ERB, then he obviously doesn't know what he's talking about. If he objects on the grounds that Joyce is so much more 'literary,' so much more complicated, and that the education to be derived from working out the FW crossword puzzle is so much broader than that from working out ERB, then he has valid objections. But I believe that ERB is as deeply 'mythic' as Joyce, although Joyce was a conscious mythographer and ERB wasn't. I submit that the unconscious mythographer may go deeper even than the conscious (and self-conscious) mythographer. He may not cover the same territory; he may not appear to claim so much horizontal territory. But vertically he is greater; his roots go all the way into the cerebellum."

The surge in Farmer's fiction and nonfiction linked to the ape-man in the first half of the 1970s continued, both in the fanbase and with professional publishers. In his Dum-Dum talk, he noted that he had completed his first anthology as editor, *Mother Was a Lovely Beast: Fiction and Fact about Humans Raised by Animals*, released in 1974. He also contributed an essay of his own, "The Feral Human in Mythology and Fiction," which, of course, included Tarzan. Farmer's role as Greystoke biographer did not end with *Tarzan Alive* and the "Tarzan Lives" interview. Farmer described further communications with his special subject, admitting that he would have to revise his biography and suggesting that his essay for *Mother Was a Lovely Beast* supplied new information acquired from the viscount. In a letter published in *Erbania* #41/42 (Summer 1977), Farmer responded to one fan's comment "that it's about time to drop this game that Tarzan really exists. For me, it's not a game. I know that there was a real Tarzan and that he still lives. I'm dead serious, though not deadly serious, I hope. Nor have I pursued this 'game' for money, as [that fan] says. If I was primarily interested in financial gain, I would never have written *Tarzan Alive*. In the time I spent on the biography I could (no exaggeration) have written four novels. And gotten bigger advances from each one than I made on the bio. The book was a labor of love, and love of labor, though lots of fun for me. If others insist it's just a game or that Tarzan is purely fictional, I won't argue with them."

Farmer enjoyed creating a tapestry of storylines that interlinked popular-culture icons. Besides his suggestion of a Tarzan/Allan Quatermain crossover, he brought together Lord Greystoke and another of his favorite characters, Sherlock Holmes, along with

Dr. Watson, in the short novel *The Adventure of the Peerless Peer* (September 1974). The Wold Newton Family provided many more opportunities that were not realized because of the press of time.

The 1976 Dum-Dum, held on 4 September in Kansas City, Missouri, as part of the 34th World Science Fiction Convention, brought Farmer back as banquet speaker. He shared speaking duties that evening with guest of honor Jock Mahoney, lead in two Tarzan films. By this time, Tarzan had been a critical part of Farmer's creative output for many years, but his growing income as a professional author was being driven by the popularity of other aspects of his oeuvre, notably the Riverworld series, where his talent with character crossovers really stood out. By the late 1970s, the Tarzan/feral man theme had to make way for more lucrative works.

But Farmer stayed connected to Burroughs fandom and Tarzan. He presented the keynote address, "I Still Live!" at the dinner closing out the 75th anniversary celebration of the book publication of *Tarzan of the Apes*. This gathering was hosted by the fan group, the Normal Beans of Chicago, capped by the formal event on 21 October 1989. Fittingly, the dinner was held at the Adventurers Club, founded in ERB's hometown of Chicago in 1911 (Theodore Roosevelt and Roald Amundsen had been members). Farmer was one of three Tarzan experts who appeared in the 1996 French Tarzan television documentary, "Moi, Tarzan," an atmospheric piece in which Farmer describes his meeting with Lord Greystoke.

He also penned the foreword for the 1996 edition of Robert B. Zeuschner's *Edgar Rice Burroughs: The Exhaustive Scholar's and Collector's Descriptive Bibliography*, a reminder of the importance of Farmer's endorsement. Despite its brevity, this foreword got to the heart of Farmer's philosophy, as this excerpt shows: "Herein is a book prepared by a lover of the works of Edgar Rice Burroughs . . . It is a labor of love, written by one who fell in love with [ERB's] semimythical beings at an early age. Bob Zeuschner did not write this for money. He wrote it because he felt, quite rightly, that there was a need for this book and because he had fun doing it . . . I know that when I go through it, and it'll be more than once, I'll recapture many of the golden moments I reveled in when these books first swam into my ken."

In recognition of his many contributions in keeping alive the memory of ERB and his creations, The Burroughs Bibliophiles awarded Farmer with their Golden Lion Award. "I choked up when I got the plaque," he confided to a fan, a meaningful statement from someone who had already won three Hugo Awards.

Back in 1956, Farmer's article, "The Golden Age and the Brass," published in Coriell's the *Burroughs Bulletin* #12, described how important ERB's books were to him as a very young boy. In the years since, his desire to pen an authorized Tarzan novel grew. Finally, in 1997, when he was nearly 80 years old, Farmer was granted approval to write a story, with the working title of *Tarzan's Greatest Secret*, that fit directly into ERB's own canon. Working with the publisher proved to be slow and tedious. The book, ultimately titled *The Dark Heart of Time: A Tarzan Novel*, did not appear until June 1999. But Farmer was finally able to go beyond his past pseudo-Tarzans.

Farmer maintained his public presence as professional fan for decades, but his private correspondence with Burroughs fans, which ran into hundreds of letters, were also very influential. Farmer enjoyed sharing ideas and discussing a wide variety of topics. He appreciated fans who were as inquisitive and dedicated as he was in thinking critically about the Tarzan mythos and ERB. John Harwood and Frank Brueckel, who published often in the fanzines, were lauded by Farmer. As noted earlier, their extended paper about Opar's past, "Heritage of the Flaming God," had given Farmer the idea for his ancient Opar series based on his own notion of a mythic Khokarsan empire. As he developed the first novel in the series, he sent letters to Harwood and Brueckel reviewing their ideas and discussing his own concerning Khokarsa. The essay finally saw print in 1999 when Waziri Publications included it in the compendium of the same title, edited by Alan Hanson and Michael Winger. Farmer provided illuminating comments about his own take on Opar in correspondence with Hanson, which Hanson applied in completing his own essay for the book.

The fact that fans have carefully preserved their letters from Farmer after all these years underscores the impact he made on them, as well as the insights they provided about Farmer the man. An example is Peter Nuro's correspondence with Farmer in the late

1990s. Farmer contacted him for help in translating the Finnish book *Vapaita Suhteita* ("Free Associations") by Veikko Huovinen, which included the essay "Tarzan and Finland." Nuro reported that it presented "musings about how Tarzan would have fared if his parents Lord and Lady Greystoke had been cast off on the wild coast of Finland, instead of Africa." Farmer's plan was to revise the translation as an article for the *Burroughs Bulletin*. Farmer confided to Nuro that for years he had wanted to learn Finnish so that he could read Finnish works himself, and lamented that he never had enough time to do so. Always a generous person, Farmer then sent Nuro a copy of *Vapaita Suhteita* as a gift.

A devoted ERB fan and editor of the fanzine *Erbivore* through the early 1970s, Phil Currie corresponded with Farmer for years. As Currie noted recently, "Phil Farmer always impressed me in a way that few other people do. He was an intellectual giant, but never let it get in the way of being a humble person with a quiet but cutting sense of humor. He was always willing to help out, even though he was also always incredibly busy. I suspect he actually had quite a deep and lasting influence on my character." Consider that, today, Currie is a world-renowned paleontologist, Professor of Dinosaur Palaeobiology at the University of Alberta, and a co-founder of the Royal Tyrrell Museum of Palaeontology. Yet he retains his high regard for Farmer. His appreciation highlights what a special person Farmer was and the strong connections he made with fellow fans and professionals.

Philip José Farmer remained an unabashedly enthusiastic fan of Tarzan all of his life. As a skilled and respected writer, he confirmed the cultural importance of the character and the unique creativity of Edgar Rice Burroughs as an author. In recognition of his indelible mark both on fandom and the literary landscape, The Burroughs Bibliophiles devoted an issue of their current journal to Farmer in 2010, the first time that an individual was so honored. Fifty years after the publication of *Tarzan Alive*, Farmer continues to speak to Burroughs fans.

Tarzan Through a Glass Darkly

Christopher Paul Carey

"In another recurring dream I was lying on a big meadow and looking up at a cloudless sky. Suddenly, a prominent constellation would begin changing shape; the stars composing it would slowly drift to new locations. I knew that the stars, when they stopped, would form another constellation, and this would be a code. If I could decipher the code, I would know all the Great Secrets, the hitherto impenetrable Mysteries; finity and infinity, time and eternity, death and immortality, the Creator's nature. Almost, almost, I grasped the meaning of the code. But I always awoke just before I comprehended All.

"Codes. Pictographs. Hieroglyphs. Runes. Exotic alphabets, syllabaries, and ideograms. Mnemonic knots. They all seemed to me, or to my unconscious, anyway, to contain secrets . . ."

—From "Maps and Spasms," an autobiographical essay by
Philip José Farmer

Perhaps it is a testament to Tarzan's universal appeal that he boasts more variant depictions in a diverse array of media than any other iconic pop-culture hero. Of the dozens of performers who portrayed Tarzan in film, on television, on radio, on the stage, and most recently in an authorized online streaming audio parody-drama, each brought something different to the character—oftentimes radically different, and so far, none of them has been completely true to the literary ape-man who comes to life in the novels of Edgar Rice Burroughs.

When one factors in comic-book portrayals, the number of variant representations of the Lord of the Jungle surely climbs well above a hundred.

Thus it is not surprising that many readers, accustomed to such Tarzanic variations, place Philip José Farmer's "biographical" version of the ape-man (as represented in *Tarzan Alive: A Definitive Biography of Lord Greystoke*, "Extracts from the Memoirs of 'Lord Greystoke,'" "An Exclusive Interview with Lord Greystoke," and other pieces found in this book) into a separate category from his fictional "Lord Grandrith" version of the character featured in what has come to be known as the Secrets of the Nine series (*A Feast Unknown, Lord of the Trees*, and *The Mad Goblin*). In fact, it has become common for readers, fan scholars, and publishers to go so far as to relegate Lord Grandrith to a far-flung alternate universe, just to make it clear—and perhaps make themselves feel more comfortable—that an impermeable wall of Harbenite stands inexorably between the jungle lord depicted in the sexually and violently explicit *A Feast Unknown* and his canonical analog who exists in "our universe."[1] As rational and ironclad as this reasoning sounds, I have always found it best to expect the unexpected when it comes to Philip José Farmer.

A Feast Unknown is an uncomfortable book to read. Everyone who has cracked its spine and eyeballed a few pages knows that. That's the point, as anyone familiar with Philip José Farmer's biography and bibliography knows. He was a literary iconoclast, though a good-natured and mischievous one. When he attended Bradley University in the 1940s, Farmer fell in with a group of pre-Beatnik Bohemians who would pass around forbidden copies of the works of Henry Miller and Frank Harris that had been smuggled into the United States, where they were banned as pornography until the 1960s. I believe it is fair to say that the direct experience of such censorship left a deep impression on Farmer. From the very outset of his literary

---

[1] Since I have mentioned canon, let me be perfectly clear in my current position as Director of Publishing at Edgar Rice Burroughs, Inc., that Philip José Farmer's only work that is considered officially canonical in the ERB Universe series is his authorized—and highly recommended—novel *Tarzan and the Dark Heart of Time* (Meteor House, 2019). Of course, everyone is free to have their own "head canon," or to draw what conclusions they wish from Farmer's research and speculations into the life of the ape-man.

career, he began breaking down walls and boundaries in the vein of Miller and Harris. The publication of his Hugo Award-winning "The Lovers" in 1952 is credited as the first story to treat in a mature fashion the subject of sex in science fiction, prompting Robert A. Heinlein to write a letter to Farmer thanking him for breaking taboos and thereby helping him with his own writing (likely his classic *Stranger in a Strange Land*, which was dedicated to Farmer). *A Feast Unknown* is without doubt another ground-breaking work in the same mold, albeit one much more graphic than "The Lovers," the latter being a work that is extremely tame by today's standards, a fact that cannot be said of the former, which is as shocking in this first quarter of the twenty-first century as when it was first published in 1969.

The preceding preamble is necessary to understand my thesis that Farmer may not have actually meant to relegate Lord Grandrith to an alternate universe, and may instead have regarded them as the same living person. A brief review of the unique methodology Farmer employed in his biography of Tarzan should begin to make my meaning clearer.

In his foreword to the book, Farmer includes the following consistently overlooked passage:

> The present "Lord Greystoke" is quite adamant about the limits to be observed in this book. Thus, his lineage and, indeed, half of the events and persons herein are not presented with the real names and places and dates attached. Half are. The other half are analogs or parallels. What I give herein is the truth but the truth looked at obliquely or in a distorting mirror.
>
> That is why the librarians and booksellers should place this work in the "B" section. That is why the reader should realize that he is reading something unique, the first analogical, or parallel, biography.

Here the reader is informed that half of the names in *Tarzan Alive* are *analogs*. A most singular pronouncement, as Dr. Watson might say. What does Farmer mean by this curious statement that the book is "something unique, the first analogical, or parallel, biography"?

Tarzan Alive is certainly not the first "fictional biography." What separates it from, say, C. Northcote Parkinson's *The Life and Times of Horatio Hornblower* or William S. Baring-Gould's *Nero Wolfe of West Thirty-Fifth Street?*

Tarzan Alive takes as its premise precisely what Edgar Rice Burroughs tells us on the first page of *Tarzan of the Apes*: that "Lord Greystoke" was a real-life person, and that the author "had this story from one who had no business to tell it" to him. The "seductive influence of an old vintage" led this unnamed individual to relate the incredible tale of the noble ape-man to Mr. Burroughs, who went on to examine "musty manuscript, and dry official records of the British Colonial Office" and corroborate the facts of the narrative. Furthermore, when Mr. Burroughs documented the story and this record was published as *Tarzan of the Apes* in the October 1912 issue of *The All-Story*, he states (much as Farmer himself has attested in the above blockquote regarding *Tarzan Alive*) that "in the telling of it to you I have taken fictitious names for the principle characters." In other words, the story of Tarzan is real, as far as the author could ascertain, but the names have been changed. It is also an admission that the story is only as true as the information he was given; he makes it crystal clear that he does not know if the story is true, though he does believe it to be so.

In *Tarzan Alive*, the reader learns of Farmer's claim that he had uncovered the true identity of the real-life "Tarzan" by pursuing leads in *Burke's Peerage*, and later even conducted an interview with him, which can be read in the present book. Then, in the foreword to "Extracts from the Memoirs of 'Lord Greystoke'" (also in this book, and please take note of the scare quotes around "Lord Greystoke"), Farmer states that "'Greystoke,' however, had promised to send me portions of his memoirs and that I could publish them. He did not say when he would send them or from where. But in May 1973, I received a package mailed from San Francisco." At first, one may think the 1973 date invalidates the idea that "Lord Grandrith" could be the same person as "Lord Greystoke" from *Tarzan Alive*. *A Feast Unknown*, which Farmer purported to be volume IX of the autobiography of "Lord Grandrith," was published in 1969, three years prior to 1972's *Tarzan Alive*. If Farmer did not receive any installments of the memoirs of "Lord Greystoke" until 1973, then "Lord Grandrith" could not be the same person as "Lord Greystoke." However, take note that Farmer doesn't specify that the package he received in May 1973 was the *first* he had gotten from "Lord Greystoke." In fact, he states in the foreword to "Extracts from the Memoirs of 'Lord Greystoke'" that "It was in 1968 that I was able to ascertain the true identity of 'Lord Greystoke' and to track him down." 1968—that is, specifically one year prior to when Farmer arranged for the publication of volume IX of the autobiography of "Lord Grandrith."

There are many similarities between *A Feast Unknown* and what is found in "Extracts from the Memoirs of 'Lord Greystoke.'" The first thing one notices is the similarity of styles. The voice in both works is the same: confident, frank, and uninhibited. Moreover, the vowelless linguistics of the Folk from *A Feast Unknown* and the n'k from "Extracts" is identical (the Folk and the n'k are clearly meant to be the Mangani, or great apes, from Mr. Burroughs' Tarzan novels).[2] Even more striking is the fact that the name of "Lord Grandrith" in the language of the Folk and the name of "Lord Greystoke" in the language of the n'k both translate in English to "Worm." These are only a few of the perfect parallels found in both memoirs, and it is quite unbelievable to think these could be coincidences. One might as well leap to the absurd idea that Philip José Farmer never met Tarzan and made it all up!

But let's back up a bit and return to the question of what Farmer meant by his claim that *Tarzan Alive* was "the first analogical, or parallel, biography," as it will help bolster my thesis and perhaps unveil a little of Farmer's mischievous trickery. In the book, Farmer makes the claim that a number of authors writing about the members of Tarzan's family tree employed code words to indicate genealogical connections and hint at the real-life basis of the stories in which they appear. But tellingly, variants of at least two of these same code words appear in *A Feast Unknown*. Thus the reader finds the code word "Appledore" in Sir Arthur Conan Doyle's "The Adventure of Charles

---

[2] On a related note, there is a race of "hairy men of the trees" in Farmer's Ancient Opar novels called the *nukaar*, which can only point toward Grandrith's n'k when one accounts for the lack of vowels in n'k linguistics.

Augustus Milverton" and "The Adventure of the Priory School" and its parallel "Applethwaite" in *A Feast Unknown*. The code word "Wilder" is found in "The Adventure of the Priory School" and its parallel "Wilde" is in *A Feast Unknown*. Moreover, another variant of Wilder, "Wildman," appears throughout *Tarzan Alive* and his novel *The Evil in Pemberley House*, the latter completed in collaboration with Win Scott Eckert.

It is almost as if Farmer is playing a clever game of algebraic substitution in *A Feast Unknown*, laying out in advance what he eventually explicated in more detail in *Tarzan Alive*. We begin to see that he is playing much the same game in *Tarzan Alive*. (Although I should be heedful of the admonition Farmer made in a letter published in the Summer 1977 issue of the Burroughs fanzine *Erbania*: "For me, it's not a game. I know that there was a real Tarzan and that he still lives. I'm dead serious, though not deadly serious, I hope . . . If others insist it's just a game or that Tarzan is purely fictional, I won't argue with them. Let the *kafir* dwell in the darkness.") This is what Farmer means by his "analogical" approach in the biography.

Similarly, *A Feast Unknown* is an analogical novel. Although Farmer is playing with real-life elements in the novel, he has clothed it in an analogical veil to disguise and protect the people he writes about. It is a veil of the outrageous, the shocking, and the obscene through which few can gain the composure to penetrate. But Farmer is poking his readers and whispering into their ears that there is a very real story that can be uncovered beneath that curtain of analogy. I shudder to think of it: that the Nine may be out there guiding—or misguiding—the course of human history.

If further proof is needed to illustrate that Farmer believed that "Lord Grandrith" and "Lord Greystoke" were one and the same, consider his statement in "The Arms of Tarzan" (see page 117 of this book) when he states, "I will tell you one thing. Tarzan's real title does not start with GR (as in Greystoke or Grebson). That initial letter cluster will, however, lead you to some of his ancestors and relatives in *Burke's Peerage*. Nor does his title contain the word *grey*. It does contain an archaic word implying grey. I won't tell you if the word is of Germanic, Latin, Pictish, or Celtic origin, however." Observe that in *A Feast Unknown*, the surname of "Lord Grandrith" is Cloamby. The root word "cloam," means "made of clay or earthenware," which, of course, certainly often implies the color gray. Now I highly doubt that Farmer would have revealed Tarzan's real name in *A Feast Unknown*, but again, it is an example of Farmer burying the bone deeper, so to say, and implying connections to Tarzan's genealogy via code words precisely as he did in *Tarzan Alive*, and as other authors like Conan Doyle did in their own works.

Whether or not one wishes to believe that the explicit material in *A Feast Unknown* portrays real events is left to the reader to decide. I, for one, being a Burroughs purist, choose to believe that Farmer layered on such graphic depictions in much the same way that so many others have depicted their own variant versions of the ape-man in assorted media. But he did so for two reasons that are quite different from the motivations of the others: Firstly, he made his depiction of Lord Grandrith so preposterously over the top to discourage anyone from believing there was a real-life basis for the character buried deep under the events of *A Feast Unknown*. In such a manner, he would protect the identity of the subject of his "novel." Secondly, he was putting his personal stamp on his own telling of this modern myth, challenging boundaries and society's knee-jerk inclinations toward censorship in precisely the same way he had broken the mold with stories such as "The Lovers," "Mother," "The Night of Light," *Flesh*, and *Fire and the Night*.

I would be remiss if I failed to point out that, from the time *Tarzan Alive* was published in 1972 until his passing in 2009, Farmer never "broke character"—repeatedly in interviews, correspondence, and public appearances, he unswervingly insisted that Tarzan was real and he had met him. In one intriguing letter published in the Summer 1985 issue of *Erbania*, he closed out his thoughts on Tarzan's genealogy and his visit the previous July to the United Kingdom by asking, "Did you know that Tarzan's father's oil portrait hangs in the National Gallery in London?" The line has stuck with me since I first read it in 1985, as I can't help but think Farmer was doling out a major clue to crack the code of his analogical approach and reveal the true identity of Tarzan. And yet I have not been able to fathom out the remark.

I keep going back to the scene from *Tarzan Alive* in which Tarzan and his cousin Lord "Bunny" Tennington discuss a portrait by Frederic Leighton that depicts one of the ape-man's relatives. Tennington remarks to Tarzan, ". . . you should see sometime his portrait of your distant cousin, Sir Richard Francis Burton. Hangs in the National Gallery, dontcha know, and if he were twenty years younger and didn't have that beastly mustache and forked beard and the ghastly old cheek scar, he and you could jolly well pass for twins, what?" But surely Farmer's statement that Tarzan's father's oil portrait hangs in the National Gallery in London can't possibly imply that Burton was Tarzan's father. The dates just don't line up, as Burton died in 1890 in Trieste, Italy, where he had lived out his remaining years, and Tarzan was born off the coast of west central Africa in 1888, some number of months after his parents were marooned there (of course, there is the alternative birthdate of 1872 for Tarzan as discussed in "The Great Korak-Time Discrepancy"; see page 90). But then again, Farmer said he was able to determine Tarzan's identity by tracing the Howard family line in *Burke's Peerage*, and Burton's wife, Isabel (née Arundell) was distantly related to the Howards according to W. H. Wilkins introduction to her memoir, *The Romance of Isabel Lady Burton*.

What could all this mean? Is this a clue to Tarzan's true identity? Perhaps I am just going down a rabbit hole of fruitless speculation, especially as Tarzan has by now doubtless concealed any trace of his whereabouts beyond any hope of discovery.

But as I said at the outset, when it comes to Philip José Farmer, I have always found it best to expect the unexpected. And so I can only revel in the fact that the mysteries left behind by the man who met Tarzan are so intriguing and provocative, and ask, who knows?

THE GOLDEN AGE AND THE BRASS

First published in the *Burroughs Bulletin*, Number 12, 1956. Although written over half a century ago, this article by Farmer serves as an excellent and apposite preface to this collection of his Tarzan writings. It also stands as testament to Farmer's adulation of that master of storytelling, Edgar Rice Burroughs, and the characters and worlds created by him.

Farmer's love for heroes, old and new, is obvious and he always strived to instil that appreciation into subsequent generations of readers. His investigations, suppositions, and pastiches of Tarzan illustrate that love very clearly and whereas this piece shines the light on the full panoply of ERB creations, it is clear the esteem he reserved for the Lord of the Jungle himself.

When I was ten, I built my personal pantheon of heroes. There were many stalwart and crafty and bold men and demi-gods among them. Hercules and Autoyous (the Greek Shadow) and Manabozho and Thor were in the front ranks. A little ahead of them stood broadshouldered Odysseus. Him I often imagined myself to be; a dug-out along the creek-bank became Polyphemus' cave, and I escaped the blind Cyclops' hands by throwing a sheep-skin (an old burlap sack) over my back and crawling out on all fours, baaing like mad.

Bright as these Greeks and Norse and Algonquins were, however, they were outshone by others, men and demi-gods who sprang, like Athena from Zeus' brow, full-grown from the mind of an American.

This man was a modern. He was Edgar Rice Burroughs, a man as fertile in the making of modern myths as his middle name indicates.

From his brow and nimble fingers—some say too nimble—sprang tall heroes and divine heroines. They were, though created by a man of our times, not the characters you would expect in latter-day myths. There was nothing of the whining, brooding, and introspective protagonist who haunts and shadows so many present day novels and whom so many novelists would have you believe bodies forth the zeitgeist of the twentieth century. Not these mighty-hewed and utterly courageous giants! These men had no qualms about what they were doing; their only concern about their destination was removing those who stood in their way. Their normal code, if rather simple and stiff-necked—even, if I dare say it, unrealistic—was still one that they did not doubt, one that did not throw them into throes of agonies over whether or not they were doing the right thing. These mighty-muscled gorilla-grapplers and sizzling swordmen were pitted against forces that they knew were evil. There were no greys or other shades in their universe; you were either black or white. The moral issues involved were few but were simple: the oppression of the good by the vicious and brutal, the forcing of good and clean and faithful women by lustful and foul men. All was very simple, and all was, after the encountering of many novel and very interesting and heart-pounding dangers, simply solved. Alexander cuts the Gordian knot; John Carter cuts down the villainous Jeddak, Tarzan breaks the Arab slaver's neck.

This, it must be admitted from a viewpoint that has now been aged and matured in the wood of time, was not an altogether admirable outlook on the universe. But for its time and for its readers it was good enough. The hero did not toss off drinks right and left and leap into buxom blondes' beds—or anybody's for that matter—nor did he take a vicious and bestial delight in shooting women in the belly. Indeed, he adhered to the code that you must not harm a woman with fist or weapon. And even though the hero was as likely as not to take justice and vengeance in his own hands instead of leaving it to the legally constituted authorities, he was not so tarred with the same brush as the villains that it was hard to see the difference between them—especially in a dim light.

As I was saying before I got off on a slight tangent, I had my personal pantheon when I was ten. Some were heroes and demigods of the Golden Age; others were not. The latter existed in a sort of auriferous limbo which, while it did not have the antiquity and prestige of the legendary men, had a glow all its own and one, indeed, that shined rather more brightly than the more legitimate Valhallas and Olympuses.

Be that as it may, I spent far more time playing John Carter than I did anything else. I "was" John Carter, late of the C.S.A., and the woods and creekbanks not too far from my house was the dying planet Mars. Armed with a lath for a rapier, I slashed through hordes of big green "dumb Warhoons" and rescued the lovely red-skinned Dejah Thoris (whom I thought of as being literally, scarlet-skinned) from various lustful Jeddaks.

When I had exhausted Mars for the time being, I shifted into Tarzan's "valence," swung through the trees and dropped in on lions and mad gorillas and Ay-rabs and broke their necks or slit their gullets. So proficient did I become in this, I was soon called "Tarzan" by all my classmates. And, incidentally, I built muscles during my arboreal activities that helped me later in my athletic career.

My favorite character, David of Pellucidar, was, for some unknown reason, neglected in my play. I preferred to sit around and dream about what Dian and he were doing. Usually, they were being chased by some dinosaur—which dinosaur, by the way, I imagined them as being, in some way, fond of. Dinosaurs, I think, dwell in an affectionate part of every science fiction and fantasy lover's heart—albeit slightly fearsome beasts. Just so, I think, did the knights of old love their dragons, and they must have been very sorry when the last dragons died.

What has the above got to do with today or even with the admitted subject for this project? Briefly, it is this. I read the Oz books and the Raggedy Anne stories, Grimm's Fairy Tales, the Mark Tidd books, Jules Verne, a series about some world-traveling, animal-collecting juveniles whose author I can't recall, and, climax, Edgar Rice Burroughs. All glowed golden, but Burroughs' books gave me the deepest and most lasting thrills. I read each one of his series at least twenty times. To get them I had to visit the local libraries, reserve them, and then, after waiting a few weeks, seize them, fondle them, and dream over them during the two weeks I was allowed to keep them out.

I saved money from my allowance, and, one by one, built up an almost complete Edgar Rice Burroughs library. My father wasn't interested in fantasy or SF, but he indulgently allowed me to purchase such with my own money. On birthdays and Christmas I would ask for, and get, at least one ERB, usually a John Carter or Tarzan, but occasionally there would be *The Moon Maid* or *The Monster Men*.

The point is, if my father had had the ERB collection I now possess, I would have blithered with joy, blown a tender young blood vessel with ecstasy. But my son is being raised in the heyday of the comics. He, in common with most of his kind in this neo-Noachian age, is being flooded beneath a deluge of crud that will last longer than forty days because there seems to be no end to paper, whereas even rain can last only so long.

(Lest I be accused of being partial, I hasten to add that some comics are quite good.)

My son, instead of living in the golden age, is surrounded by brass. Brass is notoriously easier to get than gold and is far noisier. Not that I mind the presence of brass. I can ignore it and reach for the gold.

Unfortunately, most people don't. And most can't see the gold—which they would naturally prefer—because brass glitters in their eyes and they can't see beyond it. My son looks at the John Carter, the David Innes, the Moon Maid, the Land That Time Forgot, the Tarzan books. There is an interested but dubious expression on his face. Then, after leafing through their pages—which contains so many words—he turns to the comics—full of pictures and their swiftly-read balloons. I am somewhat impatient, because I want him to know the joys I knew, because he does have the type of imagination that revels in the things that throng in ERB.

Yet, I can't force them on him, and I wouldn't want to.

Time passed, as it always did and does. I resigned myself to letting dust gather and dim the golden treasury of Burroughs.

Then one bright day in the midst of many grey, I noticed one thing that gives me hope. Among all the hundreds, perhaps the thousands, of the comics he has read, he remembers none over six months old. Except two, which he read at least eight months ago. Both these are John Carter comics, ERB transliterated. He still talks of these, and I am gently guiding him back to those dusty volumes, gently, gently, for I hope his interest leads to the day when he, too, knows the delights, raptures, and terrors that I, as a child and budding adolescent, found in the mythmaker Edgar Rice Burroughs.

THE OFFICIAL BIOGRAPHER

An Appreciation of
Edgar Rice Burroughs

First published in *20th Century Fiction*, 1985.
Unlike Farmer's preface to this collection, what follows is a less personal review of Edgar Rice Burroughs. That it spotlights Tarzan, almost to the exclusion of the other Burroughs heroes, reinforces the love and fascination he had for that character.

When almost 36 years old, with a wife and three children, disappointed in his military and various business careers, Edgar Rice Burroughs decided to try fiction writing. His first sale, later printed in hardcovers as *A Princess of Mars*, was serialized in *All-Story Magazine* in 1912. The first of a series still immensely popular, the novel illustrates most of the strengths and weaknesses of his works. Fast-paced, colorful, and often strikingly imaginative, it stimulates the sense of wonder, especially of children and juveniles. The one-dimensional characters as either evil or good, and the use of coincidence, is abused. Though his "Barsoomian" cultures are vividly presented, they are not developed in depth. The historical novel that he next wrote, *The Outlaw of Torn*, and his "realistic" stories, notably those of crime and corruption in Chicago and Hollywood, illustrate his failure to be convincing at anything other than fantasy. Tales set on Mars, in darkest Africa, or in earth's center, worlds which he nor his readers knew much about, were never-never lands that he could deal with.

Burroughs is best known as the creator of Tarzan, son of an English nobleman, Lord Greystoke, raised from the age of one in the African jungle by language-using great apes. Critics have maintained that Burroughs wrote *Tarzan of the Apes* to demonstrate his belief in the superiority of heredity over environment, and especially of the superior heredity of the British nobility. In one sense they are correct. Tarzan's human genes gave him an intelligence superior to the apes'; they gave him an innate curiosity and drive which would have taken him out of any ghetto or other underprivileged community he had been born into. But in the final analysis it was the environment which molded Tarzan's character. Raised as a feral child, he is a classic example of the outsider, one who has an objective view of human society because he has not imbibed its irrationalities along with his mother's milk. Through Tarzan's eyes, Burroughs satirizes *Homo sapiens*, as he did through some of his other heroes, notably Carson Napier of the "Venus" series.

However, Burroughs' ape-man is more than a Voltairean observer or noble savage. Though he regards pre-literates as superior in their way of life to civilized peoples, he is never quite human. He is, when in the jungle, free of the mundane, drab, wearing, and often tragic restrictions of tribal or civilized life. It is his being a law unto himself, and his extreme closeness to nature which have been part of his appeal. But Burroughs, though unconsciously, also gave him most of the attributes of the pre-literate and classical hero of fairy tale, legend, and mythology, including the Trickster. He is the last of the Golden Age heroes, a literary character who reflects the archetypal images and feelings of the unconscious mind noted by Carl Jung and Joseph Campbell.

Like Arthur Conan Doyle, Burroughs had the gift of writing adventure stories with an indefinable quality that made them endure while thousands of similar novels dropped into oblivion. Like Doyle, he created a classical fictional character of whom he wearied. The later Tarzan novels, in fact all of his works written in the latter part of his career, show a flagging invention, repetitiveness of plot and incident, excess of coincidences and improbabilities, and failure to develop fully promised themes.

AN APPRECIATION OF EDGAR RICE BURROUGHS

He never thought of himself as anything but a commercial writer of romances. His works betray the biases, conservatisms, and timidities of his social class and times, and his style is old-fashioned. With the exception of Tarzan and a few others, his characters are cardboard. His genius was in the creation of the archetypal feral Tarzan and the writing of many pseudo-scientific romances which have enthralled generations of young readers, many of whom have remained loyal to him through their middle age.

FROM **ERB** TO YGG

This article was first published in *ERBivore*, Numbers 6 and 7, in August 1973, and plays to one of Farmer's great passions; genealogy. Farmer traced his own lineage to Woden (aka Ygg) but in this piece of research, he looks at a slightly divergent branch, one that connects Burroughs to the ancient Germanic god with a few interesting inclusions along the way.

All persons of North European ancestry, and the majority of those of South European extraction, are descended from Charlemagne. Charlemagne, or Karl the Great (742–814 A.D.), was the king of the Franks and emperor of the West (Holy Roman Empire). Most Americans of African heritage can also claim the distinction of descent from this famous monarch, since very few lack white ancestors. Furthermore, those belonging to Indian tribes whose original habitat was east of the Mississippi can make a similar claim. Further, anybody whose forebears were of old British stock also has as ancestor in Alfred the Great (849–899 A.D.), king of the West Saxons. This includes many Dutchmen, Belgians, French, and Germans, since the British, in their many, many wars and travels, have left a trail of babies behind them in western Europe and elsewhere.

Unfortunately, few of us in the United States know who our great-grandfathers were. We can only show that Alfred and Charlemagne are in our lineage by arithmetic. Suppose you were born in 1950 A.D. Assuming 25 years per generation, you had sixteen ancestors living in 1850. Doubling each generation as you go backwards, you had 256 ancestors living in 1750. By the time you get to 1040 A.D., you have 23,873,978,368 ancestors.

The world population today is about 3.4 billion, the highest by far that it has been since the human species began. The world population in 1 A.D. was somewhere between 200 and 300 million. Obviously, you could not have had over 23 billion ancestors living in 1040 A.D. Marriage between cousins, near and far, is the only explanation of this discrepancy. The world is, and has been, a hotbed of incest.

It's no exaggeration to say that we're all related and that all of us have noble and royal ancestors. The difference between the majority of us and a small minority is that the latter can offer documentary proof of their descent from kings and nobility. They can give the names, step by step, ancestor by ancestor, of those in their lineage.

Edgar Rice Burroughs (ERB) belongs to this minority. His lineage is distinguished indeed. In fact, it can be traced back to the great Germanic god Woden, known in various languages as Odin, Wuodan, Wodan, Wuotan, etc. One of his epithets in Old Norse was Ygg, hence the name in the title of this essay. Ygg means "The Terrible One," and Yggdrasil, the great ashtree or worldtree of the Old Norse, means "Odin's Steed."

But let's go to a son of Odin, the man whose lineage is the subject of this article. He was born in Chicago on the first of September, 1875. Neither his environment nor his immediate ancestry smacked remotely of the divine. Yet this man, Edgar Rice Burroughs, had an imagination which would carry his readers further than Woden ruled, to the center of the Earth and beyond Earth itself, faster than Odin's eight-legged steed, Sleipnir, could travel.

His parents were George Tyler Burroughs (1833–1913) and Mary Evaline Zieger, married 23rd February, 1863. George was a major in the U.S. Army during the Civil War and a successful businessman afterwards. He was the son of Abner Tyler Burroughs (1805–1897) and Mary Rice, married 16th December, 1827.

Abner Tyler Burroughs was the son of Tyler Burroughs (1771–1845) and Anna Pratt. The ancestors of Tyler Burroughs are not known to me, though Mr. Porges, in his biography of ERB [published in 1975] may extend the genealogy in the Burroughs line.

However, it is the purpose of this article to trace ERB's lineage through the Rices. The genealogy of ERB's other American ancestors, the Ziegers, Colemans, McCullochs and Innskeeps, is not covered here.

Mary Rice (see above), ERB's paternal grandmother, was born in 1802 at Warren, Mass., and died 1889 in Chicago, Ill.

Her parents were Thomas Rice (1767–1847) and Sally Makepeace, both of Brookfield, Mass.

Thomas' parents were Tilly Rice and Mary (Baxter) Buckminster of Brookfield.

Tilly Rice was the son of Obadiah Rice (born in Marlboro, Mass.) and Esther Merrick.

Obadiah was the son of Jacob Rice (born in Marlboro) and Mary——.[1]

Jacob Rice (died 1746) was the son of Edward Rice, born in Sudbury, Mass. Mary Evaline Zieger, ERB's mother, says in her booklet on the family, *Memoirs of a War Bride* (1914), that Jacob Rice married Mary——. *Burke's Landed Gentry*, 1939, states that his wife was Mary, daughter of Christopher Bannister of Marlboro.

Edward Rice (died 1712) married Anna——, according to *Memoirs of a War Bride*. Burke says that Edward's wife was Agnes, daughter of John Bent of Marlboro.

Edmund, called Deacon Rice, father of Edward, was born about 1594 in Berkhampstead, Hertfordshire, England. He emigrated to the colonies and settled in Sudbury, Mass., in 1639. Edmund was one of the founders of Sudbury, a proprietor and selectman, a freeman and a deputy to the General Court. He had a twin brother, Robert, who followed him to America.

Edmund's father was Thomas Rice of Boemer, county of Buckinghamshire. There seems to be no record available of Edmund's mother.

Thomas' father was William Rice, born 1522 in the same town as Thomas. William was important enough to be granted a coat of arms in 1522. These arms are illustrated in color in *Burke's Landed Gentry* of 1939. Their blazoning: Argent on a chevron engrailed sable between three reindeers' heads erased gules as many cinquefoils ermine. As descendants of William Rice, ERB and his posterity are entitled to bear these arms.

William Rice was a younger son of Rice ap Griffith FitzUryan

---

[1] Old records often use a dash to indicate an unknown name.

and Katherine, daughter of Thomas Howard, 2nd Duke of Norfolk. It is through these two that noble and royal blood enters the Rice family. Let's consider the Welsh line before we go to the English line.

First, though, it must be admitted that William Rice is a weak link in the genealogical chain. *Burke's Peerage* in the section on Dynevor gives only a son, Griffith ap Rice FitzUryan, and a daughter, Agnes, as the children of Katherine Howard and Rice ap Griffith FitzUryan. *Burke's Landed Gentry* states that it is said that William Rice was a younger son of Katherine and Rice. Dr. Charles Rice of Alliance, Ohio, a genealogical writer, indicates that there is no doubt about William Rice being their son. Since Burke often does not mention children who founded "unimportant" lines, the omission in the *Peerage* may be due to this. This may also account for the omission of Obadiah Rice in *Landed Gentry*. Obadiah (ERB's great-great-great-grandfather was "unimportant" to *Landed Gentry*. This is ironic since *Gentry* lists in detail the accomplishments and novels of two of the descendants of Edmund Rice; but who today has ever heard of Cale Young Rice and Alexander Hamilton Rice? Yet, in 1939, Edgar Rice Burroughs was a world-famous writer and the creator of a character, Tarzan, whose only close rival in literary stature is Sherlock Holmes. I have no hesitation in saying that these are immortal characters, literarily speaking—the best known in the 20th century, and undiminished by time. As the years go by, they grow bigger.

Again, the family of Doyle is not even listed in *Landed Gentry*, though A. Conan Doyle came of ancient and distinguished stock from both sides. But then, neither Doyle nor Burroughs were considered to be "respectable" writers. And they are still vastly underrated by the literati.

The Welsh line of ERB's ancestry is studded with knights, princes and gentlemen. Those who are interested can refer to the section on the barons of Dynevor in *Burke's Peerage*. This begins the Rice lineage with Uryan Rheged, Lord of Kidwelly, Carunllou, and Iskennen in South Wales. He married Margaret La Faye, daughter of Gerlois, Duke of Cornwall, and he built the castle of Carrey Cermin in Carmarthenshire, Wales. He had originally been a prince of the North Britons, but was expelled by the Saxons in the 6th century and fled to Wales.

His great-grandfather's sister was supposed to be Helena, mother of Constantine the Great. However, Helena's origin as a Briton is based on legends which are not backed by records contemporary to Constantine.

Uryan Rheged's great-great-grandfather was Coel Codevog, King of the Britons. Coel, who lived in the 3rd century A.D., seems to be the original of the nursery song, "Old King Cole." (See *The Annotated Mother Goose*, William S. and Ceil Baring-Gould, Clarkson N. Potter, 1962.)

Let's return now to the English line of ERB's family tree. Katherine Howard, William Rice's mother, came of a line which had many kings in its pedigree. The present head of the family, the Duke of Norfolk, is the Earl Marshal of England and the premier noble. Katherine was the daughter of Thomas Howard, 2nd Duke of Norfolk, and of Agnes, daughter of Hugh Tilney. Thomas led the English to their great victory over the Scots at Flodden Field, 9th September, 1513.

Thomas' father, Sir John Howard, 1st Duke of Norfolk, married Katherine, daughter of William, Lord Moleyns, and died fighting for Richard III on Bosworth Field.

The 1st duke was the son of Margaret, eldest daughter of Thomas, Lord Mowbray, and of Sir Robert Howard.

Sir Robert's lineage started with a John Howard of Wiggenhall St. Peter, 1267, who married a Lucy———. Sir Robert was also descended from King John of England, Duke of Normandy, through Joan, daughter of Sir Richard de Cornwall, a bastard of Richard Cornwall, second son of King John.

Margaret, Sir Robert's wife, was the eldest daughter of Thomas, Lord Mowbray, and of Elizabeth FitzAllen, daughter of the Earl of Arundel. Her brother, be it noted, was the ancestor of Isabel Arundell, the wife of the great explorer, writer and anthropologist, Sir Richard Francis Burton. Another item of interest is that some of the present branches of the Howard family are descendants of the barons of Greystoke. (See Burke, *Extinct Peerage*.) The de Greystock blood, alas, entered the Howard veins too late for ERB to claim them as forefathers. Captain Stafford Vaughan Stepney Howard-Stepney is the present Lord of Greystoke Manor in Cumberland and a distant relative of ERB.

Thomas, Lord Mowbray, was the son of John, Lord Mowbray, and of Elizabeth Segrave.

Elizabeth Segrave was the daughter of John, Lord Segrave, and of Margaret Plantagenet.

Margaret was the daughter and heiress of Thomas de Brotherton, Earl of Norfolk and Earl Marshal of England.

Thomas was the eldest son of King Edward I by Margaret, daughter of Philip the Hardy, King of France. Philip's dynasty will be described in Part II, along with other ancestors of ERB, the rulers of Scotland, Normandy, Norway, Hungary, and the Swedish Norsemen rulers of medieval Russia.

Edward I was the son of Henry III and of Eleanor, daughter of Raymond Berengaris, Count of Provence. Edward, be it noted, was the brother of Richard, also called Norman of Torn or the Outlaw of Torn. ERB says that Richard was a legitimate son, but there is plenty of evidence that *The Outlaw of Torn* is a semifictionalized account. Richard was probably one of Henry III's "natural" children. The identity of the mother is a subject for a separate article. I may also mention that Alice Pleasance Liddell, the real-life model for Lewis Carroll's Alice, was a descendant of Edward I. Her line came through John of Gaunt, Edward I's grandson. But she, along with Old King Cole, is a relative of ERB's.

Henry III's father was King John, who's had such a bad press that no king of England has ever been named John since. Actually, John was no worse than any of the medieval monarchs and a lot better than many. His brother, Richard the Lion-Hearted, was a thorough rotter who probably couldn't even speak English, but writers (until recently) made a hero out of him.

John married Isabel, daughter and heiress of Aymer, count of the French province of Angouleme. John's parents were Henry II and Eleanor, daughter of William, Duke of Aquitaine.

Henry II's father was Geoffrey, Count of Anjou and son of John, King of Jerusalem. Henry's mother was the empress dowager of England and daughter of Henry I.

Henry I married Maud, daughter of the king of the Scots, Malcolm III, surnamed Caennmor. Maud, also called Matilda, was directly descended from Alfred the Great.

The father of Henry I was William (1027-1087), called the

Bastard or the Conqueror. He and his Normans defeated King Harold of England at Hastings in 1066 and so won the rulership of England. William was the illegitimate son of Robert I, Duke of Normandy, also known as Robert the Devil. His mother was Arletta, daughter of a tanner of Falaise, and the story is that she caught the Devil's eye while he was riding past a brook where she was washing clothes. Robert dismounted and mounted. And thus was created another link in the blood-chain which resulted in ERB. Little William was raised in Robert's house and, since Robert had no surviving legitimate sons, became Robert's heir. In those days, the upper crust often took in their natural children to rear as their own. There was no stigma attached to bastardry.

What if Robert the Devil had not happened to be riding by that particular spot on that particular day? Quite probably the Norman conquest of England would not have occurred. The world, especially the English-speaking world, would be different in many respects. The English speech would not quite be what it is today, nor would our political and social institutions. Most of us (North American and European readers) would not exist. Our places would be taken by entirely different individuals. The works of Edgar Rice Burroughs would not exist, and this article would not have been written.

William the Conqueror was the descendant of Rollo, or Hrolf, the Norseman who conquered that part of France which became Normandy. Rollo was called the Ganger, or Walker, because he was so huge that no horse could bear his weight.

William married Maud, or Matilda, daughter of Baldwin, Count of Flanders. She was descended from Alfred the Great and Charlemagne.

Skipping a few Old English kings, we come to Alfred the Great. He was the son of King Ethelwulf (died 857) and of a lady named Osburh. Ethelwulf was the son of Egbert, King of Wessex, also titled Bretwalda, "ruler of Britain," deceased in 839.

The line of descent from Offa (reigned 757-796), King of the Mercians and of all England, is uncertain. But since there was much giving in marriage of sons and daughters among all the early Old English kings, it's highly probable that Egbert was descended from Offa.

Offa, according to a traditional genealogy, was a descendant of Penda, a king of Mercia. Penda's ancestral line consisted of Wibba,

Creoda, Cynewald, Cnebba, Icel, Eomaer, Angetheow, Offa, Waermund, Wihtlaeg, and the great god Woden.

(The latter Offa is quite likely the Offa mentioned in *Beowulf*.)

No one today is claiming that a god actually begat Wihtlaeg.
This founding of a royal line by a deity was traditional and common
to all the kings of Kent, East Anglia, Essex, Mercia, Deira, Bernicia,
Wessex and Lindesfaran. But, according to some modern authorities
(Jacob Grim, among others), Woden was probably a hero of the early
Germanic peoples who became deified after his death.

He would have lived, however, somewhere between 1000 B.C.
and 800 B.C., not the 4th century A.D.

This early date means that the majority of those who read this
article are also the many times great grandchildren of that ancient
proto-Germanic speaking hero.

The descendants of ERB are living today, but the scope of this
article ends with ERB. As it is, it's been a long journey from Woden
to Tarzan.

From Woden to Edgar Rice Burroughs
A Pictorial Family Tree

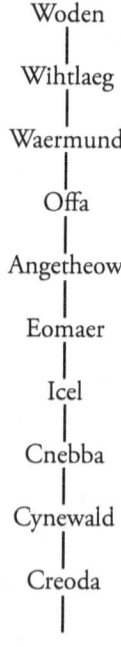

Woden

Wihtlaeg

Waermund

Offa

Angetheow

Eomaer

Icel

Cnebba

Cynewald

Creoda

FROM ERB TO YGG

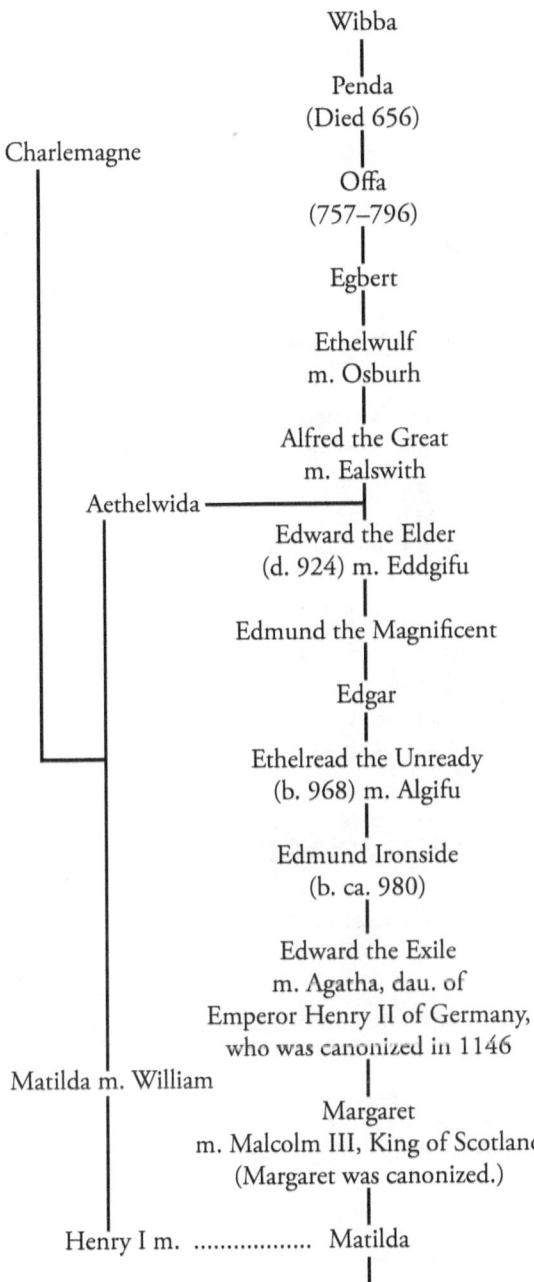

Wibba
|
Penda
(Died 656)
|
Charlemagne
Offa
(757–796)
|
Egbert
|
Ethelwulf
m. Osburh
|
Alfred the Great
m. Ealswith
|
Aethelwida
Edward the Elder
(d. 924) m. Eddgifu
|
Edmund the Magnificent
|
Edgar
|
Ethelread the Unready
(b. 968) m. Algifu
|
Edmund Ironside
(b. ca. 980)
|
Edward the Exile
m. Agatha, dau. of
Emperor Henry II of Germany,
who was canonized in 1146
|
Matilda m. William
Margaret
m. Malcolm III, King of Scotland
(Margaret was canonized.)
|
Henry I m. .... Matilda
|

Henry II
m. Eleanor of Aquitaine

John
m. Isabella of Angouleme

Henry III
m. Eleanor of Provence

Edward I
m. Margaret, dau. of Philip III of France

Thomas of Brotherton
m. Alice, dau. of Sir Roger Halys

Margaret
m. John, Lord Segrave

Elizabeth
m. John, Lord Mowbray

Thomas, Lord Mowbray
m. Elizabeth FitzAllen, dau. of Earl of Arundel

Margaret
m. Sir Robert Howard

John, 1st Duke of Norfolk
m. Katherine, dau. of Lord Moleyns

Thomas, 2nd Duke of Norfolk
m. Agnes Tilney

Katherine Howard
m. Rice ap Griffith FitzUryan

William Rice
(b. 1525)

From **ERB** to Y<small>GG</small>

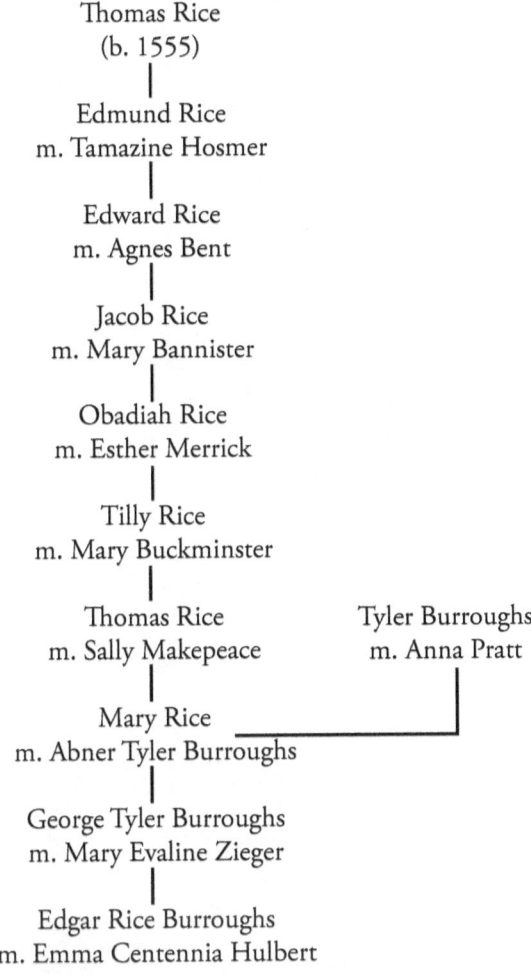

Thomas Rice
(b. 1555)
|
Edmund Rice
m. Tamazine Hosmer
|
Edward Rice
m. Agnes Bent
|
Jacob Rice
m. Mary Bannister
|
Obadiah Rice
m. Esther Merrick
|
Tilly Rice
m. Mary Buckminster
|
Thomas Rice   Tyler Burroughs
m. Sally Makepeace   m. Anna Pratt
|
Mary Rice
m. Abner Tyler Burroughs
|
George Tyler Burroughs
m. Mary Evaline Zieger
|
Edgar Rice Burroughs
m. Emma Centennia Hulbert

Note: As mentioned by Henry Franke in his introductory essay, this is Part I, Part II was never published.

THE PRINCESS OF TERRA

Charlotte Corday-Marat

This witty and entertaining piece focuses more on ERB's Mars stories than Tarzan, but does illustrate Farmer's appreciation of Burroughs' imagination (and therefore sits quite appropriately in this section of the book). That he chose to flip the perspective and take a cynical, perhaps critical, approach to ERB's 'unscientific' imagination only highlights just how inventive Burroughs was. It is compelling to consider how Burroughs' Tarzan series might have been reviewed from an extra-terrestrial point of view. In any event, this wonderfully showcases the love Farmer had for Burroughs and even if this is only tangentially related to Tarzan, it helps us understand the machinations in the mind of a master storyteller. In another nod to Burroughs imagination, Farmer uses codes and wordplay to name his characters and places.

Farmer offered no compelling explanation as to why he went for this portmanteau of a pseudonym (Marat was a physician, a scientist, and a politician during the French Revolution. Corday was his assassin). When asked, Farmer said he created that name just for the fun of it. It is worth noting, however, that Corday was an alias once used by Tarzan (see "Extracts from the Memoirs of 'Lord Greystoke'").

Note: The following is extracted from the book-review section of the Martian science-fiction and fact magazine, *Parallel*, formerly *Supersincere Science Stickler Stories* and still referred to by fandom as the *Big S*. The review was written by the prominent SF author and critic, Remlil Esspee, and was published in Vol. 69, dated (Martian style) Day of the Devout Data Digger, Week of the

Witching Wands, Month of the Muttering Mountebank, Year of the Yearning Yo-Yo, Cycle of the Psionic Seersucker.

Here we have a reprint of another book by a writer once regarded as a master of science fiction, Erb of Anazrat. *The Princess of Terra* was the first of a series written about the third planet from the sun and needs no introduction for those who read the original when it appeared fifty-one years ago. But, for the third generation of readers, who may never have heard of Erb of Anazrat or may know him only through the movies based on his character Nazrat of Sepa, the story must be reviewed.

The novel begins over a hundred years ago, shortly after the end of The War Between The Estates. The hero, Noj Notrak, is an ex-officer of the gallant but defeated Short Stick Army. While prospecting for gold in the Great South and Sandy Wastes, he is forced to run for his life from a band of wild Painted Bottoms (pretty wild in those days but now mainly concerned with operating resort areas).

He takes refuge in a cave. There, he is put under a spell by an old witch of the Painted Bottoms. Through the spell or some means (Erb is vague about this), Noj Notrak, or his astral body, or something, is released from his corpse. He soars through space and lands on the surface of Terra, the native name for the planet we call Gongoos. Notrak has a very strong affinity for this world, the pagan god of war, and it is this affinity that attracts him like a nail to a magnet.

Presumably, on this principle, if Notrak had been a great lover instead of a great warrior, he would have gone to the second planet from the sun. Notrak, however, is rather shy with women and only feels at ease when impaling somebody on his trusty and never rusty blade. (A phallic substitute?)

Why Erb chose this method of transporting his hero to Gongoos, or Terra, is a matter of speculation, if not of extreme wonder. Fifty-one years ago, it would have been scientifically valid to extrapolate interplanetary rockets. However, to be fair, rockets were not feasible in the period in which this story takes place. Perhaps, Erb was justified in using the unorthodox, even mystical, method of transportation. If it is considered as a form of teleportation, it even becomes credible. After all, many SF people, including the editor of this magazine, believe in this and other types of ESP.

Anyway, Erb wanted to get his hero quickly and without too much fuss to the third planet, and he certainly did that.

The reader who swallows the astral-corporeal method of space travel has only begun to choke. Erb paints a picture of a world based on the insufficient and sometimes incorrect data of his day. For one thing, though he correctly assumes a denser atmosphere for Gongoos than for that of our planet, he does not make the air as thick as scientists now know it to be. Actually, the gases are so heavy that beings with lungs just simply could not operate them efficiently enough to maintain life.

Erb also assumes vegetation, which probably does exist on Gongoos, but his vegetation has an incredible variety and abundance. Given the known conditions of extreme humidity and heat, only a very primitive and hardy type of flora (such as our own ubiquitous ancient sea-bottom moss) could live. Fauna, if any, would be limited to the colder polar regions.

But Erb is only out to tell a rousing good tale and to exercise the imaginations of his readers. This he does, although the present generation, accustomed to the modern "staccato" school of writing founded by Yawgnimmeh, will find Erb's style rather old fashioned, and, indeed, bad. It is far inferior to the splendid literary offerings of the authors you read every month in *Parallel*. (Note especially the current serial, "Errand of Levity," by Lah Tnemelk.)

Noj Notrak finds that he must move slowly and with some effort because of the great gravity of Terra. This is, however, no real handicap. Terran beings, though fast, are very lightly constructed and fragile. They have to be so in order to move at all against the gravity and heavy air. Attacked by a large beast of prey (four-legged!), the sturdy Notrak smashed it with his fist. The beast's porous muscles and hollow bones crumple at the first impact.

However, Notrak is taken prisoner by a tribe of dark men with only two arms when they overcome him by sheer numbers. In an effort to be colorful, Erb ignored, or was ignorant of, the fact that beings with heavily pigmented skin just could not survive on Terra. The intensity of the sun would cause a very dark skin to absorb so much radiant energy that the internal temperature of a body would be raised to a fatal level.

Be that as it may, Noj Notrak is taken to the camp of the nomads (who ride a beast called *nag*, also four-legged). There he finds a fellow prisoner, a beautiful woman called Siroth Hajed. She resembles us Martians, but she is pink-skinned and belongs to a species that bears its young alive. Despite her eggless method of reproduction (disgusting if you think about it long enough but only lightly touched on in Erb's narrative), she is soon loved by Notrak.

Siroth Hajed is a princess of Ingillan, a country entirely surrounded by water. (The astronomers of our planet designate Erb's Ingillan as Maraba, after the ancient stargazer who first saw it during one of those rare moments when its cloud cover dissipated.) She was captured by the tribe when the flying vehicle on which she was a passenger was forced to land because of engine trouble.

The vehicle does not use lighter-than-air gas. It depends on lift from extended surfaces and is driven forward by propellers turned by engines of great power. While it is true that the dense air of Gongoos, or Terra, would provide greater support than ours, it is also true that the energy required to force such a craft through the very dense air would make this method of flight mechanically and economically unfeasible.

Notrak and Hajed escape from the dark men. Several chapters are then devoted to their ordeals on the surface of the vast expanse of waters on Terra's surface. Erb describes these as being of great depth. (Scientists have evidence that they cannot be more than neck-deep.) The waters swarm with huge ferocious creatures which not only live in but *breathe* the water. He does not bother to explain the biological mechanisms that would make this possible. Perhaps, this is for the better, since there is enough to strain the reader's sense of credulity without adding this.

There is, however, a very good scene (considering Erb's prose) about the terror that Notrak feels when he is suspended in a watercraft over this abyss of liquid. Every reader will respond as Erb intended, but Erb could hardly fail with such a horrible idea.

The two finally get to London. (Perhaps, Erb chose the name of a gas as the nomenclature of a city because the element London had just been discovered in his day and was being used in dirigibles.) It is interesting to note Erb's explanation for the large splotches of light seen by our astronomers on the third planet's night surface. Notrak finds that the cities are so large and so well illuminated that their light is visible even to us.

At one time, this was a popular speculation not easily refuted. However, in the past twenty years, we have developed instruments able to detect radioactivity at a distance of over 40 million miles. In view of the sporadically high radioactivity emanating from Gongoos (Terra), it is very likely that the many glows of light are heavy concentrations of radium or similar materials spilled out onto the surface by volcanic eruptions. This, in itself, would make a profusion of animal life very improbable.

Aside from the above objection, the proximity of cities such as London to so much water would overstimulate the growth of fungus and other vegetable life. The cities would be buried under the plants.

The Londoners have no such problem. Instead, they are on the verge of defeat in their war with the sinister Hoons of Jirmani. Led by Notrak, who slays the leader of the Hoons, the Kighzar, the Ingillaners defeat and invade Jirmani. Notrak then marries Siroth Hajed.

Suddenly, the air becomes too thick. People begin to die of oxygen richness. The whole planet is doomed. Notrak, however, during one of his adventures, found the secret entrance to the supposedly impregnable air-burning plant of Terra. This building has been built as a joint effort by all nations to oxidize part of the atmosphere. If it were not for this measure, the atmosphere would become fatally dense. Now the operator of the oxidizing plant has gone mad and turned off the equipment. Notrak gets into the building, kills the insane operator, and turns the air-burners back on.

Terra is saved, but it is too late for Noj Notrak. He dies and is hurled through space and finds himself in his original body (uncorrupted) in the cave on our planet. However, those who care to do so may read the sequels, *The Gods of Terra* and *The Warlord of Terra*, and discover how Notrak gets back to the third planet and wins his beauteous pink-skinned princess.

I fear that only those of my own generation who read Erb in their boyhood and want to experience a nostalgia, or those too young to have read much modern science fiction or to know much of modern science, or the incurable romantics, will want to own these reprints.

THE STORY OF THE FERAL MAN

THE OUTSIDER

This article was first printed as part of Farmer's feral man anthology *Mother Was a Lovely Beast* (Chilton, 1974). It has been edited very lightly to remove references to other pieces in that anthology.

This piece is crammed with information and references far belying its 1700 word length and gives the reader much to digest and investigate for themselves. He also offers some incredibly insightful views on the nature of the feral man and why millennia after early feral man stories we are still fascinated by those that have been raised outside of human society.

Particularly enjoy the penultimate paragraph where Farmer displays his feminist credentials as well as living up to his trickster nature.

A feral man is a human being, male or female, who has been raised from an early age by wild animals or who has survived by himself since infancy in wild country.

The feral man theme has been popular since very early times, perhaps since the days of the cave man. Many heroes and heroines of classical myths were adopted by animals after their human parents had abandoned them. Wolves, lions, and bears were the favorite beast-parents of mythology, though goats often figured. These are also prominent in modern feral-man fiction, though the apes have become the most popular foster parents. This can be attributed to the fact that apes are closer to man in anatomy and intelligence than any other creature and are closely associated with the world-famous character of Tarzan.

The feral man theme has always had a strong appeal for several reasons. He is the only truly free man. Or at least he seems to be. He is especially liked by children and romanticists, who resent the strictures, tabus, vexations, and insecurities of civilization. He appeals to the desire to be close to Mother Nature. He is usually a heroic type or a superman and so vicariously satisfies the wish to be superior to others. Lastly, he appeals to realists when he is used in fiction to satirize the hypocrisies, stupidities, cruelties, and inhumanities of civilization. As the Noble Savage, the Outsider, the feral man looks objectively at the discrepancy between the ideal and the real in society.

Jonathan Swift did this when he depicted the Yahoos and the Houyhnhnms. He was deliberately paradoxical in making the all-too-human, truly feral Yahoos civilized man as he is and the sentient horses civilized man as he ought to be. Swift, of course, gave only half the truth. In the Yahoo, he left out those elements of compassion, tenderness, and striving-for-the-ideal that do exist in humanity. But in portraying the Houyhnhnms, he completed the painting. Man is both Yahoo and Houyhnhnm. Unfortunately, the Yahoo too often dominates.

Edgar Rice Burroughs' Tarzan books sometimes have this satiric element. Tarzan is the two-legged Houyhnhnm from the jungle, the Outsider, and we are the Yahoos. This use of satire in the Tarzan books has been overlooked by most literary critics, who regard Tarzan as a two-dimensional character in a comic book-type adventure series. But then they have never taken the trouble to study the Tarzan books. They base their misconceptions on the movies, which have little to do with the books. It is true that the Tarzan stories are largely "just adventure," but Tarzan is also a Candide wearing a leopard loincloth and is armed not only with a knife but an objective view of mankind. Burroughs, however, laughs gently, whereas Swift's mockery is savage and bitter.

Burroughs generally acts as the spokesman for the masses, who like their myths converted into folktales which deal, on the surface, with physical events. Burroughs' hero is the extension of what Joseph Campbell says is the survival of the heroes and deeds and unconscious logic of myth. The two greatest psychologists of the twentieth century, Freud and Jung, he says, have irrefutably demonstrated this.

When I use "mythical" in connection with Tarzan, I do not mean that he is only a character created by Burroughs to embody modern myth. There are two elements in the Tarzan stories. One is that of romance, the fictional feral man who represents an important persona in the collective unconscious of humanity, an archetype overlooked by Carl Jung. The second is the very real element, since Tarzan is based on a man who actually existed.

A French writer, Lucien Malson, has written a thesis about fifty-two seemingly authenticated cases of European wild children. This appeared in 1966 in an issue of the Paris daily newspaper *Le Monde*. The French film director, Francois Truffaut, was so struck by this that he made a movie about "Victor," a child discovered living alone in the forests of Aveyron in 1798. He based the film on the newspaper accounts of that time and the reports of a Dr. Itard, a famous eye-ear-nose-and-throat specialist. Itard took the child into his house to study him and to develop the latent human characteristics of Victor. Itard had some success, though Victor was only able to utter a few words imperfectly; and he could not associate a word with the referent object unless it was actually in his hands.

Truffaut concluded that man is no more than an animal if he has been isolated from human society from an early age. Without going into the implications of "nothing but an animal" I can state that the feral children who became case histories were unable to use language. They had passed through a certain necessary stage in their development without encountering human speech, and the neural centers controlling language could no longer function. The child has to learn to speak at an early age. It is presumed that Victor did know language when he was left for dead by his parents, since he must have been about three or four at that time. But he had forgotten French; and in his seven to eight years of solitude, he had passed the critical stage of linguistic development. The potential for speech exists in every normal child, but the child without any society sinks into a state equal to that of a beast. I recommend, for those interested in Victor's case, *The Wild Child* by Francois Truffaut.

I also highly recommend *Wolf Child and Human Child, The Life History of Kamala the Wolf Girl*, by the distinguished child psychologist Arnold Gesell. This is an account of two girls apparently raised by some wolves in India. It includes photographs and excerpts from the diary of Reverend J. Singh (and his wife), who raised Kamala and Amala in their orphanage after the two were dug out of the wolves' den. Gesell was convinced that the case histories were authentic. However, in 1951 (after the death of Singh), the sociologist W. F. Ogburn and the anthropologist N. K. Bose personally investigated this case. They were unable to find the village that was supposed to have been near the den where the girls were captured. They did find some witnesses who said that the girls had been brought to Singh. They gave the reverend a good character, but others stated that Singh was a well-known liar. These, however, were natives whose faith made them hostile to Singh's Episcopalianism. Nor is it unlikely that the very small village of Godamuri, isolated in the jungle, could have disappeared between 1930 and 1951.

I've read the extracts and am convinced that it's either true or Singh had missed his calling as a novelist. There are too many realistic details which one would expect only from actual observation or from a writer gifted with superb extrapolative powers.

While I was preparing my collection, I received two stories which will be the brightest items in any sequel. These are *Twish of the Kofas*, by a new writer, Tincrowdor, and *Karhun Tytär* (*The Bear's Daughter*) by a Finnish woman, Liisa Jalava. These are the only good stories I've ever read about feral females. Unfortunately, the great majority of feral human stories are about males. I suppose that this is because most of the readers of such stories are males. Another reason is that the feral environment is so demanding that it is presumed only a rugged male could survive. This is ridiculous, since it has been established that the female of the species is as deadly as the male and somewhat more rugged. Moreover, the record of authentic cases of feral humans describes many females who thrived in animal society or survived through their own efforts in solitude.

"The God of Tarzan"[1] is a fascinating account of how Tarzan taught himself to read and write English without having heard a word of English. It is a narrative of the dawning of the consciousness of God in a child raised in a society with no concept of cosmology or eschatology. And it helps illuminate some references in "Extracts from the Memoirs of 'Lord Greystoke.'"

---

[1] "The God of Tarzan" is featured in *Mother Was a Lovely Beast* but is not reproduced in this collection. However, Farmer's introduction to "The God of Tarzan" is printed later in this book.

THE FERAL HUMAN IN
MYTHOLOGY AND FICTION

Coming at the end of that erstwhile book, Farmer takes the opportunity to consolidate his thinking and theses. Although Farmer is credited as Editor on later books (specifically, the anthology Riverworld books) this is his only editorship where he fully takes the reins, where he researched and assembled the contents, and where he wrote all the connective tissue. Under Farmer's stewardship we are expertly guided through a historical tour of this peculiar facet of humankind and are rewarded with the author's own thoughts on the subject, including his conclusion as to which animals would make the best foster parents for a human child.

E very child learns at school the story of Romulus and Remus (at least, in my time they did). They were the twin sons of Rhea Silvia, the daughter of Numitor, king of Alba Longa, a city of ancient Italy. Numitor was deposed by his younger brother Amulius, who then forced Rhea Silvia to become vestal virgin. Numitor expected to keep Rhea Silvia from bearing children who would have claim to the throne, but Rhea Silvia fooled him. She bore twins whom she claimed were begotten by the god Mars. Amulius questioned both their paternity and their right to live. He had them set adrift in a boat or a trough of alderwood on the Tiber. Instead of dying of exposure, the twins drifted ashore at the site of the future Rome near the Ficus

Ruminalis, a sacred fig tree. A she-wolf and a woodpecker adopted them and fed them until they were found by the herdsman Faustulus and his wife Acca Larentis.

Finally recognized as the grandson of Numitor, the twins slew Amulius, and Numitor became king again. The twins then founded the city of Rome. Romulus built a wall around the city and Remus jumped over it to show how contemptible it was. Romulus killed him for this and became the sole king of Rome. In his old age, Romulus disappeared during a storm. The Romans said that he had been changed into a god, whom they thereafter worshipped by the name of Quirinus.

Writers of the classical age rationalized that this story evolved from a desire to explain the founding of Rome. Far from Rome being named after Romulus, Romulus was invented to explain the name of Rome. The wolf and the woodpecker were both sacred to Mars, which explains why the legend-makers chose them as the nurses of the twins. Moreover, Acca Larentia, according to Livy, had loose morals; and she may have been referred to as a lupa, which means both she-wolf and whore. And so on.

No doubt something like this is the truth. However, as Lucien Malson has shown, human infants have been suckled by wolves and some flourished and grew to a healthy adulthood.

Tales similar to that of Romulus' and Remus' feral childhood are common all over the world in folktale, legend, and myth. Stories of animals giving protection and food to lost, abandoned, or kidnapped children have appeared in such distant places as Ireland, Zanzibar, Brazil, China, Canada, Greece, Indonesia, India, and Ceylon.

Pindar recounts the Greek legend of Iamos who, abandoned by his mother Evadne, was fed honey by serpents. Ptolemy I or Soter, Pharaoh of Egypt, was raised by an eagle. (This is the literary precedent of George Bruce's *Scream of the Condor,* though Bruce may never have heard of the tale.) The Gros Ventre Indians (the Atsina of the Plains of North America) had a tale of a boy adopted by seven buffalo bulls. A medieval European story relates that a baby girl was placed in an egg shell and hatched by snakes. Alexander the Great decided to take her as a mistress, but Aristotle, suspicious of her, put her inside a ring of snake venom and she strangled on its fumes. A good thing, too, because her kisses were full of venom.

THE FERAL HUMAN IN MYTHOLOGY AND FICTION

In Greco-Roman legends, Cycnus was fed by a swan; Hippothoos by a mare; Telephus, son of Hercules and Teuthras, by a deer; and in a Celtic tale, Lugaid MacCon is nourished by a dog. Since the names of each of these heroes is obviously derived from that of the creature which fed him, these tales arc undoubtedly eponymous and based on totemic animals.

Cybele was fed by leopards, Atalanta by a she-bear, and the Tewa Indian deer-boy by a deer. Paris of Troy, abandoned as an infant, was suckled by a bear until found by some shepherds. Cyrus of ancient Persia was suckled by a cow. Goats nourished the infants Aegisthus, Aesculapius, Phylacides, and Philandrus. The baby Zeus was suckled by a goat, though Robert Graves claims that Amaltheia was, in the original form of the myth, a nymph (priestess) of a college associated with the goat totem.

These legends and myths come from very ancient times. They were probably popular for thousands of years in one form or another before they were written down. Preliterate man regarded animals as different species of human beings, or vice versa. He thought it a fact of Nature that beasts would be likely to adopt human children and that they should have speech as eloquent as his own.

Perhaps some of these tales were founded in reality. What can happen and has happened in modern times could just as easily have happened at the dawn of history.

The literary history of the feral theme is a surprisingly long and full one. Richard Lupoff, in his *Edgar Rice Burroughs: Master of Adventure*, describes a detailed and scholarly essay on this subject written by Professor Rudolph Altrocchi. Altrocchi was a professor of Italian at the University of California; his forty-five-page essay on feralism was included in his *Sleuthing the Stacks,* issued by the Harvard University Press in 1944. In this, Altrocchi refers to an essay on the history of feralism which appeared in 1603. He cites a twelfth-century Arabic story, *Hayy ibn Yaqzan,* in which a boy is raised by a deer. Altrocchi traces this work to a tale, *Salaman and Absal,* by the great Persian philosopher and physician, Avicenna (980-1037 A.D.). Altrocchi also notes a reference to feralism in Shakespeare's *The Winter's Tale,* Act II, Scene iii. The courtier Antigonus is required by King Leontes of Sicilia to take Queen Hermione's baby to some remote desert place and cast her to the crows. Leontcs gives this cruel order because he believes his wife's baby is not his. Antigonus, a kind-hearted man, appeals to the animals to spare and to nourish her.

The baby, Perdita, is not adopted by the animals, though a bear does show up just as Antigonus places her on the seacoast of Bohemia. The bear chases and eats Antigonus. The baby is immediately found by a shepherd, who raises her as his daughter. Perdita, like so many foundlings (including Tarzan), eventually comes into her rightful inheritance and all ends happily.

It would be interesting to speculate the direction *The Winters Tale* might have taken if Shakespeare had decided to portray a Perdita who had been raised by bears. He has given us the deepest of insights into humans raised by humans; what might this genius have done if he had probed into a mind which was half-infrahuman?

Altrocchi's essay demonstrates conclusively that man has always had an interest in feralism. It was, however, Rudyard Kipling who started the modern tradition of feral man stories, or at least gave it its main impetus and direction. In *The Jungle Book* (1894), he sparked off the flood of stories based on this theme. His hero, Mowgli, is an Asiatic Indian infant raised by wolves and tutored by Baloo, a honey-bear, and Bagheera, a black leopard.

This splendid and truly classical work makes no attempt to be realistic. It is as mythical in form as the tale of Romulus and Remus. Its beasts speak a common language; their societies, though simple, are even more rigidly regulated by custom than any human society. And Mowgli, like the Roman twins and Tarzan, eventually returns to human society and marries.

If Kipling is the spring from which the modern tales flowed, it is Edgar Rice Burroughs who provided the floodwaters further down the stream. A number of feral human stories owe their origin to Mowgli, but by far the greatest number have obviously been inspired by Tarzan.

Many critics have claimed that the character of Tarzan was derived from Mowgli. Lupoff's study of Burroughs quotes a letter to Altrocchi (March 31, 1937) in which Burroughs says he himself has no clear memory of how he got the idea for Tarzan. He states that the story of Romulus and Remus may have been the main genesis. He also remembers vaguely reading a story about a shipwrecked sailor who had some hairy adventures with a band of apes on a South Pacific island. This was probably *Captured by the Apes,* Harry Prentice. Lupoff gives the date of publication as 1888 (the same year in which Tarzan was born). My copy gives the copyright year as 1892.

The truth is that Burroughs was purposely vague about the literary origins of Tarzan because there were none. Tarzan was based on a living person.

The fiction about feral humans can be put into three main categories. One type can be classified as pure fantasy for one reason or another. The second is in the category of realistic literature. The Tarzan novels are in neither and yet in both. They are founded on reality but contain many fantasy elements, such as talking monkeys and gorillas, animals which do not reside in the areas of Africa in which Burroughs has put them, genetic impossibilities, an incredible abundance of lost civilizations, a race of men eighteen inches high, and so on.

The third category is represented by a single short novel which is as yet unpublished in English and is almost unknown in Finland, where it originally appeared. This is *Karhun Tytär.*

I will ignore the many and varied short stories and comic books devoted to the theme of ferality. I will describe only modern novels, and I will not by any means cover the entire field.

The fantasy class can be broken down into two subgroups: the Mowgli-derived and the Tarzan-derived, though some contain elements of both.

Shasta of the Wolves by Olaf Baker is a Mowgli novel, as the reader knows.

Hathoo of the Elephants by Post Wheeler is an openly Kiplingesque book. It takes place in India, Mowgli's locale; and its hero, Hathoo, is the son of an English noble. In this respect only, the novel is Tarzanic. Hathoo, or Charles Wilberforce Moncrief Armistead, is the infant grandson of Lord Bleyden. He is kidnapped by a tiger, Raj' Bagh, who turns him over to a herd of elephants. Though the tiger kidnaps goats to provide the baby with milk, many kinds of beasts have a hand (or paw) in raising him. In the end, Hathoo, like "Lord Greystoke," comes into his British inheritance. Post Wheeler was an elegant and poetic writer and a professional diplomat who knew and loved the jungles of India. He also believed that animals did speak some sort of language. I highly recommend this work.

In the second category, the Tarzanic, I recommend two novels by an Englishman, C. T. Stoneham. These are *The Lion's Way* and *Kaspa the Lion Man.* Stoneham was thoroughly acquainted with East Africa, loved lions, and writes in a realistic and convincing manner. The hero, Kaspa Starke, is half-Canadian, half-Danish. At the age of two or three, his parents were murdered in Africa. He wandered into the bushes, after having been hidden by an Arab servant, and was adopted by a lioness who had just lost her cubs. Stoneham maintains that an infant could be taken into a lion family and could survive to manhood. He makes a good case for his thesis in the novel.

Unfortunately, Kaspa, deprived of all contact with human beings for eighteen years or so, would have been linguistically retarded.

Lord of the Leopards by F. A. M. Webster is about Kungai, or Hector Barrabal, an English boy, son of John and Janet Barrabal, missionaries in the Belgian Congo. Hector's parents were slain by the Leopard-Men Society; the Oriental nurse of the twins, Hector and Lysander, flees into the jungle. She takes refuge in a cave but is scared off and flees with Lysander, leaving Hector behind. Hector is adopted by a leopardess who names him Kungai. Webster's book is not as well-written or as realistically detailed as Stoneham's novels, but it is dramatic and colorful. It lacks, however, the satirical picture of civilization which Stoneham paints, using Kaspa as the Outsider. Kungai also did not encounter human language during the critical period of growth and so would have been retarded.

Jan of the Jungle by Otis Adelbert Kline first appeared in *Argosy* magazine (1931). It starts with a credible premise. Jan Trevor, an American infant, is kidnapped by Doctor Bracken shortly after birth. The doctor is a psychopath who hates Jan's mother because she has rejected him. Bracken raises Jan in Florida in a large cage with an old female chimpanzee. Bracken teaches the child only two words, "Mother!" and "Kill!" and conditions him to attack a dummy fashioned to resemble Jan's mother. He plans to release the boy at a suitable moment so he can enjoy Georgia Trevor's realization, just before her death, that it is her own son who is her killer.

So far, so good. But in this story, the chimpanzees have a

language and Kline adds even more fantastic elements as the story speeds along. I don't recommend this for the reality-bound or those who insist on psychological insights in their fiction.

On the same literary, or subliterary, level as *Jan of the Jungle* is *Ka-Zar, King of Fang and Claw*, by Bob Byrd. Ka-Zar, or David Rand, is raised by lions in the Belgian Congo.

Tam, Son of the Tiger, by Otis Adelbert Kline, combines the feral man theme with science fiction and is for adventure-story lovers only.

Giles Goat-Boy by John Barth is about a boy who has been raised by goats. There is not much of the feral man theme in this except as a foil to the science fiction setting. It is, however, recommended, since Barth is one of the best writers in America and the novel is as savagely satirical as Gulliver's Travels.

A novelette I recommend, despite its rough English translation, is *The Death of an Apeman* by Josef Nesvadba, a Czech author. Nesvadba uses a man raised by chimpanzees to mirror the hypocrisies of civilization. His hero is a German nobleman who is cheated out of his inheritance by his brother. Eventually, he commits suicide. I would have liked to have included this funny-sad tale, but the rights to it were too entangled in red tape.

One of the most interesting, though not very credible, feral man stories is *Dolphin Boy* by Roy Meyers. Its hero has been exposed to radiation while a fetus and so has become a mutation. His respiratory system is similar to that of a seal's and his skin glands excrete an oily film when he is in water. An explosion throws him into a school of dolphins and he is adopted by a female who has lost her own pup. The dolphin boy eventually encounters civilization and finds that it lacks the love and honesty of dolphin society. The book is convincingly and realistically detailed, though the reader may have difficulty accepting the mutation of John Averill.

Incident at Hawk's Hill by Allan W. Eckert is a book I highly recommend. Though not a story of true feralism, it does show that there is a solid basis for such stories. This is a slightly fictionalized version of an event which occurred in 1870 on a farm near Winnipeg, Manitoba, Canada. Ben MacDonald, six-years-old, runs away from home, makes friends with a female badger, and lives with her in her burrow for two months. When he is found and brought home, the badger tracks him to his house and becomes his pet. Strangely enough, the boy's stay with the beast makes a lasting change in his behavior. Where he has previously been very shy and alarmingly untalkative, he now becomes outward going and communicative.

Orme Sackville's *The Jungle Goddess* is one of those rare stories about a feral female. Miota is a girl about eighteen years old who has lived in the African jungle since she was four or five. Apparently, her parents were explorers; she doesn't remember her father, but she does remember that her mother was killed by a lion. The mystery of her parents' identity, however, is never cleared up. She is more or less adopted by a pack of jackals. At least, they protect and feed her until she is able to fend for herself, and they maintain a loose connection with her thereafter. She is as ferally strong and as arboreal as Tarzan and talks with the monkeys. She has invented a unique weapon, a noose made of poisoned thorns. She falls in love with a member of a film company lost in the jungle, Garth Haversham; but when he leaves, she prefers to stay in the jungle. However, the implications are that Haversham will one day return and either live with her in the wilds or convince her to go with him to civilization.

The novel is adequately written, the story is nothing new, but Sackville does a realistic job of portraying an amoral feral girl. Her amoralism is, however, innocent and blameless. Deprived of human ethical guidance, she can only follow the dictates of her emotions. If she likes you, she'll help you; if she doesn't, she is likely to kill you.

The second main category, that which deals with the feral man in a rigorously realistic fashion, is represented solely by Eyton's *Jungle-Born*. Its protagonist is an Asiatic Indian infant whose peasant parents have been killed by a tiger. He is adopted by a monkey who has lost her own infant. The author calls him Nanga, meaning the Naked One, though this is only an auctorial label. Nanga and a native girl he meets go to live in the jungle and will apparently be happy together. However, the reader can draw his own conclusions about this. Since Nanga cannot communicate with Parmala except by signs and grunts, how is he going to keep her happy?

Some might doubt that it is realistic to suppose an infant could be raised by monkeys. Probably, very few would survive, but the record of authentic cases shows that some have lived through even more severe conditions. Also, the members of a monkey tribe take a tender and solicitous attitude toward the infants.

The final feral story to be described is in a class by itself. It could be classified as realistic, along with *Jungle-Born*, but it can't be said to have been influenced by Mowgli or Tarzan. It is also the only feral human story I know of which was written by a woman. This is *Karhun Tytär* (translation: *The Bear's Daughter*) by Liisa Jalava. A copy of this short novel was sent to me recently by a friend who was touring Finland. He got his copy from a Finnish friend who had inherited it from his grandfather. I'd never heard of it, which isn't surprising, since it's never been translated. It has no publication date, but the preface by the authoress indicates that it was written in 1887. She was married, the mother of three children, and forty-five years old. Apparently, it was her first and only book. My friend's investigations revealed that the publisher had gone out of business about 1906.

My ability to read Finnish is far from fluent, but frequent references to a Finnish-English dictionary have enabled me to grasp its spirit.

Karhum Tytär should be translated into English and published. It is a realistically and yet poetically told narrative, free of Victorian turgidity and moralism, sparing of adjective. Eeva Kivi, the heroine, is five years old and lives with her father, a trapper, and her stepmother in the far north of Finland, near the Swedish border. She escapes a cabin fire which kills her parents. After wandering around in the summer night, she meets a bear who has lost her cubs. In a scene reminiscent of Ben's encounter with the female badger in *Incident at Hawk's Hill*, she is accepted by the bear and lives with her until the she-bear dies. The account of Ecva's physical and mental survival is convincingly detailed and indicates that Mrs. Jalava must have lived in the northern woods herself. Eeva talks to herself, the bears, and a number of animals with whom she becomes friends or at least establishes a peaceful relationship.

Eeva's use of grammar stays throughout her childhood and adolescence at the five-year level. But she adds to her limited vocabulary by making up names for objects and feelings as she first encounters them. These are based on words she knew at the age of five or consist of nonsense syllables which follow the Finnish pattern of morphology and syntax. By this device, Mrs. Jalava enables her heroine to pass successfully through the critical period of language development. Unlike the authentic feral humans studied, Eeva is not linguistically retarded.

It's doubtful that Mrs. Jalava was aware of this critical stage in language learning. It was inspiration from her unconscious that let her hit upon this ingenious and necessary device. It is, however, possible that Jalava may have reasoned that a child cut off from human society for many years would forget her language unless she used herself as both speaker and auditor.

The words invented by Eeva caused me some trouble because they were not in the dictionary. When I caught on to what she was doing, I reread the portions I hadn't understood. Then I discovered that Jalava had clearly indicated the referents for the invented words.

Jalava's novel was ahead of its time in its portrayal of the psychology of the feral child and of the human female. Her frankness and unconventional observations must have shocked her Victorian Lutheran contemporaries, though a modern reader would find her unoffensive. She also seems to have been well acquainted with Laplander culture. Her heroine falls in love with a Lapland hunter but is unable to adjust to his culture. Pregnant, she flees back into the dark forest.

The modern novels I've described have heroes or heroines whose foster parents are wolves, jackals, bears, lions, tigers, leopards, elephants, chimpanzees, monkeys, or dolphins.

Could any of these beasts actually raise a human child to maturity? Dolphins and elephants can be dismissed at once for obvious reasons. If the well-known case of Lukas, the baboon-boy of South Africa, is authentic, then it can be assumed that chimpanzees could also rear an infant. Or, for that matter, since cases of wolf-boys seem authentic, a chimpanzee-boy seems even more possible. It is even possible that the monkeys of *Jungle-Born*, who were of a very large species, could successfully raise an infant.

Stoneham tells of a supposedly true case of an African man, exiled from his tribe, who lived and hunted with a lioness for several years. His account of Kaspa's adoption and how he managed to survive is based on the case of this man. But the man was an adult and the lioness was his partner, not a foster mother. Cub mortality is so high in prides that it seems unlikely that Kaspa could have lived to manhood.

The same can be said for the children raised by tigers and leopards in Kline's and Webster's novels. The odds would be a thousand to one against survival. But then there is Victor of Aveyron, who lived through even more natural vicissitudes than Kaspa and Kungai.

In my own judgment, it is extremely unlikely that an infant would last long in a big-cat society. He might be adopted, provided that he encountered a nursing mother who had just lost her cubs. The mothering instinct seems to be strong in many animals, as witness the validated cases of dogs who nurse kittens and rabbits and reports of wild lionesses who have nursed puppies. Most probably, however, the big cat would eat the infant. In any event, there is no authenticated case of any big cat having adopted an infant.

A nursing chimpanzee or baboon might suckle an infant. But wild chimpanzees are very shy and would probably not go near a human stranger, infant or not. Baboons are a favorite prey of leopards and a fleeing mother would be much hampered by the weight of a human baby. Moreover, when the infant had grown to a large size, he would be regarded as a competitor by the very jealous males.

On reflection, I would say that wolves and bears make the best candidates for foster parents. The accounts of authentic cases of wolf-reared children indicate that *Canis lupus* is the favorite candidate. Bears as foster parents figure frequently in folktales and legends, and it is possible that they have actually adopted infants. Still, granting that a bear might make a good mother, it does hibernate. How would a child get food in the winter?

The counterquestion to this is, How did Victor of Aveyron get food in the winters of eighteenth-century France? The climate was even colder then and he didn't steal it from humans. But he did get it and he flourished, though at the cost of loss of speech.

If Victor could survive all alone, a child with animals as companions, protectors, and mentors would have an even better chance of survival.

IRONING OUT
THE KINKS

SOME PROBLEMS IN WRITING
THE TARZAN BIOGRAPHY

This is the first of two versions of what is essentially the same article. First, we have the piece as submitted by Farmer. Included is the friendly, and interesting in itself, covering letter Phil sent to Caz (Camille Cazedessus Jr.), then editor of *ERB-dom*. The bonhomie exhibited in Phil's missive illustrates the clique that existed around the love of Burroughs and how writers, particularly Farmer, strived to explore and understand more about the heroes they revered so much.

Although there is a great deal of overlap between this piece and the one that follows, there is enough of a difference to make it of interest and it is always interesting to see the maturation of an article from submission to final publication.

Feb. 21, 1972
Philip José Farmer

Dear Caz:

Here's an article I ripped off when I should have been writing fiction. On rereading, I see it's not as polished as it should be, but out it goes.

If, however, it is too long, please send it back, and I'll cut it down. Or break it up into a series of shorter articles. I could easily write an article this long on *Untamed* or *The Outlaw of Torn* or any of a score of subjects. And I had to restrain myself to keep this from being ten pages long.

Kaor,
Phil

P.S. I've often wondered why ERB didn't tell us the great ape equivalent of "kaor"? Perhaps the mangani speech lacked a greeting; the mere fact that you were visible was enough. And speaking the name of the one you were addressing, or using a slight call, might be sufficient.

The premise that Tarzan is a living person, and not a fictional character, removes him from the rules which have governed the researches of ERB scholars up until now.

That is the basic premise of my work, *Tarzan Alive, A Definitive Biography of Lord Greystoke*, Doubleday, April, 1972, $5.95.

For one thing, this premise makes inadmissible any writings on the origin of the idea of Tarzan. ERB did not derive the ape-man from Romulus or Remus or Kipling's Mowgli or Prentice's *Captured by Apes* or any of the dozen or so sources so far advanced. ERB got the idea of Tarzan from Tarzan himself (admittedly, at first, through a second-hand source).

ERB may have stated that Romulus and Remus sparked the creation of Tarzan and that a human baby could not have lasted a week under the conditions depicted in *Tarzan of the Apes*. But we can safely ignore these remarks. As I show in *Tarzan Alive*, ERB deliberately did his best to disguise certain facts that might have led the curious to uncover the real identity of the ape-man. He also moved Opar's location around in several books, making it impossible to say with any certainty that it is anywhere except somewhere in central Africa.

I doubt that anybody would deny that ERB wrote fictionized versions of Tarzan's adventures. It remains for the scholar to separate the fiction from the verity. Fortunately, it's possible to declare certain novels as almost all fiction. Some can be shown to be almost completely true, such as *Tarzan and the Leopard Men*. Some, such as the first two, *Tarzan of the Apes* and *The Return of Tarzan*, are true in the framework of events. But ERB did not know many of the details, and some of his guesses about them were wide of the mark.

SOME PROBLEMS IN WRITING THE TARZAN BIOGRAPHY

My biography contains a chronology of Tarzan's life. A difficulty that I thought at first was insuperable was the fitting of *Tarzan at the Earth's Core* into its proper sequence between *Tarzan and the Lost Empire* (occurring April–July, 1927) and *Tarzan the Invincible* (occurring Jan.–May, 1929). The Zeppelin 0-220 took off on its maiden flight on a June morning, 1927. The chronology just won't work out, as a comparison of the above dates will show.

Furthermore, if Harbenite did exist, it would be well-known by now, considering how thoroughly explored Africa is. And if the Earth were indeed hollow, modern science would long ago have established that fact. ERB felt like writing a novel which would take Tarzan to the Earth's core, but the real Tarzan, we may be sure, was in England or Africa at this time. No doubt, he enjoyed ERB's fantasy when it arrived through the mail from Tarzana.

The Minunian part of *Tarzan and the Ant Men* is certainly fictional (and the Alalus part is probably fictional). The existence of the 18-inch high humans is theoretically possible. But the change of size in Tarzan is clearly not. The energy requirements are too high, literally of astronomic demands. The power needed to shrink Tarzan to Minunian stature could not be supplied by the sun.

However, classifying *Ant Men* as fiction, as with *Earth's Core*, solves a problem. It removes a discrepancy that's vexed Tarzanic scholars for a long time. In *Tarzan the Untamed*, Tarzan is an unskilled swordsman. In *Ant Men*, which follows *Untamed* in time, he is an excellent swordsman, having been instructed by that great bladesman, d'Arnot. (Who, no doubt, is descended from d'Artagnan or de Bergerac. Or both.) In *Tarzan and the Lost Empire*, he is again inept with the sword. How do we explain this?

Obviously, when ERB was writing the fictional Minunian story, he forgot that Tarzan was not a good swordsman. He was writing a science-fiction satire (and a very good one, too), and he did not have to pay much attention to Tarzan's character. With *Untamed* and *Lost Empire*, he was more involved with reality and so paid closer attention to the facts of Tarzan's abilities.

There are a number of contrary-to-fact elements in the two latter novels, which we won't go into here. But Tarzan's character is consistently presented in these.

Must I go into the details of the Great Korak-Time Discrepancy Controversy? Surely, all ERB aficionados are aware of the arguments that have raged about this in all the ERB-zines. Some fans have displayed an attitude towards ERB's writings that is generally only to be found in those of the very orthodox, the most fundamentalistic, towards the Bible. But those of us who regard ERB as human—albeit a genius—and not divine, know that you can't shut your eyes to certain contradictions of time implicit in *The Beasts of Tarzan*, *The Son of Tarzan* and *Tarzan the Terrible*. Korak could not be born circa 1912 (as in *Beasts*), yet be about ten years old circa 1913 (as in *Son*), and fight at the battle of the Argonne in 1918 (as in *Terrible*). Also, *Son* was written in 1915, but the events in *Son* take place over a period of about ten years. Which means that they begin in 1912 or -13 and end in 1922 or -23.

John Harwood and H. W. Starr have offered two explanations. One, which they do not advance seriously, is that *Son* may be entirely fictional. The other, the only theory so far advanced which will stand up under examination, is that the Korak of *Son* is an adopted relative. Harwood and Starr suggest that the baby that died in *Beasts* was really Tarzan's son but that ERB changed the facts because his readers would not like it if little Jack died. I reject this. Otherwise, how do you account for the "youthful" Jack in *The Eternal Lover*? (ERB's use of this adjective is not standard, since Jack would be about two years old when the Custers visited the Greystokes in June–July, 1914. But Webster's says that ERB's use is permissible.)

As an aside, *The Eternal Lover* is mainly a true book. But most of the events in it, though they did occur, did not take place outside the fantasies of Victoria Custer. ERB says that she was "an exceptionally normal well-balanced young American woman." But in the next paragraph he makes it obvious that she is a deeply disturbed woman and that the origin of this disturbance is a fear of sex. Or she is unhealthily attached to her brother, Barney. The undeniable indications are that she had a mental breakdown which was brought on by her dread of earthquakes and by her abduction by the evil Arabs of ibn Aswad. No doubt, after she was rescued, she raved in her madness about Nu of the Neocene. Nu was a sexual fantasy, created by her and desirable because of his very nonexistence and unattainability. The narrator (who certainly wasn't ERB since ERB was never in Africa) later on told ERB of these fantasies. And from these ERB fashioned *The Eternal Lover*. Other explanations are possible, and welcomed, but any statement that *Lover* is a straightforward narrative of fact can be easily demolished.

Back to *Son*. It's true that Jane says in *Son* that she fears Jack has inherited his primitive traits from Tarzan. But Tarzan says that he doubts that such could be transmitted from father to son. This conversation, and other statements indicating that Jack is indeed Tarzan's true son, are creations of ERB. Since he is fictionizing certain aspects of Korak's story, he would insert statements which would lead the reader to believe that this is Tarzan's true son. Few readers would ever deduce that there had to be two young John Claytons, one of them adopted.

My reasoning that Korak is Tarzan's cousin, the younger brother of Bulldog Drummond, is detailed in *Tarzan Alive*. Readers are free to reject this theory and to offer another candidate. But they are not free to reject the "adopted son" theory. Nor can they successfully reject the fact that the events of *Son* have to be compressed within, at most, two years, and that they probably took place within a year. These time limits bring up other problems, such as why Meriem would have forgotten her French in only a year or indeed would have forgotten being abducted by Arabs or would have forgotten her parents' name or her own name. But this can be explained as due to amnesia brought on by the trauma of abduction and her cruel treatment by the Arabs.

ERB explains certain attitudes and actions of Tarzan as due to genetic heredity. He accounts for Tarzan's rejection of cannibalism (as with Kulonga) and his chivalrous treatment of Jane after rescuing her from Terkoz as inherent traits. His noble British ancestry influenced him. But it is highly probable that Tarzan's Stone Age forefathers ate human flesh with, if not relish, gusto. As for chivalry, as for innate goodness, those familiar with the history of the English people and the English nobility just cannot believe ERB's explanation. The English are just as rotten—and as good—as any other people. No more, no less.

In looking for other explanations, we must remember that ERB had only a sketchy knowledge of Tarzan's story when he wrote *Tarzan of the Apes*. The "I" of *Apes* is not ERB, who was never in England. It is a man who learned of Tarzan in the way described in *Apes* and then related what he knew to ERB in Chicago.

ERB had the framework from "I"; the details were made up by him. At that time his knowledge of Africa was confined to what he'd read in Du Chaillu and Stanley and a few others. This is why the original magazine version has Sabor, the tiger, in Africa, which in reality knows the tiger only as an animal imported from Asia for safekeeping in a zoo. This is why the names of the animals, most of the mangani speech, and the names of Mbonga's people were made up by ERB. This is why we have lions and rhinoceroses in a part of Africa which just does not have them.

ERB was, first and foremost, a storyteller, a romanticizer. That is why, in *Apes*, whenever we see *lion* we should read *leopard*. Lions are bigger and stronger than leopards, and so Tarzan is an even mightier champion when he defeats them. I submit that anyone who can break the neck of a leopard with a full-Nelson needs no exaggeration of his prowess. According to Jean-Pierre Hallet, leopards are, pound for pound, the strongest animals in the world. And, according to Trader Horn, the Gabon jungle harbors leopards as big as some lionesses.

ERB was not satisfied with reality. Another instance of this is that the ape-man's real name is something like Zantar. This was so written in the original Ms but ERB changed it to Tarzan, no doubt because it was more euphonious than Zantar.

Despite his fictionizing tendencies, ERB never deviated from reality in portraying Tarzan's character. There is no doubt that he did not eat Kulonga or that he treated Jane much as described. My explanation for this is that he was literate. He had undoubtedly read in his father's library a number of novels and various classics, including a children's version of *Morte d'Arthur*. No doubt he was puzzled by some parts of these because of his lack of referents. But, like Don Quixote, he would have believed in the ideals of civilized society. And he would have conducted himself according to them when he met Jane.

Tarzan was indeed the "parfit gentil knight" of the Jungle, and those who sneer at his chivalry do so because they have not taken the trouble to study the epics by ERB.

I cannot describe here many of the problems met in explaining seeming discrepancies in the epics. To describe even half of them would make this article too long. I believe that *Tarzan Alive* contains strong evidence for naming Tarzan's birthdate (a few minutes after midnight of November 22, 1888), for pinpointing the true location of his birthplace, for believing that G. B. Shaw in his novel, *An Unsocial Socialist*, was portraying Tarzan's paternal grandparents in fictional disguise, for classifying *Tarzan at the Earth's Core*, *Tarzan and the Forbidden City*, *Tarzan and the Lion Man*, *Tarzan and the Ant Men*, and the novelets, "Tarzan and the Castaways" and "Tarzan and the Champion," and the short story, "Tarzan Rescues the Moon" as almost entirely fictitious. There is strong evidence advanced that others, such as *Tarzan the Untamed*, *Tarzan the Terrible*, *Tarzan, Lord of the Jungle*, are based on true events but highly romanticized in the telling.

Knowing this should not detract from any reader's entertainment. Indeed, the closer a Tarzan book is to reality, the less entertaining it is (generally speaking). Thus, *Tarzan and the Leopard Men*, the truest, is the dullest. (This excepts *Forbidden City*, which, in my opinion, is an abomination and should never have been published. Why ERB permitted this work to go into hardcover without correction of the many errors made by the magazine editors in their rewriting is beyond me.)

One problem which I have not yet been able to solve is that of the red tarry poison used on the arrows of Mbonga's tribe. I have found a description of such a poison in Du Chaillu's *Explorations and Adventures in Equatorial Africa*, Harper, N.Y., 1861. (It's highly probable that ERB read this.) The poison was used by the Fän (Fang, Fon) people, but its origin and preparation were kept secret by the Fän. My perusal of many books on Africa, botany, and poisons and my written inquiries to a number of authorities have resulted in a blank. Has any reader come across any information about this poison?

Many of the findings and explanations in the biography are mine. Others I owe to articles or letters written to me by ERBian scholars.

Where this is so, I give credit. Sometimes, I formed theories or made discoveries only to find that I had been anticipated in some ERBzine years before I started to subscribe to them. Thus, I had independently arrived at the conclusion that Tarzan was born at 2° S latitude, not 10° S. In such cases, I felt no obligation to give credit, though I sometimes did so anyway. This biography is peculiar in that, due to space limitations, and to a consideration for the general reader, I did not always give reasons for my conclusions. Thus, instead of basing a book on articles already written, I will have to write articles after the publication of the book. This reverses the general procedure.

I expect much controversy after the publication of *Tarzan Alive*. Whether or not I am vindicated, the controversy should generate a flood of articles and pour fresh blood into the sometimes jaded arguments published in ERBzines. I've gone over the four manuscript versions of the biography and the galleys many times. But last week I reread the final Ms version and detected several errors. I also found a number of things that I wish I'd changed somewhat. If a revised edition can be brought out a few years from now, I'll make the necessary changes. The book is not perfect by any means. It is a tour de force, and it took an immense amount of labor and time on my part. But it would not be as good as it is, whatever "good" means in this case, without the labors of other workers in the field.

I'd like to stress again in closing that ERB did produce fictionized versions of Tarzan's true adventures. But he never deviated from a consistent portrayal of the unique character of the immortal ape-man. Throughout all the epics, Tarzan himself rings true.

THE GREAT
KORAK-TIME DISCREPANCY

One can only imagine the conversations (verbal or written) that were exchanged between Phil and Caz following Farmer's submission of his letter and this article, which appeared about a month later (in *ERB-dom*, Number 57, April 1972). But one can deduce from what was actually printed in *ERB-dom* that Caz took Phil up on his offer to split the article and expand on a specific element, and so this article concerns itself solely with the Korak conundrum. Much of the facts here replicate those Phil published in *Tarzan Alive* but this is a fresh retelling of his conclusions.

The tone, too, is different between the two pieces. What was a more genial conversational style has changed to reportage and thesis.

In "The Great Korak-Time Discrepancy," Farmer presents the questions left inadvertently unanswered by Burroughs in *The Son of Tarzan*. Was Tarzan born in 1872 or 1888? Is Korak the adopted son of Tarzan? How could Tarzan's friend d'Arnot be a French naval lieutenant in 1909 and yet an admiral in 1914? The answers may not please all Burroughs scholars, but Farmer's love and enthusiasm for these stories and characters will.

Tarzan is a living person.
  This is the basic premise of my *Tarzan Alive, A Definitive Biography of Lord Greystoke* (Doubleday, 1972).

This premise that Tarzan is not a fictional character makes inadmissible any speculation about the literary origin of Tarzan. Romulus and Remus, Kipling's Mowgli, Prentice's *Captured by Apes* and the dozen or so other sources so far advanced as the sources from which Burroughs derived his idea of Tarzan have no relevance to reality.

Since this premise removes Tarzan from the realm of fantasy it requires that the stories about him be examined for their fidelity to fact. Or to what we can classify as fact, admitting that evidence may be uncovered in the future which will force us to reclassify.

With this in mind, we can reread the Tarzan epics by Burroughs. And we can place some in the category of largely fictitious, some in the half-true, and some in the nearly all true. Few, for instance, would deny that almost all of *Tarzan at the Earth's Core* and most of *Tarzan and the Ant Men* is fiction. The reasons for these conclusions will, however, be dealt with in separate essays.

This essay is devoted to the epic about which the most controversy has raged in the world of Tarzanic scholarship: *The Son Of Tarzan*. This storm is not due to ambiguous or obscure statements by Burroughs or lack of pertinent data. No, certain facts are clear enough. But certain scholars have refused to admit these facts, and they have done so because of emotional factors.

These people cannot admit that Jack Clayton, or Korak, cannot be Tarzan's son.

The Great Korak-Time Discrepancy Controversy must be old ground for most of the readers of this publication. For the benefit of the new, I'll go over the familiar material. However, I'll introduce some aspects not considered before. And I'll then go on to an examination of other features of the book. (My textual source is the 1918 A. L. Burt reprint edition.)

The Son of Tarzan, written in 1915, is a sequel to *The Beasts Of Tarzan*. In *Beasts*, Tarzan's and Jane's son is a babe in arms, and, from all internal evidence, is less than a year old. Burroughs does not say so, but it is evident that Jane is nursing the baby she carries with her in her flight from Rokoff. This baby is the same age as little Jack.

The events in *Beasts* must take place in 1911 or, at the earliest, in late 1910. In *Son*, Sabrov, a Russian, is rescued after ten years as a captive in an African cannibal village. Burroughs says that his real name was Paulvitch, though he does not say how he could have known that. Sabrov never told anyone that his real name was not Sabrov. Thus, if Burroughs is writing a novel based on certain events which did, in fact, happen, he had no way of knowing that Sabrov was Tarzan's old enemy. But it would make for a fine dramatic point to have Sabrov be Paulvitch, and Burroughs, first and foremost a storyteller, would not be likely to let such drama go by.

Burroughs does state that it is ten years since the events in *Beasts*. This means that Sabrov is rescued from the cannibals circa 1921.

In *Son*, Jack (Korak) must be ten or eleven years old. He is a remarkably powerful youth, since he can subdue his young male tutor with ease. A few months after this, he strangles to death with his bare hands an adult native. This man is presumably much more powerful than the tutor and is fighting for his life.

A year later, Korak, himself only eleven or twelve years old, throws the eleven-year old Meriem across his shoulder and leaps nimbly into the lower branches of a tree. A year or two later (Burroughs is vague about the exact time), Korak fights a mighty mangani male with his bare hands and teeth and rips open the great bull's jugular vein. Immediately after follows a scene in which it is obvious that both Korak and Meriem are well into puberty. This is succeeded by a scene in which Korak uses fists to beat another giant bull into near-unconsciousness.

All of the above except one are just barely credible. It's possible that Korak could carry Meriem as easily as Burroughs says, that Korak and Meriem were coming into sexual maturity, and that Korak was skilled enough and powerful enough to hammer a bull great ape into submission. But it is difficult to believe that any human's teeth, let alone a twelve year old male's, could bite through the hair and thick skin and jugular vein of a massively muscled anthropoid the size of a gorilla. Especially while the anthropoid was tearing away with his hands at Korak. The great apes are described by Burroughs as being equal to a gorilla in strength, and a gorilla's strength has been estimated as equal to at least ten men's strength.

I don't doubt that Korak did win in his fights. But I think it's likely that Burroughs was gilding the lily for story purposes and that Korak used his knife and may even have had some help from Meriem and her spear. Even so, these feats would be remarkable and would need no exaggerating to get our admiration and respect.

Meriem, or Jeanne Jacot, is ten years old when Korak is forced to flee London with Akut, the great ape. When the book ends, she is sixteen. Thus Korak would have been in the jungle for almost six years. He was also sixteen. It would not be discreet to ask why Korak's parents permitted their son to marry at such an early age.

It is permissible to wonder about the Honourable Morison Baynes. He must have been at least 21 years old and was probably at least 25, judging from his considerable hedonistic experience on the Continent and his sophistication. Yet he estimates that Korak was his own age or possibly older. This can be explained as due to Korak's unusual large size, an accelerated maturity due to the rigors of jungle living, and the possibility of a beard. Burroughs says nothing about Korak shaving, so we can at least speculate that he could have had facial hair. Some youths do get rather heavy beards at sixteen. Tarzan didn't; he does not seem to have had to shave until he was about twenty.

In *Tarzan The Terrible*, Korak is old enough to fight during the Meuse-Argonne operation (Sept-Nov, 1918).

Peter Ogden, editor of *Erbania*, has published a theory to account for the Korak-Time Discrepancy.[1] He says that Burroughs could have given the wrong date for Tarzan's birth in *Tarzan of the Apes*. He would have done this as one more cover for the true identity of Lord Greystoke. And, working backwards from 1914, so that the chronology of *Son* will be consistent with reality, Ogden figures that Tarzan was probably born in 1872.

(It's not relevant, but is interesting, to note that 1872 was the year of Phileas Fogg's amazing dash around the world and of the mysterious case of the *Marie Celeste*. I am presently working on a book which will tie the two together.[2])

Thus, Tarzan could have met Jane by 1893 and married her in 1895. Korak would have been born in 1895 and would be ten years old in 1905. He and Meriem would've married in 1911.

Ogden's theory raises more problems than it solves, and these will be dealt with in my essay on *Tarzan of the Apes*. However, after all the evidence for the 1888 or 1872 theories is in, neither can be "proved." The reader is free to choose whichever he prefers. What he is not free to choose as the truth, if he insists on being logical, is Burroughs' version of *Son* in its entirety.

The central insurmountable fact that *Son* was written in 1915

---

[1] This is further explored in the next article, "A Reply to 'The Red Herring.'"

[2] This was published by DAW in 1973 as *The Other Log of Phileas Fogg*.

means that all events in *Son* have to have taken place before Burroughs started writing it. Korak married Meriem before 1915, when both were sixteen. If Korak was sixteen in 1914, he would have been born in 1898. Tarzan did not meet Jane until Feb. 1909 (see *Tarzan of the Apes*).

The Burroughsian has two choices. Believe Ogden's theory or believe Harwood-Starr's. If you choose the latter, then you must accept as a fact the adoption of a boy born about 1898 by Tarzan and Jane. Probably, he would have been a close relative who had been orphaned. In my book *Tarzan Alive*, I opt for Bulldog Drummond's younger brother, John. (That is, for the younger brother of the man on whom the fictional character of Bulldog Drummond was based. Do not, however, be misled by the statement of McNeile that this man was Gerard Fairlie.) My reasons for this are developed in *Tarzan Alive*; to present them here would expand this essay to too great a length. But the reader may examine the evidence presented in my biography and say yea or nay to it.

Harwood and Starr also suggest that Tarzan's son really was the baby who died in *Beasts* and that Burroughs suppressed this and distorted other facts to give the book the happy ending which he knew his readers would demand. I reject this. Otherwise, how do you account for the "youthful Jack" in *The Eternal Lover*?

I believe that Tarzan's real son lived but that we shall never know anything about him except what Burroughs tells us in *Beasts* and *Lover*. Because of having presented Korak as Tarzan's true son in *Son*, Burroughs was obliged to leave out any reference to the true son thereafter in the novels. At the time, Burroughs may have thought that this was a small price to pay, since Jackie was a baby and it would be many years before he, too, could have adventures and so become a worthy subject of Burroughs' fictionalized biographies. But I wonder if, around the time of World War II, he did not regret this. Surely, the real Jack Clayton III, first in line to the title of Greystoke, must have been a remarkable man in his own right. Nor do we have to suppose that Tarzan and Jane had no other children after him just because Burroughs does not mention them. If the Claytons had daughters, for instance, we may be sure that they would have been tall, lovely, and grey-eyed and very capable of taking care of themselves.

The Son of Tarzan has to end in 1914, before August of that year. From August on, Tarzan was looking for Jane until after the end of World War I. The chronology of *The Eternal Lover* indicates clearly that the Custers were visiting the Greystokes at their plantation in 1914 not too long before WWI broke out. Tarzan's baby son and Esmeralda were present then; Korak and Meriem, if present, are not mentioned by Burroughs. But they were undoubtedly still in Europe, visiting Meriem's parents. Tarzan and Jane would have accompanied them to England first, as indicated at the end of *Son*, and then would have returned to Africa, where they were visited by the Custers. For some reason, Esmeralda took young Jackie to England, since the two were not at the plantation when it was destroyed by the Germans (in *Tarzan the Untamed*). Perhaps the "business" which Tarzan was attending to in Nairobi when *Untamed* opened was sending Esmeralda and Jackie away to England or France.

Beasts seems to have ended about the middle of 1912. Since *Son* would have started not too many months later, it is obvious that Paulvitch could not have been a prisoner of the cannibals for ten years. And it is obvious that Sabrov is not Paulvitch. Harwood-Starr's surmise that Burroughs identified Sabrov as Paulvitch for dramatic reasons is the only reasonable theory so far advanced. Even if Paulvitch had disguised his appearance, he would not have been able to conceal his individual body odor, and Tarzan would have identified him immediately.

What did happen to Paulvitch?

We'll never know. If his name had been Pyotrvitch (Peterson), I'd be inclined to think that he had made his way back to Europe, had become a master at disguise, no doubt to ensure that Tarzan would never hear of him, had become as powerful as the late Professor Moriarty, and died (supposedly) in a flaming dirigible in 1927 after he'd tangled once too often with Korak's older brother.

Paulvitch, by the way, is not a standard Russian name. It should be Pavlovitch or Pavlitch. However, it is possible that Paulvitch's grandfather was a Frenchman, perhaps a captured French soldier who settled down in Russia after Napoleon's defeat, and Paulvitch was his hybrid Gall-Russian name.

Many opponents of the "adopted relative" theory point to the numerous references in *Son* to Korak's inheritance of his father's traits. But Burroughs would have made these up and inserted them in the novel to strengthen the premise that Korak was Tarzan's issue. The novel is consistent within its own framework, though there are some curious things to consider.

Captain Jacot, Meriem's father, is a grey-haired general at the end of the book, an "old man." In nine years he has gone from a seemingly vigorous young man and captain to an aging general. And d'Arnot, a naval lieutenant in *Apes*, which ended in 1909, is, in 1914, an admiral.

John F. Roy, in *ERB-dom* #18, has explained the latter promotion. He says that Admiral d'Arnot could be the father of Tarzan's good friend. As for Jacot, it is true that Burroughs does not specify his age at the time when Meriem (Jeanne) was kidnapped. He could have been a vigorous fifty or so. And that he could see further than his men, that they called him for this reason the Hawk, may have been due to the long-sightedness brought on by middle age. And it is possible that a combination of fortunate events, good connections, and his outstanding military record, did advance him to a generalship.

Another problem. How did Korak, who was only ten, when *Son* began, according to Burroughs (but fourteen according to my estimate) manage in one day to get false passports for himself and Akut? He had the money to flee England, but how did he make the necessary connections with the criminal world?

Also, Burroughs says that Tarzan would not tell Korak the location of his African plantation? Would not a boy with Korak's driving interest in such matters have found out?

The *Marjorie W.*, which picked Sabrov up, was chartered by a scientific expedition. Why would the scientists aboard have permitted Sabrov to walk off with Akut, obviously a specimen of a hitherto unknown genus of great ape? (Or, if my theory is right that the mangani were hominids akin to Australopithecus robustus, the uniqueness of Akut would have been even more apparent.)

It is probable, however, that the scientists were botanists and chemists so unqualified in anthropoid identification. And Sabrov's claims to Akut as his property could easily have prevented any attempt by the scientists to obtain Akut for their uses. But Sabrov and his property did have considerable publicity after getting to

London. It is difficult to understand why scientists there would not have known that Akut was something new in the zoological world. Perhaps they did, but, again, Sabrov refused to recognize anything but the jurisdiction of private property.

This matter can be cleared up by examining the London *Times* of this period (say, from 1911 through 1913 to cover a broad enough area). If no such case is mentioned in the papers, then the next step is to admit that perhaps Ogden's theory of Tarzan's birth in 1872 is right. *The Times* for the period of 1893 through 1896 should be covered for items about Akut or a reasonable facsimile thereof.

Would anyone, even in the slums of London, have taken in such a lodger as Akut? Especially when Akut does not seem to have been locked up in a manner to satisfy the public as to its safety? Would not the police have been called in by the terrified tenants of the house where Sabrov and his "pet" lived?

Perhaps not, if Sabrov had greased enough palms. And it is possible that Akut was much more restrained during transit between the East End lodgings and the theater than Burroughs implies. It was only during the theater shows and in Sabrov's room that Akut had any comparative freedom.

Another problem is Jane's concern about Korak's clothes after hearing that he has been found. She wants Tarzan to take to Korak one of his "little suits" that she has saved. This would indicate that a long time has elapsed, since Tarzan says that Korak has grown so big that he would fit only into one of Tarzan's own suits. But this little scene is, again, one of the fictions of Burroughs to make the novel consistent in its own framework. Even so, it's doubtful that Korak, big enough at the age of ten to overpower his tutor would have been wearing a little suit when he disappeared.

The ability of the monkeys and the baboons (who are really monkeys and not apes) to speak should be examined. But this will be taken up in a separate essay.

There are some problems about the location of the Greystoke plantation, but this will be dealt with in the essay on *Tarzan the Untamed*.

Meriem, at ten, is the Sheikh's prisoner in a small native village "hidden away upon the banks of a small unexplored tributary of a large river that empties into the Atlantic not so far from the equator . . ." (*Son*, p. 63). Here the Sheikh's tribe collects goods and twice a year carries them on camels to Timbuktu. An examination of the (Michelin) maps of Africa fails to locate any river which will fill the above requirements. The only large river near the equator which empties into the Atlantic is the Congo. Any small tributary of the Congo which emptied into the Atlantic would be about 1800 miles on a straight line from Timbuktu. A caravan route would cover two or three times that distance, perhaps four times 1800 miles. Moreover, no camels could traverse the thousands of miles of heavy jungle, rugged hills, and many rivers between the tributary and Timbuktu (which is in the present nation of Mali). Burroughs could not have meant that the tributary was one of the Congo's inland rivers, because Korak found Meriem in a village near the coast. The text clearly indicates this.

However, about 1500 miles from the equator (northwards), in the German Kamerun (the Cameroons), ibn Khatour's tribe might have had a headquarters. They would have been fairly close to Korak, who probably disembarked at Douala. Even so, the tribe still would have had to travel through considerable jungle and it would have been about 1200 miles (in a straight line) from Timbuktu. A year later, both Meriem and Korak were on the other side of Africa, near the Greystoke plantation. To get there, they had to round the great lake of Victoria and cross steep mountains. What ibn Khatour's tribe was doing in this area is not explained. Probably it had been driven out of western African because of its criminal activities and was headed for fresh opportunities for ivory poaching and slave raiding.

But on page 325 of *Son* is a phrase which seems to indicate that the tribe and Meriem, after a few days' march, are back at the village on the tributary of the Congo, back on the west coast. Meriem is brought back "to the familiar scenes of her childhood . . ."

Obviously, this is impossible. Burroughs must have meant for the reader to interpret this as the people and type of buildings with which she had been familiar during her childhood. But it could not have been the same location.

Why did not Tarzan recognize Malbihn when he showed up as Hanson? Meriem might have failed to recognize him because Malbihn had changed his appearance. But Tarzan should have recognized his odor. On the other hand, his contact with the Swede had been very brief. And no doubt Malbihn as Hanson not only bathed frequently when he was to be with Greystoke, he used a strong cologne.

The river on which Meriem escaped and on which Malbihn was wounded could be the Mara river of lower western Kenya and upper western Tanganyika. It is not, however, "a great African" river (p. 333) nor is it in jungle territory. But inasmuch as it seems the only candidate reasonably near the Greystoke plantation and since *Untamed* indicates the plantation is in southwestern Kenya, then the river should be the Mara. That it is a jungle river in *Son* can be due to Burroughs' tendency to romanticize. Also, Burroughs often deliberately confuses locations so that the true site of the Greystoke plantation cannot be found from a reading of the novels.

In conclusion, I sympathize with the fundamentalists' desire that Korak be Tarzan's real son. But I do not find that the Harwood-Starr theory of an adopted relative spoils *The Son of Tarzan* for me. It is one of my favorites, and it contains several scenes which still bring tears. Such as Meriem's joy on finding a mother's love again in My Dear's arms or in Korak's reunion with Jane. When I am not reading *Son* to analyze it, I read it as a novel. And I accept, for the time being, the internal premises of the story.

No reader should be disappointed that Korak is not Tarzan's real son. After all, as Korak himself says,

"THERE IS BUT ONE TARZAN . . . THERE CAN NEVER BE ANOTHER."

A REPLY TO "THE RED HERRING"

D. Peter Ogden was the editor of *Erbania* and the author of an article called "The Red Herring" in which he questioned some of the key facts concerning Tarzan's timeline. Farmer's reply, published in *Erbania*, Number 28, December 1971, and written just after the completion of *Tarzan Alive*, challenges Ogden's position that Burroughs deliberately altered Tarzan's birth date to protect his identity.

What is perhaps as fascinating as the debate itself is Farmer's explanation of the process he adopts to differentiate between fact and fiction when studying fictional works which are not always fully, and accurately, biographical.

I've re-read your article on Tarzan's and Korak's age ("The Red Herring"—*Erbania* 27) a number of times and also studied Harwood's and Starr's, which I knew fairly well before your article came to me.

It looks like a tossup, as far as validity goes. Either you accept Harwood and Starr's adopted-relative theory to explain Korak or you push the date of Tarzan's birth back to 1872. Whichever theory you choose, you do violation. You have to change a number of things in the novels and say, "No, ERB didn't present the truth here. But, of course, he had good reason. Now, here is what we believe is the truth . . ."

You make a good case, and if I had thought about it more, I might have used 1872 and proceeded from there. I would have satisfied very few people, the various schools of thought would all have jumped on me. Not that I mind that. But it was too late to rewrite the book[1] from the 1872 viewpoint; the work I did on the version now in Doubleday's hands was enormous and changing it to start from 1872 would have required an equal amount. Just about every page would have to be rewritten, many cast out and entirely new ones written. And I would still have felt that I was departing from the truth.

Yet—would ERB have given the true date of Tarzan's birth? Would it not have been simple then to look into the records of that year, including the sailing dates of ships from Dover in May, 1888, and locate the young nobleman and his wife who sailed out, never again to return?

No, the answer is, it would not be simple. Because I wrote to the Dover Port Authority two years ago to ascertain this point, and I was told that the records are not available. I deduced that they had been destroyed in the bombings (WWII), though the Authority didn't say so. BUT—what if money and influence has been used by—guess whom?—to make sure that these records are not available? Or no longer available, I should say.

I wrote two letters to the Freetown, Sierra Leone, Port Authority, inquiring about ships that put out in the May-July, 1888, period, especially those sailing ships that went southwards along the coast with the intention of setting a young English nobleman and his wife on shore on the west coast. Or, I said, I'd be satisfied with just the lists, let me do the searching. But the Freetown Authority never bothered to reply or else the mail is such that it didn't get my letters.

But it must be remembered that ERB could have shoved the true date of sailing from England a year or two ahead or behind. More probably behind, because the exploitation of the Congo by Leopold had really not begun yet. Also, from what British colony were the Belgians seducing the natives for their armies? Look at the map of Africa, 1888. I believe that the truth is that Greystoke was sent to investigate what the Germans were doing on the Kamerun-Oil Rivers. This is the only thing he could have been sent to investigate at that time. ERB knew this, of course, but deliberately misled the reader about the true destination and mission of Greystoke.

---

[1] *The Private Life of Tarzan*, by Philip José Farmer, due from Doubleday April 1972. (The title of the book, when published, was *Tarzan Alive*.)

A Reply to "The Red Herring"

If you take 1872 as the true date, then you have to think up an entirely new reason for the Greystokes going to Africa. You would end up by theorizing that the two were really just taking a trip to South Africa, or that Greystoke was an amateur explorer and injudiciously took his wife along, or that he was sent to investigate the illegal slave trade but first meant to accompany his wife to S. Africa and leave her there to visit relatives while he returned to the tropics. Or he may even have gone to Gabon, with his wife, because she wanted to find out what had happened to her uncle. (It's my contention that Trader Horn's George T—— was Alice Rutherford's uncle. The reasoning for this you will read in *The Private Life of Tarzan*.)

As you know, I have gone through Burke's vast *Peerage* in an effort to find a candidate for Tarzan. I think I know who the real Tarzan was, but I can't reveal that at this moment. To make sure I'm not in error, I'm going to have to go through Burke several times more and search the records of births from 1872 on. Inasmuch as Burke contains over 1250 pages of small close-set type of genealogy, I won't be finished with my study for some time to come.

Another point. Besides the wrong date of sailing, ERB might have given the wrong port.

And perhaps Tarzan's parental ancestors weren't nobility after all but just baronets. ERB made the Greystokes even more distinguished than they were, made them viscounts. (Though, as you know from my Detroit speech,[2] Tarzan couldn't have been a viscount, or, at least, if he were, he must also have been either an earl or a baron or both.)

The possibility that Tarzan's ancestors may have been baronets extends the search through Burke, extends it very much, since baronets take up much of the space therein. The chances are that his ancestors were of the lesser nobility or of the baronetage, since it would have been difficult to hide from the press the fact that a long-lost heir to a dukeship or marquessate or even an earlship had been found in the jungles of Africa. On the other hand, if enough money were spent in the right places, it might be done. But not very easily.

You say that the idea that Korak might be adopted, not Tarzan's real son, spoils *The Son of Tarzan* for you. This book is one of my favorites; I've read it many times and it doesn't spoil it for me to think

---

[2] "The Arms of Tarzan," published in this collection.

that Korak is adopted. The way I look at it, there are two Tarzans, the real Tarzan and the fictional Tarzan. The fictional Tarzan is based on the real Tarzan that ERB knew, and, undoubtedly, ERB drew the longbow now and then in his "biography," added some things, left others out, and even wrote several Tarzan books that were total fiction, such as *Tarzan at the Earth's Core*, or only partly true, such as *Tarzan and the Ant Men*. Knowing this doesn't spoil them for me. When I read them, I read them as I would any other book of fiction and enjoy them as they are.

When I study them as biography, then I differentiate to the best of my ability and knowledge between the fact and the fiction. This is not always easy to do, but it's a lot of fun and rewarding in many ways. Thus, when I read *The Son of Tarzan*, I know that Korak is adopted (or I should say, I believe he is). My own theory is that he is the younger brother of Bulldog Drummond, reasons for which theory I give in the *Life*. I believe that Korak's career in the jungle did not last more than a year, or two years at most. A proper chronology of Tarzan's life demands this. But this doesn't bother me. In the first place, Korak was an extraordinarily strong and adaptive individual, but he wasn't Tarzan, as he was the first to admit. There is only one Tarzan, and Korak, mighty though he was, was not his equal. Undoubtedly, John Drummond was an unusually strong person, like his older brother, who, as you may remember, in his first recorded adventure, snapped the neck of a half-grown gorilla with only his fingers. (I think it was a gorilla. On the same page, the beast is called a gorilla, a baboon, and a monkey. McNeile wasn't very strong on zoology.)

Anyway, when I read *Son*, I forget the facts behind this story and read it as ERB wrote it, knowing that he had to fictionize the true story and that, as you suggest, he did want it to be regarded as fiction.

By the way, what are your thoughts regarding ERB's killing of Jane in the magazine version of *Tarzan the Untamed*? Was she really killed but ERB realized that an investigator could find out her identity and thus Tarzan's, by looking into the deaths of plantation owners' wives killed in western Kenya in 1914, and so brought her back to life in the book version to throw any such investigator off the trail?

A Reply to "The Red Herring"

As far as I know, your idea that the person who first told ERB about Tarzan was D'Arnot is original. It seemed a likely one, but there are problems about it.

In the first place, the "I" of the first few pages of *Tarzan of the Apes* (*TOTA*) could not have been ERB. ERB was never in England. What happened, I think, is that the "I" was a man, or woman, who got the story from the "convivial host" and then told it to ERB who was, I believe, living in Chicago in 1911. ERB was inclined to give the narrator his own identity, as you will recall from *A Princess of Mars*, where the "I" could not possibly be ERB. (I mean, of course, not the "I" of John Carter but the "I" of his supposed nephew.) Besides, ERB couldn't read French and so wouldn't have been able to read the elder John Clayton's diary.

Was D'Arnot the person who told the story to the "I" of *TOTA*? If he were, he must have been in England, since he and "I" went to the Colonial Office to dig through the "musty manuscript, and dry official records." And why did he have access to British Colonial Office records? He was neither British nor a member of any secret agency which might have gotten permission to look into the records. Especially since, it seems to me, the Clayton family would have made sure that the records were not accessible to anyone except the highest authority.

But there is the matter of Clayton's diary. The last we see it is in Chapter XXVI of *TOTA*, in which the police official is reading it. Did he give it back to Tarzan or to D'Arnot? Tarzan left for America the next day, so I think it likely that D'Arnot kept it for further perusal while he waited for M. Desquerc, the fingerprint expert, to arrive. The "I" of *TOTA* read the diary, so he must have gotten it from D'Arnot or his "convivial host," whoever he was.

Would D'Arnot reveal to anybody, without authorization from the Claytons, the story of Tarzan? Undoubtedly not. What happened, as I reconstruct it, was that Tarzan, or a member of the Colonial Office, placed the diary with the records of Clayton's mission to West Africa. The "musty manuscript" must have been the summary of the story of the Claytons and their son. It was written by a Colonial Office clerk. The "I" was a visiting American who got loaded over a bottle with a British official who was one of the few who knew the story. The official must have been a very vain man to have insisted on "I" seeing the Greystoke material just so he could prove he wasn't lying. And he must have been unethical, too. I suspect that "I" may have used a bribe to get the official to show him the records. What the nature of the bribe was I don't have the slightest idea, of course.

Fortunately, the "I" told ERB the story and then either forgot about it or was prevailed upon not to disclose the truth after the first book about Tarzan came out and was such a hit. Perhaps, "I" died shortly after revealing to ERB what he had learned about the "Greystoke" case. ERB, of course, took care to conceal the true identities of the "principal characters," though there is evidence (as H. W. Starr has pointed out) that ERB only changed the titles of the noble persons concerned and retained the family names. Clayton and Rutherford are, after all, not unusual names in *Burke's Peerage and Landed Gentry.*

The reconstruction, based on the above: Tarzan never picked up the diary again, though he made sure that he could see it whenever he wished. The diary was transferred to the Colonial Office for keeping with the records pertinent to the Greystoke case. A clerk made a summary, in handwriting, of the story. (Unless "I" means that the "musty manuscript" is also the diary, since a diary is written, or was in those days, in handwriting.) The manuscript was never, for some reason, typed out. Perhaps because it was a summary for the eyes of some high authority only. (The French Naval Intelligence would also have a report, you may be sure of that. D'Arnot was Tarzan's best friend, but he would have been required, as a matter of duty, to report on the "incident." His report, plus those of other personnel of the cruiser, and the policemen's report about the fingerprints, would have been put in the secret files of the French Navy, where, no doubt, they still are.)

The "I" of *TOTA* then learned about the British records and the diary and got his egotistical and probably corrupt host to let him see whatever he wished to see concerning the Greystoke case.

THE LORD MOUNTFORD MYSTERY

The last article in this section (published in *ERB-dom*, Number 65, December 1972) sees Farmer as literary investigator, using his skills to identify, and explain, the connection between characters seen in the novels of Edgar Rice Burroughs and H. Rider Haggard. The inference being that they may have colluded to complete the story of the 'fictional' Mountford family and to give some resolution to those left wondering what Gonfala's backstory is. Burroughs' *Tarzan the Magnificent* may now be seen as a sequel of sorts to Haggard's novel *Finished*.

As almost everybody knows, Tarzan does live, and most of the stories told about him by Edgar Rice Burroughs (ERB) are true. However, ERB did mix some fiction in his biographies of the immortal apeman. H. Rider Haggard (HRH) was also not above falsifying some accounts of Allan Quatermain. Unlike ERB, though, he never concocted a story. His deviations from reality were confined to giving some of his real-life people fictional names or falsely locating the fabled cities which the great hunter and explorer of Africa found. Just as ERB used pseudonyms to protect some persons from unwanted publicity and gave hopelessly confused directions for finding Opar, so HRH used fake names and made it impossible to track down Kor, Zuvendis, and Waloo by following clues in *She*, *She and Allan*, *Allan Quatermain* and *Heu-Heu*.

The American, ERB, and the Englishman, HRH, never met. HRH probably heard of ERB as they both had stories in *New Story*

Magazine in late 1913. It's highly likely that ERB had read some of Haggard's very popular works, and he probably did research on one of HRH's minor protagonists before writing one of his Tarzan tales.

It's the purpose of this essay to show just where a work by each intersected in a certain English noble family.

"The Lord of the Jungle is abroad" in *Tarzan the Magnificent*. He's far north of Lake Rudolf (which is near the northern border of Kenya) on a mission for Haile Selassie I, King of Kings, Lion of Judah, and emperor of Ethiopia (Abyssinia). (As an aside, Tarzan, like Selassie, is descended from King Solomon, as may be seen by referring to addendum 3 of my *Tarzan Alive*. Greystoke, however, is lord of far more than Selassie can claim, since all Africa is his domain.)

Tarzan finds a skeleton of a message-bearer and in the runner's cleft stick, a nineteen-year-old letter. Since *Tarzan the Magnificent* occurred in 1934, the letter was written in 1915. Its writer, Lord Mountford, and his wife had disappeared twenty years before while exploring this vast arid, and mountainous area. Mountford says that he and his wife were captured by a tribe of white women who live on the plateau of Kaji. Kaji, ERB says, is not far from where the Mafa River empties into the Neubari River. A study of detailed maps of Ethiopia and several encyclopedias and atlases fails to locate these. We can assume that ERB is using fictional names for real rivers. The only large river in the area northwest of Lake Rudolf is the Omo (sometimes spelled Umu). The Omo forms the eastern border of the northwest area. The only town of any consequence in this area is Maji, which has an airport now. The similarity of Kaji to Maji is no doubt a coincidence.

Possibly, the confluence of two rivers which ERB described may be, in reality, the point where the Akobo River branches into two streams. Certainly, this territory is rugged and unpopulated enough to still conceal the cliff dwellings of the Kaji and the small village and two-story building of the Zuli, the enemies of the Kaji.

Lord Mountford says in his letter that his wife bore a daughter a year after they were captured. His wife was killed by the Kaji because she had not delivered a son. The Kaji amazons needed white males to keep the "white blood" in the tribal veins. This murder seems to be illogically motivated. Why not allow Lady Mountford to have more babies, some of which might be male? However, as we know, all societies, literate or preliterate, often proceed on illogical and non-survival grounds, and this seems to have been the case with the Kaji.

A little later, Tarzan finds a refugee from the Kaji. He is Stanley Wood, a travel writer who has capitalized on his "natural worthlessness, which often finds its expression and its excuse in wanderlust."

It may be that ERB put these words into Wood's mouth. Every now and then, in his books, ERB pokes fun at his own profession.

Wood and a friend had led a small safari to search for the long-lost Mountfords. On the way, Wood finds Mountford, who has just escaped from the amazons and their chief, a male witch doctor. After some delirious statements, Mountford dies. He is a man well under fifty, and so, if he's in his early forties, would have been born circa 1892. This point is made here because it's relevant to the chronology of my theory.

Tarzan later encounters Mountford's daughter, a beautiful nineteen-year-old blonde. She is known only as Gonfala. After many adventures, aided by Tarzan, Gonfala and Wood escape to civilization and are, presumably, married there. They'll be wealthy, since Tarzan is going to give them the enormous emerald of the Zulis or some share of it.

Tarzan the Magnificent does not give many details about the Mountfords. It says nothing, for instance, of their family background or history before their disappearance. Nor are the Mountfords mentioned in the other Tarzan epics.

But Allan Quatermain, in *Finished*, Haggard's 1917 novel, meets a member of the Mountford family in 1877. And from this story, we can fill in the background which ERB left blank.

Quatermain, while in Pretoria, then a frontier town, runs into a Maurice Anscombe. He is a younger son of Lord Mountford, one of the richest peers in England. He is tall and loosely built and between thirty and thirty-five years old. He has steady blue eyes with a humorous twinkle. His face is attractive, though the features are too irregular and his nose is too long for good looks. He served in a crack cavalry regiment, resigned, and went to South Africa to hunt big game. He is brave, but a bad shot.

Anscombe has inherited much money from his recently dead mother. His father is also dead. An older brother is the present Lord Mountford. None of his brothers have any children.

Anscombe goes to the Kashmir in India to hunt wild sheep but returns on October 1, 1878 to hunt with Quatermain. While they're tracking a wounded gnu, they run into the alcoholic and terrible-tempered Marnham and his sinister partner, Doctor Rodd. These recruit native labor for the Kimberley mines but get most of their money from smuggling diamonds and running guns for rebellious natives. Marnham once served with Anscombe's father in the Coldstream Guards but was cashiered for striking a superior officer during a card game. He had married a beautiful Hungarian, but she died a year after giving birth to a daughter, Hedda.

The daughter is almost twenty-one, is tall and slender, and has auburn hair and large dark-grey eyes. Rodd is in love with her but is killed while trying to do away with Anscombe and Quatermain.

A weird dwarf, the wizard Zikali, the Opener-of-Roads, the Thing-that-should-never-have-been-born, predicts that Hedda will have five children. Two will die, and one will give her so much trouble she'll wish it had died, too. Inasmuch as all of Zikali's prophecies come true in other Quatermain tales, it can be assumed that this one is valid.

Zikali then makes a strange statement. "But who their father will be I will not say."

Whatever this means, Anscombe and Hedda do get married. After many years, Quatermain hears they're still alive and spend most of their time in Hungary, where Hedda has inherited property.

"Lord Mountford" is as fictional a title as "Lord Greystoke." Mountford, to the best of my knowledge, is not to be found in any book on extant or extinct peerages. The real title is a matter for future research.

But ERB, when writing of the peers who figure in *Tarzan the Magnificent*, decided to use HRH's title, since they were both writing of the same family.

Since Maurice Anscombe's brothers would have died childless, he would have inherited the title, perhaps late in life. One of Hedda's sons, born when she was about thirty-four, would have become Lord Mountford when Maurice Anscombe died. It was this son who was the Lord Mountford of *Tarzan the Magnificent*.

It is possible that, since he was raised in Hungary a good part of this time, he married a girl of that country. Their daughter, Gonfala, could be one of the beautiful Hungarian blondes typified by the Gabors. Probably, Gonfala's mother was of that ancient aristocracy which, like Baroness Orczy, biographer of *The Scarlet Pimpernel*, traces its ancestry back to Árpád, the Magyar conqueror of that area to be called Hungary. (Lord Greystoke himself, as shown in *Tarzan Alive*, could do the same through the founder of the Scots family of Drummond, a Maurice by the way.)

Whether or not Gonfala could lay claim to the title is not known. When her father disappeared into Africa, the title may have gone to a male relative, a brother, a nephew, or cousin. If there were no male relatives, the title may have become extinct. If, however, the patent permitted a female in the direct line of descent to inherit the title, as some English patents do, Gonfala could have become a peeress.

If this were not the case, she probably went to the USA as just Mrs. Stanley Wood. The latter seems more likely, since there is nothing in the various chronicles of the years circa 1934 indicating that the daughter of a long-lost peer suddenly appeared out of Africa.

In any event, there is evidence that Henry Rider Haggard did write the story of the parents of Edgar Rice Burroughs' Lord Mountford.

A KERNEL OF TRUTH

This letter appeared in *Erbania* 41/42, in the summer of 1977 and is Farmer's reply to a previously published letter from James Cawthorn (1929–2008), UK illustrator, critic and author. Farmer's robust defense cements his assertion that the Tarzan stories, as written by Burroughs, are based on a real character and tries to explain why proving that has been such a difficult but rewarding experience.

Kaor!

R e Cawthorn's comment that it's about time to drop this game that Tarzan really exists. For me, it's not a game. I know that there was a real Tarzan and that he still lives. I'm dead serious, though not deadly serious, I hope.

Nor have I pursued this "game" for money, as Cawthorn says. If I was primarily interested in financial gain, I would never have written *Tarzan Alive*. In the time I spent on the biography I could (no exaggeration) have written four novels. And gotten bigger advances from each one than I made on the bio. The book was a labor of love, and love of labor, though lots of fun for me.

If others insist it's just a game or that Tarzan is purely fictional, I won't argue with them. Let the kafir dwell in the darkness.

As for the controversy about Barsoom. Was it in a parallel universe or its entrance through a time gate? This is a game. The game is based on the assumption that there was indeed a John Carter and a Barsoom. I personally think that the Barsoom stories are fiction (and minor classics in world literature). So was everything else that ERB wrote, that is, they were one hundred percent fiction. Except for the Tarzan stories, which, though often fictionalized and exaggerated, contain a kernel of truth.

A thought concerning the 1888/1872 controversy. If Tarzan was born in 1872, then the fingerprints on the diary would have been examined, and his identity as Greystoke proved, in 1893. The identification was done in Paris. But it wasn't until 1891 that identification by fingerprints was removed from the field of theory and made practical. This was the system introduced by Vucetich[1] of Argentina. Not until 1900 did this system become used in Great Britain. To be more precise, Sir Edward Henry published his book on the use of fingerprints in 1900, and the Metropolitan Police Fingerprint Bureau was established in July 1901.

Somewhere in my still unorganized collection of books is a statement about the French Sûreté's first use of fingerprints. I'll send you the information when I find the book. In the meantime, I have a vague and possibly incorrect memory that the French preceded the English in the use of fingerprints. But if they didn't, then it's doubtful that a Tarzan born in 1872 could have been identified by his thumbprint.

Not by the French anyway.

This is a matter to be ascertained later.[2]

In any event, the question is irrelevant if there is a true Tarzan. Obviously, if Tarzan had succeeded his cousin, or, rather, ousted the false claimant, then worldwide publicity would have resulted. We would know exactly who Tarzan was, his real name and title.

But this didn't happen. There was no publicity in real life. So— Tarzan must be fictional right?

No, because ERB did not give us the true sequence of events. As "Lord Greystoke" says in his "Extracts from the Greystoke,'" Tarzan took his cousin's role after his cousin died. Nobody except a very few

[1] **Juan Vucetich Kovacevich**, born **Ivan Vučetić**; July 20, 1858–January 25, 1925) was a Croatian-Argentine anthropologist and police official who pioneered the use of fingerprinting.

[2] No evidence can be found to support Farmer's memory on this.

confidants knew about this. This is the way it was, and this is how Tarzan avoided publicity. This is also the reason why it is so difficult to determine the true identity of "Lord Greystoke" from a perusal of *Burke's Peerage*.

So, there wasn't any telegram from Paris proving that Tarzan was the real heir. Nor was there any notice of a British Peer dying on the coast of West Africa.

Nor is Tarzan's name "John Clayton." ERB makes that clear in *Tarzan of the Apes* in the very beginning of the narrative. He says (page 2 A. L. Burt ed.) "we learn that a certain English nobleman, whom *we shall call John Clayton, Lord Greystoke . . .*" (italics mine.)

It's possible that "Clayton" wasn't even a member of the nobility. His father may have been a baronet, which is a sort of hereditary knight. But he would have been descended from nobility, as are many of the landed gentry and baronetcy. And it's possible that "John Clayton" earned a noble title in his middle age for his services to the king.

Enough of that. Unlike some of your correspondents, I thought *The Land That Time Forgot* was a bad movie. It only looks good in comparison with *At the Earth's Core*. Here I am, having waiting all my life for the splendors and colors and great adventure of these two books to be transferred to the screen, and they were blown, wasted, ruined. Maybe it is impossible to put the essence of ERB's qualities on film. It's never been done yet. The Tarzan movies were fun, but they weren't the real Tarzan.

Best,

Philip José Farmer (Peoria, Ill.)

PARSING THE LEGEND

THE ARMS OF TARZAN

(The English Nobleman whom Edgar Rice Burroughs called John Clayton, Lord Greystoke)

Farmer was not content with just proving that Burroughs' Tarzan was based on a real man. Having established as much to his own satisfaction, he also spent considerable energy and thought enhancing our understanding of the jungle lord; the myth and the legend. His knowledge of genealogy led him to heraldry and what more noble task in this regard than to devise a coat of arms for the man known to the world as Tarzan.

The background to, and the description of, the heraldic image was originally presented as a speech at the Dum-Dum banquet on Burroughs' Day, 1970 and first published in the *Burroughs Bulletin*, Number 22, in the summer of 1971. It is the printed version that is reproduced here with very minor edits to enhance the reading experience.

Scholars of Tarzan will be gratified to know that the original artwork for the Coat of Arms was donated by Farmer to the Edgar Rice Burroughs Memorial Collection in Louisville, Kentucky.

Note from Philip José Farmer: The speech published here is not quite that given during the Dum-Dum banquet on Burroughs' Day, September 5, 1970, in Detroit, Michigan. Some changes have been made and insertions and additions worked in due to corrections of errors on my part and a failure to resist the temptation to gild the lily. It is, however, in the main, the same speech.

Ladies and gentlemen, mangani, tarmangani, gomangani, and bolgani.

I'm happy to be here. Whether or not you will be happy remains to be seen. I warn you that what I am going to say has little "relevance." I'm all for relevancy to the problems of our time. I belong to the ZPG (Zero Population Growth)[1], have worked in the Write For Your Life campaign, and have consistently tried to combat prejudice and inhumane thinking in my writings. I've been working for some time on a book concerning the need for an economy of abundance. I've just finished two short stories about pollution in our times. I'm writing a novel, *Death's Dumb Trumpet*,[2] about the effects of pollution twenty years from now.

But you won't be getting any of that today. Men must have hobbies, otherwise they go mad. The works of Edgar Rice Burroughs (ERB) are, to me, a gate into parallel worlds where there are problems, but none that my hero, and, therefore, me as the hero, can't handle. There I can relax and forget, for the time being, the noisy, stinking, dusty, and hostile world that exists outside my window. And, too, often, inside the window.

It's not my purpose today to justify my love for ERB's worlds. You know why I love them, otherwise you wouldn't be here.

I propose today to inspect a very small segment of the world of Tarzan, one that has been left entirely unexplored, as far as I know. For that purpose, I've had some images of the subject for today, the Greystoke coat-of-arms, prepared.

Please show the first image.

I furnished the original research for these arms, the first rough sketches, and the blazoning. But Bjo Trimble did the actual execution, which I consider to be superb. She took a keen interest in the project and put in much time she could ill afford in research of her own and in the actual calculations and drawings. The result exceeded my expectations; her visualizations surpassed my own.

---

[1] Founded in 1968, Population Connection (formerly Zero Population Growth or ZPG) is the largest grassroots population organization in the United States.

[2] Although *Death's Dumb Trumpet* was also announced in *Luna Monthly* (1970) it was never published.

NOTE: This illustration is at present, September, 1971, scheduled to be part of the jacket illustration of my *The Private Life of Tarzan*.[3] This is a biography of Lord Greystoke along the lines of W. S. Baring-Gould's *Sherlock Holmes of Baker Street* and *Nero Wolfe of West Thirty-Fifth Street*, and also of C. Northcote Parkinson's *The Life and Times*

---

[3] *The Private Life of Tarzan* was published as *Tarzan Alive*.

of Horatio Hornblower. The latter was issued after the Ms. for the Tarzan life had been turned in to the publisher, Doubleday.

The Tarzan books describe, or hint at, many things. But in none is there any reference to the coat-of-arms of the "Greystoke" family. There is a reference in *Tarzan of the Apes* to the family crest on the great ring which Tarzan's father wore. But the crest is not described. Greystoke, as you know, is not the actual title of the noble family that engendered the immortal ape-man. Greystoke is a pseudonym used by ERB to cover the real identity of a line of English peers. I intend to speculate about the real title. But Greystoke has been associated too long with Tarzan for any of us to be at ease in using any other title. This is the way it should be, and this is why I have placed the legend, GREYSTOKE, under the arms.

However, though Greystoke is not Tarzan's real title, he is descended from the de Greystocks, the ancient and distinguished barons of Greystoke, Cumberland, England. I refer you to Burke's *Extinct Peerages*, Sir Nicholas Harris' *A Synopsis of the Peerage*, and George Edward Cokayne's *The Complete Peerage* for their history. This descent of Tarzan through several lines of this family is one of the reasons ERB chose Greystoke for a pseudonym.

Now—the blazoning, I'll give it to you as it would be in *Burke's Genealogical and Heraldic History of the Peerage, Baronetage and Knightage*. *Burke's Peerage* (to use its short title) has over 2475 pages of very small, closely set print devoted to genealogy.

After the blazoning, I'll explain the technical terms I used. Then I'll go into the history of each family represented here. I'll demonstrate that Tarzan, king of the tribe of Kerchak, chief of the Waziri, a member of the English peerage, lord of the jungle, demigod of the forest, has a noble genealogy indeed. In fact, no one in Europe, not even Queen Elizabeth of Great Britain, can boast of a more ancient and varied lineage.

The Blazoning:

ARMS—Quarterly of six: 1st, GREBSON OF GREBSON, *argent*, on a saltire *azure* drinking horns in triskele *gules*; 2nd, DRUMMOND, *or*, three bars wavy *gules*; 3rd, O'BRIEN, *gules*, three lions passant guardant in pale, per pale *or* and *argent*; 4th, CALDWELL, *sable*, a torn *or*; 5th, RUTHERFORD, *gules*, a wild bull's head cabossed, eyes of the first, otherwise of its own kind, between the horns a wild man's head affrontée, eyes of the first; 6th, GREYSTOCK, barry of six, *argent* and *azure*, over all three chaplets of roses *gules*.

CRESTS—A sleuth-hound *argent*, collared and leashed *gules*, for DRUMMOND; issuing from a cloud *azure* an arm embowed brandishing a sword *gules*, pommel and hilt *sable*, for GREBSON; a spear *or* transfixing a Saracen's head *gules*, for GREBSON.

SUPPORTERS—Dexter, a savage wreathed about the middle with oak leaves, in the dexter hand a bow, with a quiver of arrows over his shoulder, all *vert*, and a lion's skin or hanging behind his back; sinister, a female great ape guardant, all proper.

MOTTOES—"Je Suys Encore Vyvant"; "Kreeg-ah!"

The explanation of the technical terms:

Quarterly of six. Quarterly originally meant the four equal parts into which the shield was divided for showing four arms. But some people added even more, and the family of Dent, the Baronage of Furnivall, has a quarterly of ten. The Greystokes could add a hundred, if they wished, since they are descended from that many different noble families. But the shields generally are restricted to a reasonable number.

Argent is a heraldic term for silver or white. Azure is blue. A saltire, or St. Andrew's cross, is a cross in the form of an X. The St. Andrew's cross is usually found in the field of a Scots family but not always. Gules is red. In triskele indicates a figure composed of three usually curved or bent branches radiating from a center. Triskele, or triskelion, is from a Greek word meaning three-legged.

Or is gold. A bar is a horizontal division of the shield occupying one-fifth thereof. Wavy means undulating. Passant is a term for beasts in a walking position with the right forepaw raised, although I've seen the left front paw raised, for instance, in the lion passant of the crest of a branch of the English family of Farmer.

Guardant is front or full-faced. In pale indicates that the charges, in this case, the lions, are arranged beneath one another. Per pale indicates the particular manner in which a shield or field or a charge is divided by a partition line. Thus, the lions, in pale, per pale *or* and *argent* are arranged in a vertical column and each is half-gold and half-silver, as you see.

Sable is black. A torn is a heraldic spinning wheel. Torn was an archaic English word for the early type of spinning wheel used in the late 13th century.

A wild bull's head cabossed. Cabossed, or caboshed, indicates the head of any beast looking full-faced with nothing of the neck visible. "Of the first" means that the color is the first one mentioned in the blazoning. In this case, of the first means gules. The eyes of the bull and the wild man are bright red, giving the Rutherford charges a fierce and sinister look. Making the eyes red was Bjo's idea, a stroke of genius on her part, as far as I'm concerned. Of its own kind, or proper, are terms applicable to animals, trees, vegetables, etc., when they are their natural color.

A wild man's head affrontée. Affrontée is a term applied to full-faced human heads.

Barry describes the field or charge divided by horizontal lines. Thus, GREYSTOCK, barry of six, *argent* and *azure*, means six horizontal bars alternately silver and blue.

Crests over coats-of-arms were originally derived from the actual crests of helmets worn by the nobles. The only term used for the crests so far not explained is *embowed*. (Pointing to the center crest.) An arm embowed. Embowed means bent or bowed.

The Saracen's head originally indicated an ancestor who went to the Holy Land on one of the crusades. The head is gules, instead of a proper or natural color, because of a story associated with Tarzan's crusader ancestor. The story will be told in the genealogy of Tarzan in *The Private Life of Tarzan*.

Regard the two supporters, the figures holding the shield up. One is dexter; the other, sinister. Dexter means the right-hand supporter. Right and left, in heraldry, are as seen by the man behind the shield. Sinister, of course, has no evil meaning in heraldry; it merely indicates the left-hand position.

The savage, or woodman, or wildman, is all *vert*, that is, green.

The upper motto is French in archaic spelling. *Je Suys Encore Vyvant.* Translation: *I Still Live.* Or *I am Still Living.* Or *I Yet Live.*

Tarzan, as you no doubt recall, said these words more than once in seemingly hopeless situations. In *Tarzan the Untamed*, Bertha Kircher, the supposed German spy, and Tarzan are about to be caught by the insane Xujans and their hunting lions. She says to Tarzan, "You think there is some hope, then?"

"We are still alive," was his only answer.

And in *Tarzan the Terrible*, when Jane and Tarzan are soon to be sacrificed, Jane asks, "You still have hope?"

"I am still alive," he said, as though that were sufficient answer.

Thus Tarzan echoed the motto of his ancient family, the old war cry his fighting ancestors used to rally their men around them when the battle seemed to have turned against them.

I probably don't need to point out that "*I still live*" is also the motto of another great fighter, John Carter of Mars.

The lower motto, "Kreeg-ah!" is, of course, the warning cry of the great ape. (As an aside, I'd like to suggest that it's long past time for the great ape to be given a scientific classification. And since Tarzan's father was the first European to describe the great ape—in his diary, of course—I propose that we honor him by terming this new genus *Megapithecus greystoki*. This would also honor his son, who knows more of the great ape than anyone in the world, civilized or uncivilized.)

The lower motto, "Kreeg-ah!", was added by Tarzan to the family arms when he assumed the title in late 1910 (according to my reckoning). The great ape supporter is also Tarzan's idea. The original supporter was a heraldic Sagittarius, a centaur with a bow. But Tarzan wanted to honor his foster mother, Kala, and so he replaced the Sagittarius with a female mangani. This changing of supporters in a coat-of-arms for personal reasons is not unprecedented. The 10th Duke of Marlborough, for instance, replaced both supporters on his family's arms. However, this type of arms is usually regarded as a personal coat-of-arms, a variation on the family's, and other members of the family may use the older type if they desire. I would imagine that Korak would keep his father's arms, inasmuch as he was also closely associated with the mangani.

While I'm at it, I might as well say that these arms are not complete or even accurate from the strict viewpoint of the College of Heraldry. All of the quarters except the first and fourth should have little symbols, such as a crescent or mullet (a five-pointed star) or others to indicate that these are different branches from the main Drummond, O'Brien, Rutherford, and Greystock lines. However, the symbols for difference are not always used, and Tarzan's noble forebears never got around to conforming to strict usage.

Also, the Drummond crest, the sleuthhound (that must be Sherlock Holmes' crest, too) should be on the sinister side. The crests of the primary family, the Grebsons, should occupy the dexter place of honor and the center. But these crests entered the Greystoke arms a long time before heraldry became regulated by a college of heralds or by royal authority. The crests should be somewhat smaller and all placed above the shield, but, again, they were drawn thus in the distant old days, and the Greystoke family has never seen fit to change them.

The headpiece you see on top of the shield is the coronet of a duke, not to be confused with the ducal or crest coronet. It has a circle, or coronet, of gold surmounted by eight golden strawberry leaves, of which only five are visible, and by the red golden-tasselled cap with the ermine under-rim you see. I know that some of you are thinking: Why the coronet of a duke? Tarzan, according to his own statement in *Tarzan, Lord of the Jungle*, is a viscount. And several other Tarzan books assert that he is a viscount.

Is he? My own theory is that he may have been a duke, a marquess, earl, baron, or baronet (a baronet is not a noble but a sort of hereditary knight), or any combination of these. But he would not be a viscount. Or, if he were, it would be only one of his titles. ERB took great pains to conceal the true identity of "Lord Greystoke." He would have altered the reply Tarzan really made when asked (by Sir Bertram of the city of Nimmir) what his rank was. ERB knew that Tarzanic scholars would search through the some 120-plus viscounts listed in *Burke's Peerage* for evidence that one was Tarzan. So he directed them down a blind alley.

I don't want to go into this theory in detail at this time, but the feudal society Tarzan found in a lost valley in Ethiopia was supposed to be descended from two shiploads of Englishmen who had set out with Richard I on the First Crusade. This was in 1191, but viscount, as an English title, was not used until 1440. If Tarzan had "truly" said he was a viscount, Sir Bertram wouldn't have known what he meant. Obviously, Tarzan did not say that. Or, if he did, seeing that Sir Bertram did not understand him, he went on to his other titles. Sir Bertam would have heard of "earl" and "baron" since these were the only English titles of nobility extant in Richard's time.

From the above argument, we can assume, with a good amount of reasonableness, that Tarzan is an earl or baron. Given the ancientness and honourableness of his line (stressed by ERB in the first Tarzan book), the chances are that he is both.

On the other hand, very few Englishmen, that is, men of Old English descent, actually accompanied Richard. Most of his crusaders were Normans, and it is doubtful that Richard had enough Englishmen to fill one ship, let alone two. (Accounting at least 60 knights per ship as a shipload.)

This would mean that the people of the valley were descended from Normans and so spoke an evolved Norman. This leads to developments that I don't have time for here but will lay out for the interested reader in *The Private Life of Tarzan*.

It is, however, incredible that the man we know as Lord Greystoke would not be a duke. If Peter Wimsey's father was Duke of Denver and Lord John Roxton's father was Duke of Pomfret, then surely Tarzan must be a duke, regardless of how many other titles he holds. Don't forget that Tarzan is referred to as a "dook" twice, once in *Tarzan and the Foreign Legion*. I do have more solid reasons than this for placing him in the highest rank of nobility. But I have to expound these elsewhere, due to lack of time here.

Please show the second image.

To arms. The first, first. GREBSON OF GREBSON. Am I revealing, for the first time by anyone anywhere, the true name and title of Tarzan's family?

Not exactly.

The present Lord Greystoke wishes to have his identity stay hidden, and I respect his reasons. (Besides, I would not think of offending the Lord of the Jungle.) So I have picked a title and a coat-of-arms which reveal certain facts about him, or come close to the facts, without disclosing his genuine identity. The title and the arms are analogs. They are not the real title and arms. But they are near enough to give an idea of what the genuine items are.

Some of you know that ERB, in the original Ms of *Tarzan of the Apes*, used Bloomstoke as Tarzan's title. Then he changed it. Why? For one thing, Greystoke sounds more aristocratic than Bloomstoke. Also, Tarzan *is* descended from the Greystokes. (So is half of the

peerage of England as you may ascertain if you care to take the trouble to trace them through Burke.) But the Grey in Greystoke was also provided by ERB as a clue for some scholar who might want to tackle the formidable hunt for the real Tarzan. (We know that ERB was fond of codes and sometimes used them in making up names or disguising real names for his characters and places.)

Following this coded lead (among many others), I hunted down and identified the real-world Tarzan. The project took me two and a half years and involved reading every word of the lineages in 2,475 pages of *Burke's Peerage*. However, all the work I put in would not have led me to the real Tarzan if I had not stumbled across a certain clue through sheer good fortune. Only a highly improbable sequence of events could permit another to follow the trail I followed. I am sorry, but I cannot supply the necessary clue, since "Lord Greystoke" himself has asked me not to. Therefore, I am compelled to suppress everything I know for sure and behave as if I were as ignorant as everybody else in the matter. I have to proceed by analogy, and if you choose to dispute my theses, you have a perfect right to do so.

I will tell you one thing. Tarzan's real title does not start with GR (as in Greystoke or Grebson). That initial letter cluster will, however, lead you to some of his ancestors and relatives in *Burke's Peerage*. Nor does his title contain the word *grey*. It does contain an archaic word implying grey. I won't tell you if the word is of Germanic, Latin, Pictish, or Celtic origin, however.

Grebson, our analog family name and title, comes from the Old English Graegbeardssunu. This means The Son of the Grey-Bearded One. And who was the Grey-Bearded One? He was Woden, the chief god of the Anglo-Saxons or Old English, the same as the Othinn of the Old Norse or the Wuotan of the Old High Germans or Othinus of the continental Saxons. According to the Norse *Edda*, the great god had many epithets. To read off all his titles would take several minutes, so I resist the temptation.

Tarzan's real title contains an epithet for Woden, though not the one I give here, which is an analogous epithet.

Note the argent field and azure saltire of Grebson's arms. Argent and azure are Woden's colors. Note the three drinking horns with interlocking tips. This ancient sign for Woden (or Odin) is found carved on rocks in many places in Scandinavia and a number of places in the British Isles. In Old English it would be called the *waelcnotta* and in Old Norse is the *valknutr*. It means the "knot of the slain" and stands for Woden (or Odin) in his aspect as the god of the warriors who've died in battle. Hence the gules, or red, color of the drinking horns.

You won't find this symbol on Tarzan's real shield. But you will find something analogous, if you are persistent enough and wildly lucky.

Apparently, the founder of Tarzan's family, the original Grebson, claimed to be descended from the god Woden. The Queen of England makes exactly the same claim, as you can find out by reading "The Royal Lineage" section of *Burke's Peerage*. She is descended from

Egbert, King of Wessex (died 839 A.D.). Egbert, like the other kings of English states at that time, Mercia, Deira, Kent, Eastanglia, etc., had a traditional genealogy which went unbroken back to Denmark of circa 300 A.D. and to the great god Woden.

Those interested can refer to page 165, Vol. 1, of Jacob Grimm's *Teutonic Mythology*, Dover Books.

I submit that a human being can't have a more highly placed or illustrious ancestor.

That Tarzan's arms bear the ancient symbol of Woden indicates that his ancestors clung to the old religion long after their neighbors were Christianized. Originally, their shields bore only the drinking horns gules in triskele on an argent and azure field. Then the saltire was added to convince others that the family was truly of the new faith. History tells us of the tenacity with which parts of rural England held on to the ancient faiths. And ERB, in *The Outlaw of Torn*, says of the peasants' love for the outlaw, "Few . . . had seen his face and fewer still had spoken with him, but they loved his name and his prowess and in secret they prayed for him to their ancient god Wodin and the lesser gods of the forest and the meadow and the chase . . ."

Second, DRUMMOND. Drummond comes from the Gaelic *druim monadh*, meaning *back of the mountain*. This Scots family is presently represented by the Earl of Ancaster and the Earl of Perth. The family was founded by Maurice, the son of George, a young son of Andreas, King of Hungary. Maurice came to Scotland in 1066 and settled there. He, in turn, could trace his ancestry unbroken back to Árpád, the Magyar chief who conquered Hungary (died 907 A.D.).

Third, O'BRIEN. A prominent member of this ancient Irish family is the Baron of Inchiquin. In an unbroken line it descends from Brian Boroimhe, chief Irish monarch in 1002 A.D. and victor of the battle of Clontarf, though he himself was killed by the Danes. This line can actually trace itself back to Cormac Cas, son of Olliol Olum, King of Ireland, circa 200 A.D.

Fourth, CALDWELL, *sable a torn or*. Some of you pricked up your ears when I first blazoned these arms. You remembered that Tarzan, in *The Return of Tarzan*, used the pseudonym of John Caldwell when he was a French secret agent traveling on a liner from Algiers to Cape Town.

Why would he use that pseudonym? Obviously, he picked the first name that came to mind, that of his illustrious ancestor, John Caldwell. No doubt, Tarzan had been reading in *Burke's Peerage* about the Greystoke lineage and the story of John Caldwell was fresh in his mind.

Another reason you pricked up your ears was the mention of the torn, the heraldic spinning wheel. You recalled Richard Plantagenet, son of Henry III, he who would later be called Norman of Torn or the Outlaw of Torn. You probably asked yourself, "What does Farmer mean by that? The Outlaw of Torn is Tarzan's ancestor? But Norman killed one of Tarzan's ancestors, a Greystoke!"

Did he? ERB did not say that this particular Greystoke was an ancestor of Tarzan. That's an assumption by some of his readers. Perhaps the slain Greystoke was a member of the genuine de Greystocks of Greystoke Castle, Cumberland. He may or may not have been Tarzan's forefather, but I'm inclined to believe that Norman of Torn certainly was. Tarzan would certainly have the greatest warrior of the Middle Ages in his family line.

The Outlaw was born in 1240 A.D. and was 15 years old when he slew Greystoke. This would be in 1255, the 39th year of Henry III's reign. So the Greystoke whom Norman killed was probably the son of Baron Robert de Greystock (died before 1253) and the younger brother of William de Greystock. William's son, John, was the first Greystoke summoned as a baron *by writ* to Parliament. This was in 1295 A.D. in Edward I's time. This, by the way, was the first regular parliament, recognized as such.

We know that Henry III finally became aware that the famous, or infamous, outlaw was his long-lost son, Richard. But Henry died in 1272, and his son, Edward I, called Longshanks, was, though a very good king for those days, proud, jealous, and suspicious. His younger brother Richard, too popular with the common people, would have been forced to flee on a trumped-up charge of treason (nothing rare in those days). By then Bertrade de Montfort, his wife, had died, probably in childbirth or of disease, very common causes of fatality then. Richard would have taken a pseudonym again, that of John Caldwell, landless warrior. In the North of England he met old Baron Grebson. The baron had no male issue, and so, when his daughter fell in love with the stranger knight, he adopted him. This was nothing unusual; you will find similar examples throughout *Burke's Peerage*. The family name became Caldwell-Grebson, though the Caldwell was later dropped. Similar examples of this also abound in Burke.

John Caldwell could not use the same arms as the Outlaw of Torn, of course. So, instead of *argent* a falcon's wing *sable*, he used *sable* a torn *or*. That he chose the torn showed he could not resist an example of "canting arms," a heraldic pun. One, indeed, that proved as dangerous as might be expected. Edward I heard of the appearance from nowhere of a knight who bore a torn on his shield, and he investigated. The king's men ambushed John Caldwell, and though he slew five of them, he, too, died.

How can we be sure of this?

An obscure book on medieval witchcraft, published in the middle 1600s, describes the case of a knight who was, for reasons unknown to the writer, slain by Edward I's men in a northern county. When his body was laid out to be washed, his left breast was found to bear a violet lily-shaped birthmark. This was thought to be the mark of the devil. But we readers of *The Outlaw of Torn* will recognize the true identity of the man suspected of witchcraft.

This theory could be wrong, of course. I propose an alternate to consider. You may have noticed the remarkable resemblance between the Outlaw and Tarzan. Both were tall, splendidly built, and extremely powerful men. (Anybody who can drive the point of a broadsword through chain mail into his opponent's heart is strong enough to crack the neck of a bull ape.) Both men had grey eyes. Both wore their hair in bangs across their foreheads. Neither knew the meaning of fear.

But the description of the Outlaw could also apply, except for a few minor points, to John Carter of Mars. What if the Outlaw did not die, as I first speculated, but had somehow defeated the aging process? What if, like Tarzan, he had stumbled across an elixir for immortality? During his wanderings in rural England, he came across a wizard or witch, actually a member of the old faith, who had a recipe for preventing degeneration of the body. If a witch doctor in modern Africa could have such, and give it to Tarzan, then a priest of an outlawed religion in the Middle Ages could give such to the Outlaw of Torn.

Sometime during the following six centuries, the Outlaw suffered amnesia. This was either from a blow on the head (again recalling Tarzan, who suffered amnesia many times from blows on the head) or because loss of memory of early years is an unfortunate by-product of the elixir. Thus, on March 4, 1866, the Outlaw, a long-time resident of Virginia, an admitted victim of amnesia, left a cave in Arizona for the planet Mars. ERB called this man John Carter. Notice the J. C. I suggest that he may have been Richard Plantagenet, Norman of Torn, John Caldwell, and, finally, John Carter.

It is possible that John Caldwell was not killed, that he slew all of Edward's men, who actually numbered six, mangled the face of one tall corpse, and stained a violet lily mark on the corpse's left breast. And, once again, he disappeared into pseudonymity but gained immortality as the Warlord of Mars.

It's true that the Outlaw's hair was brown and Carter's was black. But hair gets darker as one ages (until it starts to grey), and 626 years are long enough for anybody's hair to get black.

If this theory is correct, the Outlaw of Torn is not only John Carter of Mars but Tarzan's ancestor by about 600 years. But John Carter may have been the ancestor of Tarzan many times over. He may have followed the fortunes of his descendants with keen interest and, every now and then, remarried into the line and begat more powerful, quick thinking, fearless, grey-eyed men and fearless grey-eyed beautiful daughters. I wouldn't be surprised if he were not only the ancestor of Tarzan's father but of Tarzan's mother, Alice Rutherford. Perhaps this regular insertion of Carter's genes into the line is why ERB insists so strongly on the influence of heredity in Tarzan's behavior.

And I point out, as something for you to chew on, that Sherlock Holmes, Professor Challenger, Raffles, Richard Wentworth, Lord Peter Wimsey, and Denis Nayland Smith were all grey-eyed. And, though some were slim, all had very powerful muscles. Could these, together with Tarzan, be descendants of John Carter of Mars?

Their relationship, with those of Doc Savage, Kent Allard,

Korak, Lord John Roxton, Nero Wolfe, and The Scarlet Pimpernel, will be described in a separate essay. Oh, yes, I almost forgot Bulldog Drummond.

Fifth, RUTHERFORD.

As we know, Tarzan's mother was the Honourable Alice Rutherford. The *Honourable* indicates that she was the daughter of a baron or a viscount, though ERB does not tell us what the title of her father was. The Rutherfords are an ancient and once-powerful Scots border family. Its name comes from the Old English *hrythera ford*, meaning *wild cattle of the ford*. The arms you see here, the wild bull cabossed and the wildman's head between the horns, are the arms of the lords of Tennington. Internal evidence in *The Return of Tarzan* convinces me that Tarzan's mother was the aunt of the Lord Tennington who married Hazel Strong, Jane Porter's best friend. The reasons for this conclusion will be given in a separate essay.

Sixth, GREYSTOCK.

Tarzan is descended through at least half a dozen lines from the barons of Greystoke. At present, the barony is in abeyance, the last male heir having died in 1569. The Earl of Carlisle, the Baron of Petre, and the Baron of Mowbray, Segrave, and Stourton are co-heirs. The Earl of Carlisle bears the Greystoke arms on his shield, and a cousin of the Duke of Norfolk resides in Greystoke Castle. I have a letter from the cousin in which he says that he was very fond of the Tarzan books when he was young. But, he adds, ". . . as you know, I am not Tarzan."

What he doesn't say is that he is a relative of Tarzan's.

About all that remains to explain in the arms is the dexter supporter. Aside from it being green, it looks like the usual savage or woodman supporter. Actually, it represents the son of John Caldwell. After his father's supposed death, the son had to flee into the wilds of northern England to escape the King's officers. There he adopted a green costume and used a green-painted bow and green arrows. Because of these, he was known as The Green Archer or, sometimes, as The Green Baron. His legend was combined with that of Robert Fitzooth to create the Robin Hood legend.

The golden lion skin which he wears here was added by Tarzan to honor Jad-bal-ja.

THE ARMS OF TARZAN

So you can see that the baby born in a little log cabin on the West African coast, raised by apes, naked until twenty and then wearing second-hand clothes, yet came from a lineage few can match and eventually inherited the golden coronet and crimson miniver-edged mantle of a peer of the realm.

Before I close, let me summarize the illustrious ancestors of Tarzan.

First, the nonhuman founder of his line, Woden, chief god of the Old English tribes.

Henry III and through him William the Conqueror and Rolf the Ganger (the Viking who conquered Normandy). Through Henry III's wife, Alfred the Great, Egbert, and Charlemagne, Charlemagne could trace his ancestry back to Pepin the Short, died 768 A.D.

Also, through Henry III, the Outlaw of Torn and his son, The Green Archer, one of the two men whose exploits contributed to the Robin Hood legend.

And possibly, many times over, the genes of the Outlaw of Torn, later known as John Carter of Barsoom.

Through the Scots Drummond family, Tarzan is descended from Árpád, the Magyar conqueror of Hungary.

Through the O'Briens, from Olliol Olum, Irish King, early 200s.

I don't have time to go into the many other famous ancestors of Tarzan, such as Sir Nigel Loring (whose story is told in Doyle's *The White Company* and *Sir Nigel*). Or such as William Marshal, the Earl of Pembroke, who served Richard I and King John and was undoubtedly the greatest warrior of his time and probably of the entire Middle Ages (outside of the Outlaw of Torn). These will be described in detail in the lineage of Tarzan, which will be in my, *The Private Life of Tarzan*.

I hope you have enjoyed this visitation into Tarzan's ancestry via his coat-of-arms.

I thank you.

TARZAN THE REASONER

This piece is a perfect example of how Farmer condenses his extensive knowledge, based on a lifetime of study, into a short but idea-packed article. Originally written as in introduction for a reprinting of the short story, "The God of Tarzan" (in *Mother Was a Lovely Beast*, Chilton, 1974) it is included here for the references Farmer gives and for reminding us that Burroughs, like Farmer, was interested in more than just Tarzan's adventurous exploits. Tarzan is not only a real man, he is one with a prodigious talent to reason and extrapolate.

"The God of Tarzan" is not reproduced here but readers conversant with that story will smile when they recall, or revisit, the last line and will marvel at Tarzan's god-like ability to question the world about him.

The best feral human stories try to illuminate the mind of the man or woman who has been raised in a dark world, the nonhuman world. The nervous system of the child is cast into a human mold by reason of its heredity, but the environment has shaped it otherwise. The mind has two parallel world-lines which, in a Lobachevskian fashion, never quite meet. In Lobachevsky's geometry, parallel lines don't meet; but they do approach each other asymptotically. The distance between them becomes less as they are extended. Just so, the feral human's mind has adopted a half-animal world view and may keep this unchanged unless it encounters the human world. Then it becomes more human. But it never becomes all human.

Throughout his Tarzan stories, Edgar Rice Burroughs was more concerned with adventure than with psychology. But every once in a while he would try to extrapolate the feral human mind. He came closest to success in the first novel, *Tarzan of the Apes*, and in a collection of short stories, *Jungle Tales of Tarzan*. The latter describes in physical and psychological detail the ape man when he was nineteen, just before he met white Westerners and shortly after he had encountered Africans of an isolated community. In a sense, Tarzan had previously encountered the Western world, since he had taught himself to read English and had gained some fluency in reading the books in the cabin of his long-dead parents. So he was not altogether the innocent. But his knowledge of the Western world was necessarily confused and vague. He had no referents.

My favorite among the *Jungle Tales of Tarzan* is "The God of Tarzan." In this we see the ingenious method by which he taught himself to pronounce words he had never heard. He comes across references to God, the Creator, a concept unknown to the subhumans he grew up among. He becomes obsessed with eschatology, ontology, and cosmogony without, of course, having as yet come across these philosophical and theological terms. Like George Bernard Shaw's heroine in *Adventures of the Black Girl in Her Search for God* and Amos Tutuola's heroine of *Simbi and the Satyr of the Dark Jungle*, Tarzan goes forth to track down the Creator.

He fails in this quest, of course. But he discovers something in him that at least brings him closer to his Creator and, hence, to humanity. He discovers compassion.

A Language for Opar

In this essay Farmer explores the anomalies that Burroughs' description of La and Opar gave us. He explains that Burroughs, not being a linguist, was more interested in telling the story and so took short cuts. Of equal interest is Farmer's speculations on the religious history of Opar and how it might have come to have the hierarchy it does.

First published in *ERB-dom*, 75 in 1974 it exemplifies the painstaking thought processes (physical, cultural, and linguistic) Farmer went through to support his contention that Tarzan, and the majority of his adventures as described by Burroughs, are based on a real person and real events.

In *The Return of Tarzan*, Tarzan is captured the first time he enters the city of Opar. He is placed on an altar to be sacrificed, and the high priestess, La, recites a "long and tiresome prayer." At least, Tarzan presumes it's a prayer, since the language is unknown to him. Later, La addresses him. Tarzan replies in five languages, none of which she understands. The last is "the mongrel tongue of the West Coast," a *bêche-de-mer* or pidgin spoken in the ports and along the shoreline of West Africa.

So far, I've been unable to identify this pidgin, though no doubt it exists and my research has not been extensive enough. The surprising thing is that Tarzan knows it. He's had the time to learn French, English, Arabic, and Waziri (to some extent, anyway). But when and where did he have opportunity and leisure to learn the West Coast pidgin? During the events of *Tarzan of the Apes* and *The*

Return of Tarzan, he has been very busy and had very little contact with the natives of the West Coast.

But seek and ye shall find. Tarzan must have learned at least its rudiments while he and d'Arnot were in the port-town they found at the end of their wanderings in *Tarzan of the Apes*. Tarzan, always a magnificent linguist, could have picked up the *bêche-de-mer* very quickly.

During the ceremony at the altar of this lost outpost of Atlantis, Tha, an Oparian priest, makes a complaint. Tarzan is surprised to hear him speak "his own mother tongue." This is the speech of the Mangani—"the low guttural barking of the tribe of great anthropoids." La answers Tha in the same tongue.

Burroughs could not have meant that the two Oparians were emitting dog-like barks. Possibly, a language could consist of clusters of long and short barks, a barking Morse code, in other words. But humans would never adopt such a speech.

Besides, Burroughs makes it evident throughout the Tarzan books that the Mangani speech has definite words with consonants and vowels and that these are arranged in syntactical order. Intonation also plays an important part in the meaning. It determines whether "kagoda" means, "Do you surrender?" or "I do surrender." And intonation in a barking language is impossible.

The only way to reconcile Burroughs' two contradictory descriptions of the Mangani speech is to assume that he meant something that did not accord with the conventional definition of "barking." Perhaps the force with which the words were uttered suggested to him the "barking" metaphor. Thus, in English, a drill sergeant can "bark" orders.

Burroughs' use of the adjective "guttural" must mean that the Mangani used sounds not found in English and seldom found in other languages. I believe that he meant by this one of the definitions of "guttural" given by Webster: "being or marked by utterance that is strange, unpleasant, or disagreeable." Burroughs was no linguist and hence did not use "guttural" in a truly linguistic sense.

Note that the original language is "a grunting monosyllabic" tongue. What Burroughs means by "grunting" is open to speculation. He does not define the term. "Opar" and "Oah" (Cadj's fellow conspirator) are not monosyllables. But Opar must be a heritage of the period in which the language was not monosyllabic. Oah, instead of being O-ah, could be a diphthong, pronounced as our English "aw" or "oy." Burroughs doesn't tell us its pronunciation.

Whatever the sounds of the Mangani language, they are not out of the range of human speech. Apparently, the Mangani have teeth, oral cavities, larynxes and pharynxes much like those of human beings. And this tells us that the Mangani are not as ape-like as Burroughs depicts them.

After Tarzan kills the madman Tha, he and La have a long conversation in Mangani. La tells him of the origin of Opar and summarizes its history. And we're confronted by a problem at once.

Both La and Tarzan use many words which the Mangani tongue just would not have. In the paragraph beginning "You are a wonderful man . . ." La uses "city" and "civilization." Tarzan, in his reply, uses "religion" and "creed." Some of the other non-Mangani words in the following dialog are "priestess," "temple," "ten thousand," "gold," "ships," "mines," "slaves," "soldiers," "sailed," "fortress," "galley," "rituals," "sacrilegious," and "God."

It is probable that La used these words. But they would have been loanwords from the Oparian tongue and hence unintelligible to Tarzan. He knew only the Mangani of the west coast of Africa. This, as chapter IV, "The God of Tarzan," of *Jungle Tales of Tarzan* indicates, had no concepts of, or words for, any words to do with religion. And what would the Mangani among whom Tarzan had been raised know of gold, galley, mines, slaves, civilization, etc? Doubtless, the Oparian language had a word for "ten thousand." But the preliterate Mangani would not. For most preliterates, a word signifying "many" has to represent numbers above twenty. Some can count above that, but not very far.

How Was Tarzan Able to Understand La?

One explanation is that he interpreted the unfamiliar words from the context. Another, the most likely, is that he interrupted La many times to ask her for the definition of a word. This would not have been easy for La, since she would have had to use the limited Mangani vocabulary to make the definition. Apparently, she was successful. Tarzan's acquaintance with the vocabulary of several civilized peoples enabled him to grasp her meaning quickly.

In any event, the dialog did not proceed as reported by Burroughs.

This linguistic difficulty may have been described to Burroughs. In this case, Burroughs just ignored the facts and described the dialog as if it had gone smoothly. He did this for the benefit of the reader, whom he thought (rightly or not) wouldn't be interested in the mechanics of the conversation. Burroughs discarded realism for the sake of speed of narration. The essential thing was to communicate the basics of La's history of Opar.

Since the humans and the Mangani of Opar were in such close linguistic contact, it is likely that some of the personal names of the humans were borrowed from the Mangani. La doesn't seem to be one of these. Since she is the inheritor of a priesshood and queenship many thousands of years old, it is probable that "La" came from the other tongue. It might have originally been a title. Perhaps every chief priestess was named La. On the other hand, Oah, during her brief tenure as the chief priestess, did not adopt the name of La. Or perhaps Burroughs did not tell us that she did because he did not want to confuse the reader with two La's.

Some ERB scholars have speculated that La might mean, simply, She. That is, The She, Ayesha, the immortal queen and high priestess of the city of Kor (see H. Rider Haggard's *She, She and Allan,* and *Ayesha*) is addressed as "She" or "She-who-must-be-obeyed."

It's my theory that the city of Kor was founded by refugees from the same great civilization which gave birth to Opar. After the cataclysm which destroyed the mother-culture, survivors fled to various parts of Africa and founded their own tributary cultures. The cities of Athne and Cathne, Xuja, and Tuen-Baka may have been built by the refugees, and the wild Kavuru may also have been descendants of the refugees.

John Harwood and Frank Brueckel have originated this latter thesis, and it will be expounded in their forthcoming article, "Heritage of the Flaming God, an essay on the History of Opar and its Relationship to Other Ancient Cultures." This will be published by Vernell Coriell in a *Burroughs Bibliophiles.*[1] Harwood and Brueckel originated the idea that the lost cities of the Tarzan books may have been built by survivors of the destroyed mother-state. It is my own

---

[1] This article was not printed as indicated here but did become the titular essay in a collection printed in 1999 by Waziri Publications.

idea that Kor (and the civilization of the Zu-vendis, see Haggard's novel *Allan Quatermain*) were also founded by refugees.

One final speculation. The religion of Opar seems to have been monotheistic. This means that it was the end-product of thousands of years of civilization. It has gone through the polytheism which is an inevitable stage of early cultures and now has one deity, the sun, the Flaming God.

The Flaming God is a male, and yet the head of the theocracy is, and apparently always has been, a woman, La.

This situation is unlike any other of which I have read. Where the dominant deity (or deities) is male, the chief theocrats are males, and almost always the temporal ruler is male. In the pre-Indo-European and pre-Semitic civilizations around the Mediterranean, the chief deity was a chthonic mother-goddess, and her chief vicars were women. Then the Indo-Europeans and Semites of the patriarchal male gods won out. Men became the chief vicars; priestesses assumed a subordinate role.

Yet, in Opar, a woman is the head of the state and the chief of a religion which worships a male god. Does this singular situation reflect a long struggle between the priestesses of a mother-god and the priests of a father-god in ancient Opar? Was the sun-god originally a son of the Great Goddess, and did he finally rise from the rank of a secondary deity to that of the primary and, finally, that of the only deity? Such seems to have been the case with the male gods in Greece and other Mediterranean countries.

And was the struggle in Opar solved by a compromise? Did the son-sun become the only deity but the priestesses retained their position as the head of the religion?

This seems the only explanation to account for the unique Oparian religion. And this indicates that the mother-state, the mighty empire stretching from sea to sea, was a matriarchy, and its chief deity at that time was an earth-goddess.

However, it is possible that she was the sun in the beginning, and that in the end the sun had to become masculinized.

In Kor (according to *She and Allan*), the struggle was still going on. She, priestess of the moon, had long been challenged by Resu, priest of the sun. Only because of the intervention of Allan Quatermain and his mighty Zulu ally, Umslopogaas, were the worshippers of the moon (a female deity) able to triumph.

The question of the ancientness of religious sacrifice of human beings in Opar is not answered in the Oparian novels of Burroughs. Apparently, it had been going on for a long time. But this does not mean that human sacrifices were a part of the religion of the moth-er-state at the time of the cataclysm. In ten thousand years much will change, and the Oparians had degenerated in many respects.

I Still Live!

75th Anniversary Dinner Keynote Address

On October 21, 1989, Phil was a member of a hearty group of Edgar Rice Burroughs enthusiasts to travel to Chicago, Illinois to commemorate the 75th anniversary of the first hardcover publication of *Tarzan of the Apes*. The event was hosted by a group known as the "Normal Beans" of Chicago ("Normal Bean" being ERB's tongue-in-cheek pseudonym when he wrote his first novel, *A Princess of Mars*, misprinted by his editor as "Norman Bean") and a dinner was held, appropriately enough, at The Adventurers' Club. Chicago was chosen as the setting of the gathering for a number of reasons. Not only was it ERB's birthplace, but it was also where he penned *Tarzan of the Apes*, as well as being the city where the book was published by A. C. McClurg & Co. in 1914. But there was one more reason the location was so very appropriate, as Phil would reveal here for the first time.

Ladies and gentlemen (if you'll pardon me this now old-fashioned form of address), Mr. Tom Willshire, who's the organizer of this festive occasion, Normal Beans and all gathered here who don't fit into the three categories above:

Greetings from Lord Greystoke, a.k.a. John Clayton, Tarzan, Lord of the Jungle, the River Devil, The Apeman, Munango-Keewati, John Caldwell, and a dozen other more-or-less fitting titles!

This salutation does not come directly from Tarzan. I am assuming that, if he knew of this gathering, he would transmit greetings through me. However, since I last talked to him, I have not heard from him. That was in 1970, when I briefly interviewed him. Our meeting did not take place in Libreville, Gabon, West Africa as I described in an article for *Esquire* magazine and in my biography, *Tarzan Alive*. Because of security reasons, Lord Greystoke asked me to say that the meeting was in Libreville. But he told me that, after a few years, I could reveal that the meeting actually occurred in a motel room in Chicago. I don't know why security demanded that the truth be held back for a while. I didn't ask His Lordship, and I'm sure he wouldn't have given me any specifics if I had asked. It may have been more for my safety than his that he made this request. Probably, he was involved in some British government work, undercover, of course, or perhaps some personal enemies were after him.

Some day, we may find out just why this deception was necessary.

In any event, it was in Chicago, not far from here, that I talked to Tarzan. It was appropriate that this city be the place where I met him. His chief biographer, Edgar Rice Burroughs, was born in Chicago on September 1, 1875.

Thus, it's fitting that we celebrate here the Diamond Jubilee of the printing of ERB's 1st hardcover book, the 101st birthday of Tarzan, born Nov. 22, 1888, and 114th birthday of Edgar Rice Burroughs. We're a little premature in gathering here for Tarzan's birthday and a little late for Burroughs'. But nothing is perfect except in our imaginations.

However, we're not far off the mark in celebrating on this date the first appearance in print of *Tarzan of the Apes*. This was in the October issue of *All-Story Magazine*, 1912. And, remember, it was in Chicago that Burroughs first heard of Tarzan from the unnamed man who told Burroughs about The Apeman, the last incarnation of the heroes of ancient mythology.

As a side note, I did ask Lord Greystoke about his wife, Jane Porter. He replied briefly that she was still living and in good health. I assume that she, too, still looks young and is the gorgeous blonde undiminished by age, whom he married. Height, 5 feet seven inches, bust, 38; waist, 19; hips 36. What used to be called an hour-glass figure. And she's still the same courageous, tough and strong-minded lady.

I wish I could reveal just how I discovered who the "real" Tarzan was. I had plans for describing this complicated procedure—which used mainly *Burke's Peerage*—in the revised edition of *Tarzan Alive* (not my title[1].) The book is out of print just now, but I have hopes that, in a few years, it'll appear in a corrected and up-to-date edition[2]. I would prefer that it also give Lord Greystoke's real identity. But, until I get his final permission, I can't do that. I mentioned a minute ago that Tarzan was the last incarnation of the heroes of ancient mythology. I'll get to an elucidation of this statement in a moment. First, however, allow me a digression that is really not a digression. I have here some pages of a report from a professional astrologer, Susan Gillis, on the horoscope of a certain individual. This was done after the biography, *Tarzan Alive*, was published. Just for kicks, I had a friend who believes in astrology—I don't—act as middleman in the preparation of this horoscope. The astrologer was given the birth date and birthplace of an unnamed person. Using this data, she came up with the pages I have here, some of which I'll read to you.

Not until after the horoscope had been prepared was she told the name of the individual. While I'm reading this, keep in mind Tarzan's, Lord Greystoke's, characteristics as revealed in Burroughs' semi-biographical, more than somewhat fictionalized chronicles of the Apeman's life.

Interpretation of Horoscope
[With Farmer's commentary in square brackets]

PERSONALITY

The Native [*est. but he's an African native*] is a powerful individual who demands independence and freedom. He resents authority. There is a great persistence and determination. He finishes what he sets out to do. When he makes a promise he feels obligated to carry it through and will do so. [*right*] However, the Native tends to shun responsibility; [*prefers jungle life*] therefore he avoids committing himself. In other words he knows that he will feel an obligation to carry through any promise that he makes, and so prefers to avoid making a promise. [*right*] His feelings are likewise with other responsibilities. He has great self-control. He truly knows himself and can determine

---

[1] Farmer originally titled the book *The Private Life of Tarzan*.

[2] An updated version of *Tarzan Alive* was never printed.

his own fate. He is a humanitarian [*not in large sense, just towards those he knows*] but at the same time demands his own privacy. The native feels a need to get away from people to think things out and contemplate. [*Jungle Tales—ponders on Nature of Creation & the Creator, searching for identity as a human & formulation of his own philosophy*] What one sees of the Native's surface personality is not what is within. The Native outwardly presents a light and bolder type of personality. His true inner personality is extremely deep and intense. His mind works in a deep and intense fashion as well. The native enjoys intense research, delving, and learning. [*teaching himself to read when he didn't know English*] When he finds something that interests him, the Native will carry through to a successful conclusion. He has this tremendous self-control. He does not like to show his emotions outwardly, so people are not aware of the intensity of the emotions with the Native. However, the Native does get involved with the emotions and problems of friends. The Native will never lay his own emotions out on the table, or his own problems, for friends. The Native is intelligent, curious and skeptical to a healthy degree. [*right, Jungle Tales of Tarzan*] There can be disappointments in friends, though, due to misplaced trust. The Native is analytical and critical. Deep within there is a basic lack of emotional security and self-confidence. [*wrong*] He is an extremely physical person. He loves the outdoors, sports and animals. He has extreme physical coordination and dexterity. He has tremendous energy, and a love for travel. There is writing ability, as he communicates better through the written word than he does through the spoken word. [*silent—again learned to read—taught himself*]

LOVE LIFE

The Native is more physical than the emotional in his sex life and love life. This is due to his physical and emotional makeup, as previously mentioned. He is not quick to settle down and marry, but when the Native does marry, it is for good. There is no divorce shown in the chart. There is a broken marriage engagement shown in the chart of the Native however. [*not quite true—unless we talk of La of Opar, Nemone, the Countess de Coude or Teeka*]

HOROSCOPE
by
SUSAN GILLIS

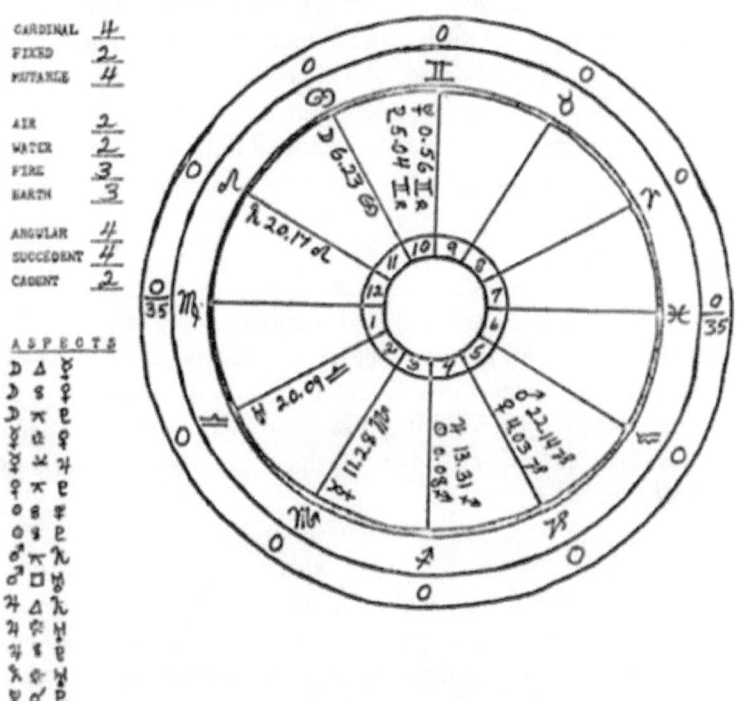

Name __TARZAN__   Sidereal Time at Noon or Midnight _28:07:36_

Birthdate _NOVEMBER 22, 1888_   Born how much before or after
                                   Noon or Midnight _11:55_

Time of Birth _12:05 A.M._   Sidereal Time at Birth _16:12:36_

Corrected Time _12:05 A.M._   Noon Mark at Birth Place _0:36 P.M._

Place of Birth _Coast of Gabon, Afr._ Born how much before or after
                                       Noon Mark _12:31_

Latitude _2°S_ Longitude _9°E_   Constant Logarithm _.2827_

CARDINAL _4_
FIXED _2_
MUTABLE _4_

AIR _2_
WATER _2_
FIRE _3_
EARTH _3_

ANGULAR _4_
SUCCEDENT _4_
CADENT _2_

ASPECTS

HOME

The Native does not know his father due to the death of the
father or a separation from the father when the Native was very
young. There is a stepfather in the Native's chart. There are problems
relating to the Native's parents. No specific problem is indicated in the
Native's chart, but general difficulties are indicated. These difficulties
could include an early separation from the natural parents, and/
or the Native's resentment towards the stepfather. [*Tublat—Dum-
Dum, Tarzan 13 years old. Tublat goes mad, corners Kala, Tarzan kills*

him with his real father's knife. In a sense recreated the original oedipal situation]

CAREER

Upheavals in the Native's career are indicated. [*plenty of those, one great danger after another*] Conflict is indicated between the Native and his employers or superiors. [*Tublat and Kerchak*] The Native attracts public attention through his career. [*ERB's books and movies*] His financial status is never on an even keel. [*loses money in investments more than once, back to Opar to refill his exchequer*] The Native can go back and forth between financial stability and financial chaos many times in his career. The Native has a potential for acting, [*posing as aged, his various pseudonyms and identities assumed*] as well as an ability for writing. There is career potential for the Native's great physical coordination and dexterity. [*not an Olympic contender—too much publicity.*]

HEALTH

The Native is extremely health conscious. He strives to keep himself physically fit. He would be aware of a proper diet and would use health foods. The Native knows that good nutrition keeps him healthy. [*A Feast Unknown*] Any health problems would most likely be in the Native's legs; particularly the thigh and knee regions. [*? mostly his head, concussions*]

As you can see the astrologer came close to the mark on most counts.

While writing *Tarzan Alive*, I did my own research in astrology. I'm a mere tyro in it, but there were enough reference books available for me to figure out the horoscope. And, amazingly or not, the astrology did work out. Tarzan, a Sagittarius, but born on the cusp between Sagittarius and Scorpio, also has many of the characteristics of the Scorpio. The persona of Tarzan, as described by Burroughs, and the natal chart as worked out by the astrologer, agreed in most respects.

Once, I got a letter from a reader of *Tarzan Alive*. He had the brass to accuse me of having worked out Tarzan's birth date from the characteristics and life of Tarzan. That is, I did it backwards in order to find the most suitable birth date and, hence, the astrological data.

I Still Live!

I was hurt and somewhat indignant for a while at this accusation. But I've cooled off since then. After all, a healthy skepticism is to be admired, and both Tarzan and myself are skeptics. But I assure you that the birth date came first. I got it from Lord Greystoke himself. Of course, he could have been misleading me, but I see no reason why he should have.

We return to the statement that Tarzan is the last incarnation of the heroes of ancient mythology. Mythology, as those familiar with the works of Joseph Campbell and Carl Gustav Jung know, derives ultimately from the archetypes in the mass unconscious mind of human beings. Not just in the minds of Westerners but in the minds of all races, tribes, and nationalities.

There's not enough time here to develop this theme, but those who have read my *Tarzan Alive* have been given enough to highlight this theme. Allow me, however, to read a paragraph relevant to this premise, one which I pursue in a number of sections in the book.

> Tarzan was indeed magnificent. He looked like the hero of classical myth, and, like them, he had been hidden in a far-off corner. He had been biding his time until he had fully developed his powers. Then he would come out to astonish the great world and perform feats of wonder and be the savior of peoples. He was like Hercules, Samson, Theseus, Achilles, Hiawatha, Gilgamesh, Finn McCool and the young Arthur. Burroughs may or may not have been consciously aware of the similarity of young Tarzan to the heroes of old. But there is no doubt that in his unconscious, where artistry is born, where archetypes live, he was aware. He was reporting on the last of the heroes, the final great son of Mother Nature, her gift to the twentieth century, and her reminder that the demigods were not yet all dead.

One of the appeals of the Tarzan books is to our unconscious, where dwell the gods, and goddesses, the spirits, the succubi and incubi, the djinns, the monsters of Chaos, the wizards and witches, the wise old man, the Great Mother, the great enchantresses and seductresses (ERB's La of Opar and HRH's She-who-must-be-obeyed to name only two), Old Man Death Himself, and the saviors and heroes of old.

This is not the only appeal. A strong fascination is the image in the reader's mind of living like Tarzan in the jungle, free of inhibitions, constraints, obligations and responsibilities of civilized life, freedom from traffic, traffic lights, traffic jams, paying taxes, paying off the mortgage, hospital and doctor bills, free of doing what your neighbors and the government, which also lies to you, requires you to do. Freedom! Being your own ruler, living in a state of blissful anarchy.

This freedom is doubtless an illusion, but it glows brightly in the imagination and makes us envy Tarzan.

There are also the adventures Tarzan experiences. We live in them vicariously, and we have fun, without the danger. Let's not forget fun.

However, the evoking of archetypal images while reading Tarzan is a very strong one. I gave some space to that in the biography. But a professor of Classics at the University of Iowa, Doctor Erling B Holtsmark, devotes much more space to this theme—and others—in his *Tarzan and Tradition: Classical Myth in Popular Literature*, Greenwood Press, CT, first published in 1981. It may still be available from Greenwood Press. I strongly recommend this study, which not only stresses the classical and preliterate myths evident in Tarzan's life but also makes a keen literary analysis of Burroughs' writings.

Holtsmark claims—and cites evidence—that Burroughs is much more than the inspired hack writer so many critics and academics think he is.

Allow me to quote briefly from the description in the front inner flap of the dust jacket.

"Holtsmark finds Burroughs' own extensive classical education evident in the Tarzan books. The first six books that is. Burroughs' language and narrative style reflect the central premises of ancient Greek and Latin literary technique. His thematic concerns also parallel those of the classical authors. Tarzan himself is a surprisingly complex literary persona whose clear roots in the mythical heroes of antiquity, notably Odysseus, are combined with features borrowed from American Indian traditions . . . Holtsmark also explores the erotic and Darwinian elements in Burroughs' thematic structure."

Holtsmark has an extensive bibliography. He seems to have covered all items re Burroughs and Tarzan that he could find. Strangely enough, there is no mention of my book, *Tarzan Alive*, which preceded his by nine years. I don't know how he missed it. But our conclusions re the thematic elements in the Tarzan books and the development of Tarzan's character—he does change in his attitudes and behavior during the course of the early books and in the final chronological volume—Holtsmark and I find the same elements, come to the same conclusions.

However, Holtsmark's study also stresses the literary elements and analyses them almost to the molecular level. Again, I highly recommend this book. Not just to readers of the jungle saga but to academics who make comments about Burroughs and Tarzan which display their own ignorance despite their claim to be scholars.

Now, in the same vein, I'll read a copy of a letter of mine which appeared in the editorial column of the *Philadelphia Inquirer*, April 29, 1972. The *Philadelphia Inquirer* is not connected to the *National Inquirer*.

BOOK CHARACTER DISTORTED

Tarzan Still Lives – and is no bigot

To the Editor:

I read Art Peters' column of April 14 concerning my book *Tarzan Alive* and Peters' stand against comic books. If Mr. Peters had read my book, he'd know that there is almost no connection between the Tarzan of Burroughs (the book Tarzan) and the movie, TV, and comic book images of Tarzan.

If Mr. Peters had read my book, he'd know that Tarzan is not racially prejudiced. How could he be? Prejudice is judging before you know the facts. Society establishes an emotional bias towards certain subjects in the infant. The adult continues to reinforce his early-life conditioning with rationalizations that have no basis in reality.

Tarzan never saw a human being until he was an adult. And, as Burroughs makes clear in the 24 books about him, Tarzan could care less about skin color. Black or white, man or beast, it was the individual that counted.

If Mr. Peters had read my book, he'd know that Tarzan had a Jewish grandmother. This won't set well with the many anti-Semites among whites and Blacks. But Tarzan also had Black forebears. And he was descended from Mohammed, who, you may remember, was an Arab.

Contrary to what Mr. Peters says, Tarzan did mature. (The book Tarzan of course; I'm not speaking of the movie or comic book person.) In the beginning, he's a simple ape-man, sometimes cruel, prone to solve problems with violence. But he is highly intelligent, and though he makes mistakes, he learns.

He not only matures; he evolves. He learns the rules of civilization, though he doesn't always obey them nor does he ever groove on civilization.

In the final book of his adventures, it is he who restrains an American soldier from slaughtering surrounded Japanese troops. It is he who says that hate never does any good. It is he who has learned to laugh at many things, including himself.

He is still, in one sense, the Noble Savage, but he is also an ideal civilized man, that is, he is a true gentleman. Of course, he'll still eat worms if he gets a chance, but that's because he has no prejudice against eating them.

American readers are too likely to confuse the present white-black situation here with the relations between Tarzan and Blacks in Africa. There is no correlation.

Just as there is no correlation between my book and Mr. Peters' comments on it.

Philip José Farmer
Peoria, Ill.

So, there, you asshole! I thought as I finished that letter.

I have a few tag ends re *Tarzan Alive* that you might find amusing.

One, when *Tarzan Alive* came out, a Boston TV station called the publisher to get my address. The station wanted to invite me to Boston for an interview about Tarzan and, mainly, about his being a real, that is, nonfictional character. The dolts at the publicity department of the publisher told the caller that the book was a hoax! This really pissed me off. The least the publicity people could have done was phone me and ask if Lord Greystoke really did live. That incident, by the way, was one more in the long list of things I had against this particular publisher.

Two, several years ago, I got a call from a would-be Olympic athlete who wanted Tarzan's address. The athlete desired training tips from Tarzan, whom he figured, rightly, was the world's greatest athlete. And all without steroids, too.

I had to tell this athlete that I did not have Tarzan's forwarding address. I still don't.

I also received a number of letters, one from as far away as Australia, inquiring about getting in touch with Tarzan.

Once, at a convention, an attendee asked me if I really believed that Tarzan did exist. I replied, "You believe in God, don't you?" I let him figure out the ambiguities in that statement.

But I say to you, in one sense or another, TARZAN STILL LIVES!

FROM FORNE TO FARMER

Another short piece but brimming with Farmer's wit and mischief. Published in *Erbania* 53/54, in the summer of 1985 Farmer looks at his own lineage and reveals he is a distant relative to the man known to all as Tarzan.

Today's my 67th birthday (Jan 26th), but I'm busier than I have ever been what with four book contracts, overwhelming fan and business correspondence, and just living. Plus putting in a little time now and then on an Esperanto translation of *Tarzan of the Apes*, a Latin translation of "The God of Tarzan," and a Munchkin translation of *The Wizard of Oz*.

During my genealogical research, going on for six years now, I've discovered that President George Washington was a direct descendant of the barons of Greystoke. Just recently I've found out that President Abraham Lincoln and his mother, Nancy Hanks, were direct descendants of the early lord of Greystoke. And so am I. I'll be happy to send a chart if you're interested in publishing it along with an article. Rather, charts. I figure there are 36 generations from my grandchildren to Forne, the earliest recorded Greystoke.

In fact, there must be over fifty million people in the U.S.A. alone who are descended from the early Greystokes. But most of them can't prove it or, alas, aren't interested in doing so.

When I was in England last July, I saw a taped film of a British film-documentary, *The Making of Greystoke*. Someday, maybe, it'll be on PBS here. Ian Johnstone, a British TV reporter-editor, flew to Peoria to interview me, and some of that is in the film. It's certainly gratifying, though unexpected, to see the skyline of Peoria, Illinois in a film made about the filming of the movie. Johnstone had read my biography of Lord Greystoke, so he did the documentary on the assumption that Tarzan was a real person. Did you know that Tarzan's father's oil portrait hangs in the National Gallery in London?

Philip José Farmer (Peoria, Il)

In His Own Words

EXTRACTS FROM THE MEMOIRS OF "LORD GREYSTOKE"

Farmer's foreword to this piece originally appeared in *Mother Was a Lovely Beast* and, as here, served as an introductory and explanatory commentary on what was to follow.

It should be noted that American spellings are used. Presumably this was due to minor amendments made by Farmer, or his Lordship, knowing the audience, adopted US spellings and writing conventions.

The footnotes are those added by Farmer in the original publication of this piece. Some very minor edits have been made to fit it more comfortably into this collection.

FOREWORD BY PHILIP JOSÉ FARMER

This is the only valid example of first-person reporting by a feral man himself.

It is composed of selections from memoirs written by a man who was raised from the age of one by beings halfway on the scale of evolution between the great apes and modern man. His parents, English aristocrats, were marooned on the coast of Gabon, then French Equatorial Africa, in 1888. His mother died a year after he was born, and his father was killed the same day. Fortunately, he was taken from the cradle and raised by a female "anthropoid" whose own baby had just died.

In 1909, "Lord Greystoke" made his first contact with whites and was taken to France. After a series of adventures, he assumed his British inheritance, which included a title. He also married an American woman of an old Virginia and Maryland family. In 1912 an American writer, Edgar Rice Burroughs, heard some garbled accounts of "Greystoke" and used these as the basis for a novel which now ranks among the world classics of literature. This was *Tarzan of the Apes*, a highly fictionalized narrative which nevertheless was essentially true.

In 1968 I was able to ascertain the true identity of "Lord Greystoke" and to track him down. I did this through a close study of *Burke's Peerage* and another source I am not free to divulge. I got in contact with "Greystoke," and he agreed to give me a fifteen-minute interview. An abridged version of this was printed in the *Esquire* magazine of September 1972. The meeting supposedly took place in Libreville, Gabon. But I have now been given permission by "Greystoke" to reveal that this actually occurred in a motel near Chicago.

The interview was so short that I was not able to ask nearly all the questions I had hoped to. "Greystoke," however, promised that he would send me some portions of his memoirs and that I could publish them. He did not say when he would send them or from where. But in May 1973, I received a package mailed from San Francisco. Part of it is printed herein.

I was happy to learn just how "Greystoke" managed to come into his inheritance and title. Burroughs, referred to as "B" in these memoirs, wrote that "Greystoke" was revealed as the true heir after his cousin died. I knew that this could not be true. Such a spectacular event would have been widely publicized, and the world would know exactly who "Greystoke" was. The account here explains how "Greystoke" managed to avoid all publicity and exposure. I had suspected that something such as he describes had occurred, and I am glad that my suspicions were valid. The beauty of this revelation is that even now, without a certain clue which I discovered quite by accident, the identity of "Greystoke" remains a secret.

I was also happy because this is the only account that I have ever read which gives an insight into what it is like to be a feral man. It tells in authentic detail just how he was raised; it gives the mundane details, in short, the days in the life of a truly wild man. It also offers some insight into the psychology of a human raised by nonhumans. Or, to be exact, a human raised by creatures as close to beasts as to humans.

In one sense, "Greystoke" is not a true feral man. The beings among whom he grew up were language-users, and this differentiates him from all the other authentic cases of feral men. He was not linguistically, and hence mentally, retarded. He grew up in a society which was less than human but which had enough human elements to enable him to adjust to the culture of *Homo sapiens*.

The wording herein is not always that of "Greystoke." It is frank enough as it is, but I have substituted Latinisms for his "Anglo-Saxonisms" in his references to sexual and excretory matters. "Greystoke" has no emotional reactions to the use of "tabu" words and felt free to use them in his memoirs. I have made the substitutions necessitated by the recent Supreme Court ruling on obscenity and pornography, which is a step backwards toward Victorian darkness and idiocy.

The order of the sections here is not necessarily as arranged by "Greystoke."

How it was with J

I looked out of the cabin window, and there was the ship.

I'd seen ships in pictures. But this was a real sailing ship, an enormous thing of beauty and awe.

I knew it was artificial, but I never thought of it as such. It was a living being, as much alive as an elephant and even stranger than my first sight of an elephant. I never was to get over that deeply ingrained assumption that anything that moved was alive. I've traveled on a hundred ships, driven dozens of automobiles, and piloted scores of airplanes, and I always feel that I am on or in a living being.

And so I waited for the great creature to come to a stop and let the smaller creatures, human beings, from its back. My heart was thudding, I was dry-skinned, my mouth was dry, and I was quivering. At last! To see, not pictures, but the flesh! To face, to talk with, beings of my own kind!

Still, I did not run out to greet them. My experiences with the natives had taught me that humans might be hostile no matter how friendly I was. I retreated from the cabin to the bush, and there I spied on them. Presently, a longboat was let down off the davits (I was proud because I knew what *davits* were, though I couldn't pronounce the word, of course).

After a while, the boat beached, and some men got out onto the sand. A few minutes later, one of them was murdered during a quarrel.

I was wise to hide in the bush. They were dangerous.

When I saw J[1] step out of the boat, I was thrilled. I had never seen anything so beautiful except for my foster mother, and that was a completely different kind of beauty, of course. I also got an erection.

This was the normal response of a twenty-year-old human male and of an adult male n'k. B never mentioned this in his novel for several reasons. One, he did not know of it. Two, if he had guessed that it did occur, he could not have described it. Such references were forbidden. He might have said that I was "inflamed with lust," but then the literary conventions required that the hero be "pure in thought and deed." "Purity" required that his mind and body be unconnected with his genitals. Every adult reader knew, of course, that the hero would have an erection, but this was ignored. Or perhaps every adult reader did not know this. The ignorance of sexual matters among the female population of English speakers circa 1909 was amazing. And often tragic.

I did know, from my reading, that the characters in the novels were never described as having genitals nor was the sexual act described except by the most circuitous route. And only the villains were ever "inflamed with lust."

I knew that if I were to display myself to the woman, she would be shocked and repelled. But even if I had done so, I was wearing an antelope-skin loincloth. This was one I'd taken from a local villager and habitually wore because I *knew* that humans did not expose their genitals. I was mistaken in this, since a number of preliterates, various

---

[1] I don't know if this stands for Jane, Jean, Jill, June, or some other name. "Greystoke" has the annoying, but necessary, habit of using initials only to designate individuals whose identity needs shielding.

Sudanese natives, and Australian aborigines, etc., go completely naked. Or did so at that time.

The males who had first landed seemed to be in control of the woman and her party, so I did not venture out. I was afraid, rightly, that the sailors would try to kill me if I revealed myself. I intended to watch until I got a chance to rescue the woman and her party. I wasn't sure whether or not the sailors intended to butcher their prisoners and eat them. Though none of the novels or histories I'd read had said anything about cannibalism being accepted in human civilization, I assumed that it was tabu. The article on cannibalism in the encyclopedia stated that the custom was prevalent among certain groups of Africans, and I knew that the natives near the n'k territory were cannibals. Perhaps the practice existed among some groups of whites.

In any event, I did know that rape was common among all groups of men, and I was determined that the woman was not going to be raped. Not unless, of course, she accepted it. I understood that there were certain women, prostitutes or whores, who sold their bodies for use by men. The woman did not seem to be one of those, but then I did not know exactly how one recognized a whore.

I kept a close watch on the tall beautiful blonde with the large grey eyes. Events for the next few days occurred somewhat as B described them, including my posting a warning note on the door of the cabin after it had been ransacked by the mutineers. I was capable by then of writing simple English sentences. Contrary to what B wrote, however, I did not sign my n'k name. This would have been impossible, since I did not know the correlation of n'k sounds with the Latin alphabet. I printed the English translation of one of my n'k names: WHITE BOY. Rather, I gave the translation I preferred. As I've said elsewhere, my name could be translated as Worm, Hairless Boy, and others even more derogatory.

B was also correct when he described me as breaking the neck of a big cat with a full nelson when it tried to get into the cabin window after J and E.[2] However, the cat was a leopard, not a lioness, and it was an old male. One of the extraordinarily large leopards that existed in that area, it had become a man-eater, preying on the local

---

[2] J's mother surrogate, the servant of J's father. J's mother died at J's birth, and E raised her. E was J's chaperone on the treasure hunting expedition.

villagers. Actually, it was my fault that it was a man-eater, since I had thrown the body of one of the men I'd killed to it and so enabled it to acquire a taste for human meat.

On that day when J and E bathed in a pool and J was carried off by Tks, I heard her screaming and tracked the two down. Tks had become king of the tribe after I'd abdicated, but he had been driven out because of his cruelty and his disdain of the tribal laws. He was, I believe, a psychopath. His aberrations may have been caused by being dropped on his head when he was an infant. In any event, he was wandering around when he saw J bathing. He grabbed her and ran off. He did not swing through the trees with her as B described. He was too heavy to have progressed in monkey fashion even if he had been alone. He ran with her in his arms until he got winded and then pushed her ahead of him.

I arrived before he could rape her, and I killed him with my knife. This would have happened sooner or later, since Tks hated me, and I was happy to have it over with. Besides, it made me look good in J's eyes.

She, however, had a short-lived relief. I scooped her up and kissed her all over, as was the n'k custom when making love. This panicked her, and she fought and screamed. I stopped, since I did not want to offend her, though I did not understand why she was so frightened. After I released her, she insisted that we return to the pool so she could put her clothes on. I did not understand her words or gestures, though the gestures were plain enough. I think now that I did not want to understand her. I wanted to keep her for my own, and I was sure that in a short time she would get over her fright.

As B said, I did not return her to the cabin until the next day. She got over her fright somewhat, though my evident tumescent state ensured that she could not relax completely. When night came, I tried to hold her in my arms to keep her warm (also hoping by this to overcome her objections). But she would have none of that. She preferred to sit against the trunk of a tree and shiver all night.

Our relations were not quite as idyllic or as innocent as B portrayed.

Next day, I took her back to the pool, where she donned her clothes. I wanted to watch her, but she made it evident that I must not do so. After a while, I got the idea and turned my back. I did not understand why she was so embarrassed by her nakedness. After all, she had been completely naked for twenty-four hours.

Now that I look back on it, I am surprised that J did not become so disgusted with me that she found it impossible to love me. My eating habits must have repulsed her, and my lack of Western toilet training horrified her. But she understood that I was a feral man and that I was in no way responsible for my behavior. She also understood that I was restraining myself from making love to her and so I got some credit as being a basically decent human being.

I wonder what she would have thought if she had known that I'd mated quite often with some of the n'k females? I was unable to tell her about this at that time, and it was just as well. Though she was a liberal-minded woman despite her Victorian conditioning, she might not ever have forgiven me for having three wives. Having had, I should say. When I abdicated the kingship and left the tribe, I also divorced the three females, since I did not want them as companions.

Some years later, I told her about them, and her only response was to laugh and to ask me if I had had any children by them. I answered, truthfully, that I had not.

Since these females had babies by n'k males after I'd left them, it was evident that they were not sterile. I don't know whether it was impossible for a human to fertilize a n'k or whether I am just not very fertile. I've had only one child by J, though we've never used any birth control methods. So I presume that I am at fault.

But, as J has several times remarked, thank goodness virility has nothing to do with fertility.

The way it was with O

In his second novel about me, B gives a somewhat bowdlerized and distorted account of my "affair" with O, Countess C. (Lovely woman, she is dead now. After her much older husband died, she remarried and had four children, one of whom I met while he served with the Free French in World War II.)

B says that O and I were alone in her house, though our assignation had, in the beginning, no sexual intent. But we were in each other's arms when her husband, warned by that despicable blackmailer, her brother, entered with intent to kill.

I don't know what would have happened if he had not burst in on us. I myself was not sure what my conduct should be, since I was not sure of the rules in this particular case. I suspect that I would have followed my natural inclinations unless O had said no, and she did not seem likely to do so.

I was neither engaged nor married and was on the rebound from J. As far as I knew, J and I would never see each other again. But I did want to follow the rules of society. The trouble here was that I did not know what the rules were in this particular contest.

Adultery was illegal, but I had observed that humans often did what was illegal and did not consider adultery immoral. At least, not very immoral.

I myself had none of the moral objections to sexual conduct by which humans are supposed to guide themselves. Though adultery is frowned upon by the n'k, everybody practices it. If caught, they suffer physical punishment, not the pangs of conscience or ostracism from society. Once the beating is over, the thing is done.

I was in Paris, and I knew that the rules depended upon the situation. Some French men would kill you if they caught you with their wives. Others accepted it as long as the business was conducted discreetly.

So what, I wondered, was the context of the situation with O? To which group did her husband belong?

While I was wrestling with this problem, O was preparing to disrobe. Whatever her husband's attitude, she was getting ready to mate with me.

I wasn't, as B implied, "loath" to mate. But I did intend to ask her what her husband thought about this.

Then he burst in with a loaded cane and tried to kill me with it. I lost my temper, and I reverted to my normal state of the threatened n'k. If O had not cried out so vehemently, I would have killed him as a terrier kills a rat. But I stopped; and then, cooling off, I felt that I should abide by the human rules. I had made a mistake and must suffer the consequence. Hence, the duel which B describes wherein I refused to fire back at him. Hence, my lie about the seriousness of the intentions of his wife and myself.

A number of B's critics have said that I acted as if I had been born in King Arthur's court. No real human being would have acted as self-sacrificingly as I did. What they overlooked is that I felt obligated to obey the rules because I was not thoroughly human.

Later on, after I had comprehended the extent of the hypocrisy of humans, I would not have behaved so chivalrously. I would have lied to save O, taken the blame, but I would have shot the count in the arm and rendered him hors de combat.

But then I would never have gotten into the situation in the first place.

How I escaped Publicity

If events had been exactly as B described them, the whole world would have been cognizant of me, and nobody would now think of me as a fictional character. The publicity would have turned my life into hell. My only escape would have been to plunge back into the jungle.

D[3] was well aware of what would happen if my story became known. He was afraid that publicity might destroy me.

My cousin had already inherited the title, and I did not wish to file my claim on it. As B says, I sacrificed my rightful inheritance because I thought that J wished to marry my cousin. I was willing to give up everything if it meant that J would be happy.

I know that this sounds like the noble act of the hero of a romantic novel. But it happened. Perhaps it happened so easily because I had read such novels and thought that I should abide by the rules expressed and implied in them. But I don't really think so. I loved J, and I loathed my cousin because he had, I thought, won out over me. But I did not hate J because she had rejected me. I could understand why she, a highly cultured person, would not want to marry a man raised by beasts. (She thought the n'k were some kind of apes, but even if I had been raised in an Amazonian Indian tribe, she would have hesitated. Or so I thought.)

B says nothing about my difficulties in getting a passport in Port-Gentil[4] and taking passage to France. But D knew that there

---

[3] D is presumably the French naval lieutenant who brought Greystoke to civilization.

[4] A town in Gabon, an area on the west coast of equatorial Africa.

would be much trouble when I entered the town unless a suitable story was prepared. Otherwise, the authorities would have thrown me into gaol while they investigated my unauthorized presence in the French territory of Gabon.

While I waited in the jungle outside Libreville, D arranged with some of the bribable authorities to get me a passport. My borrowed identity was that of a Monsieur Jeanne Charles Corday, a Norman trader. Corday's post was far up the Ogooué River, but he was at that time in Port-Gentil. For the sum D promised him, Corday was quite willing to surrender his passport. It was arranged that Corday would be smuggled out of Gabon and back to France at a later date. Corday would then pick up the passport in France as if he had had it all along. By then I was to have assumed a new identity, that of an Englishman.

All this cost D much, but he was quite wealthy and willing to spend much for the man who had saved his life.

As it turned out, after we got to France, D received word that Corday had died of a fever and had been secretly buried by a man in on the deal. So I remained Corday for a long time. Corday had no relatives and had been out of France for fourteen years so there were no problems in the familial area.

My imperfect French and unfamiliarity with French customs was explained to those authorities not in on the plot as the result of an accident A blow on the head had impaired my mental functions, and I was returning to France for treatment.

Events transpired somewhat as B has described them. I lived in Paris, studied the English and French languages and the people, read books on many subjects, learning to read while I read, smoked cigarettes, drank absinthe, beat up some thugs who attacked me and then some policemen who tried to arrest me, went through the affair of O and the count, and then traveled to America. There I drove to Wisconsin, saved J from a forest fire, was rejected by J, and received the telegram that told me that the fingerprints on my father's diary were indeed mine. I was the rightful heir to the fortune and the title. Though I must add that I was neither the viscount B said I was nor the duke and earl that F[5] facetiously said I was.

---

[5] Your editor.

EXTRACTS FROM THE MEMOIRS OF "LORD GREYSTOKE"

I am titled, and I am descended from viscounts, dukes, and royalty. But I am only a b————[6]

F constructed a highly romantic and grandiose lineage for me in his "biography."[7] He claims to be more of a realistic writer than B, but he is a romantic who clothes his fantasizing with the trappings of reality. He could have told more of the true story in his biography without disclosing my real identity, but he couldn't resist the temptation to gild the lily more than a little. However, I am in *Burke's Peerage*, though not under Greystoke, of course. I am descended from the historical Barons Greystoke and related to the Howards. But that can be said of hundreds of people or, for all I know, thousands.

There was only one way I could have gotten the title and the money without publicity. Nor do I know why B did not tell the real story in his account of how I became . . .[8] Perhaps he felt the publication of the novel was too close in time to the real events. He may have felt that somebody might have investigated and have been lucky enough to detect the fraud. After all, all one had to do was to reread the English newspapers of a few years back. However, he would not have found that a young English————[9] had been shipwrecked off the coast of Africa and, after some hardships, had been rescued. T's[10] yacht, contrary to what B said, was only disabled, not sunk.

On the other hand, my father had been on a secret mission for the British government, and when he and his wife disappeared, the government gave out a totally misleading report. So I can't be tracked down through that account

Even if some determined person did come across the proper clues, he wouldn't find me. I have already faked my death. Nor would he dare make a public accusation. He would be laughed to scorn and undoubtedly sued by my family. B has done me the inestimable favor of establishing once and for all in the minds of the public that I am a purely fictional person.

---

[6] The rest is deleted by Greystoke. B could stand for baron or baronet. If it is the latter, Greystoke would be addressed as Sir, not Lord. Nor would he be a noble. Baronets are a sort of hereditary knights.

[7] Philip José Farmer, *Tarzan Alive*, (New York: Popular Library, 1973).

[8] Deleted by Greystoke.

[9] Deleted by Greystoke.

[10] T is Greystoke's cousin.

Half of the events told in B's second novel had their parallel in reality. It is not true that J was abducted by men who would have had to trail me across half of Africa if B's account had been true. Actually, though I did find that lost city, those Cold Lairs inhabited by a few survivors of an ancient Caucasian people, that "rose-red city half as old as time," before I returned to the west coast, I was not to visit it again until some years later.

I did find my cousin[11] dying on the west coast, and he told me how he had been aware that I was the true heir but had concealed it from J.

After he had died, J told me what would happen if I stepped forth to make my claim. I would never know a moment's privacy while I lived in the civilized world.

"I wouldn't either," J said. "As your wife, I'd be subject to just as much publicity."

"Then I won't claim it," I said.

"No," she said. "You have a right to it."

She looked at her dead fiancé and said, "We've commented on how much you look like him. So. . . ."

My cousin was only an inch shorter than I and had an athlete's physique. His features were much like mine, which wasn't surprising considering that my grandfather and his father were brothers. And he had the same black hair and grey eyes.

"Technically, it's illegal," she said. "But it's not a criminal fraud. You wouldn't be getting anything you aren't entitled to."

So that is why we buried him there and journeyed up the coast to where the rest of the shipwrecked party was. Nobody there who knew my cousin was fooled, of course. But after J had explained what I was going to do and why, they agreed to keep silent. D was the only one from the French ship that rescued us who knew my identity, and he thought that the deception was a splendid idea.

N[12] remained to be dealt with. He would have been glad to keep silent, too, if I would pay him blackmail. Of that we were all sure. But he had no idea that my cousin had died, and we did not tell him.

---

[11] This is not T but WC, Greystoke's nearest relative.

[12] O's brother, a member of the party but under an assumed name and wanted by the French police.

He was put in the ship's brig and turned over to the French police at Marseilles. I returned to England as my cousin.

We were taking a long chance, though not as long as it might seem at first sight. My cousin had been out of England for a year, taking a sort of Grand Tour before he went to Oxford. He was only nineteen and hence might reasonably be expected to have grown another inch in a year's time. The scars on my forehead and body could be accounted for as a result of the accident to the ship and the jungle hardships. Since I am a gifted mimic, I had no trouble imitating his voice, the timbre of which resembled mine somewhat in any case. His parents were dead, and he had seen no close relatives for years. The servants at the ancestral hall and the villagers nearby were a sticky problem. But they were described to me, their photographs shown, if available, and I was filled in on them by my third cousin, Lord———[13] He was, as B said, a member of the party, in fact, the owner of the yacht which had sunk. He was marrying J's best friend, and he was very sympathetic when he heard my story. He furnished me with all the information he had about the servants and the villagers.

He also told me as much as he knew about my cousin's friends and his schoolmates. He had gone to Rugby, too, though he was three years ahead of my cousin. He had kept in contact with him after school. They ran in the same circles and belonged to the same clubs.

Still, I was bound to run into friends and relatives of my cousin about whom I would know nothing. So it was thought best to pretend that I had suffered partial amnesia as a result of the shipwreck.

This story got me through a number of difficult situations.

The servants and the villagers must have thought that my African experience had made me rather odd. But if they suspected that I was not who I was supposed to be, they did not bruit it about.

About a year later, N escaped from the French prison. He looked up his old crony in crime, P, and they came to England. Why, I don't know. But somehow they found out that I had taken my cousin's place. They were in a position to blackmail me and would have done so if they had not known that I would kill them regardless of the consequences. Instead, they kidnapped my baby and J and carried them off to Africa. J was to be sold to some desert sultan, and my

---

[13] Deleted by Greystoke.

son was to be raised as a savage. In this respect, B was correct. But much of the third novel is grossly exaggerated, and many things he describes never happened.

My son died of a jungle fever; N was killed much as B describes. P escaped but was never heard of again, though B used him as a character in the fourth novel. I imagine he died in the jungle shortly after escaping.

And that is how I was able to claim my inheritance with only a few people knowing that I was not my cousin.

HIS EARLY LIFE IN THE RAIN FOREST
"In the beginning was the Word."

True perhaps for the creation of the world. But not true in my case. In the beginning was a pair of large soft brown breasts with enormous pink nipples. These constitute my earliest memory, which goes back, I believe, to when I was two or three years old. I was not completely weaned until I was about six years old; and when my mother (foster mother, rather) told me I could suckle no more, I went into a screaming rage. I felt that I was no longer loved, that I had been rejected by the only person I loved. She expected this and was prepared. Instead of cuffing me, as she often did when I was mis-behaving, she took me into her arms. She explained that I couldn't expect to be treated any longer as a baby, since I was not a baby. I had to become independent of her. She had suckled me for a far longer time than any infant of the tribe was suckled. My playmates were jeering at me because I was still taking her milk, and this added to my burden of being different from the others. I needed to become as much like them as possible. This was one more step toward making them forget my alienness.

Moreover, to nurse me so long, she had given up mating, and while she had no particular desire for any male of the tribe, she was suffering from lack of sexual intercourse. Also, the women and the male elders were urging her to mate again. The tribe needed every infant it could get in order to keep its numbers at a constant level.

That she refused me her breasts did not mean that she no longer loved me. She was doing this for my own good and for the good of the tribe.

None of this except the statement that she still loved me meant anything to me. I would have seen the whole tribe dead before I would have given up the delicious and warm and cozy feeling of suckling. In fact, if I had been big enough and strong enough, I would at that moment have scooped up my mother and run away with her into the forest. And I suppose that if I had been that big and strong, I would have mated with her. There was a diffuse element of sexuality in this suckling. At least, I always got an erection when I suckled. My mother took no especial notice of this, though some of my playmates commented on it. Erections were common among both adults and children of the tribe and accepted with a blaséness that human beings would have regarded as shockingly immoral. Civilized human beings, anyway. There are some preliterate peoples who regard this as natural. Among some peoples of the Sudan area, where the male is naked, if a male should happen to pass by a female and get an erection, the female looks upon it as a compliment. And if no one else is around, the two are liable to go into the bushes.

So it was with the tribe, though there was seldom a chance to commit adultery. Its members felt uneasy when out of sight of the tribe, which is why expulsion was the worst thing that could happen to a member. If he or she could not quickly find another tribe and be adopted into it, he or she just sat down and within a few days grieved themselves to death. This happened far sooner than starvation can account for. The heart was broken and simply quit beating.

I never felt this uneasiness; and if I had been exiled, I would have reacted with rage, not depression. This stemmed from my feeling of alienness, of course, but it was a healthy expression. Better to be mad than sad. Though this feeling of alienness sometimes made me unhappy, it was in the long run a survival factor. Certainly, without it, I could never have spent those days by myself in the cabin teaching myself how to read English. Nor would I have been able to leave the tribe, forever, I thought, when I finally did find people like myself.

I've read Freud and the other great interpreters of the human psyche, Jung, Adler, Sullivan, and so on. On first reading Freud, I believed that every word he said was true. The Oedipal situation seemed to me to be a universal phenomenon. But that was because Freud had certain personal attitudes that coincided with mine. My attitudes came about because of the similarity of his familial situation and mine. I had a mother who was the center of my universe. Or, at least, the only other center of which I was aware. I don't think anybody ever gets over the infant feeling that he is truly the focus of the world. Not completely, anyway. Maturity is a relative state; the most mature are those who have traveled the most distance from that infantile attitude. But nobody has ever gone over the horizon and out of sight of it.

My mother loved only me and I loved only her, outside of our own selves of course. My stepfather hated me, and I knew from an early age that if I didn't kill him first he would kill me. And I was, of course, intensely jealous of him. He was always importuning K'l to mate with him, and though she would always say no, I was afraid that someday she would weaken and say yes. That meant that I'd be sharing her with him, which would have been as traumatic for me as losing an arm or leg or going blind.

Thus we had a sort of *Oedipus Rex* in the jungle, with P/t as King Laius, K'l as Jocasta, and myself as Oedipus. P/t was no king and never would be. But I fantasized from an early age that I would be king someday, which meant that I would have to kill the king, Kck, in combat. Kck tried many times to get K'l to slip away into the bushes with him, and since he knew that she would do so if it were not for me, he hated me almost as much as P/t did. So, in a sense, both P/t and Kck represented King Laius.

I don't want to strain this analogy too far. My readings of Freud and his critics, plus my own observations of many human societies, have convinced me that Freud often applied his own peculiar familial situation as a general principle to all of humanity. I don't think that the majority of male children hate their fathers because of any sexual jealousy. Nor do I think that any but a small minority of female children have penis envy. They might envy the physical superiority and the economic and political benefits that having a penis automatically confer upon the male. There is as much evidence that males might have a vagina envy. That is, very little evidence at all.

On the other hand, Freud did bring the concept of the unconscious mind to its fullest fruition; and he did discover that sexuality is much more diffuse than previously thought, that it pervades and influences most of the elements of human behavior. Sexuality is, in short, a field that stretches far beyond the genital; or, put differently, the genital invades every area of human behavior. The Westerners of his day were loath to accept this, and there are still many who reject this concept.

This rejection is founded on hypocrisy. In fact, society is founded on hypocrisy (among other things). It is my belief that if hypocrisy were eliminated overnight as if it were fecal matter, and people became completely honest, society would fall apart. This dictum applies to all human societies, literate or preliterate.

Hypocrisy has caused much misery and injustice, in fact, the deaths of millions of people over a period of perhaps a million years. But hypocrisy is one of the bonds that keeps human society from collapsing like an old castle in a hurricane.

I loathe and abominate hypocrisy; yet, when I am among humans, I have to practice it myself to a certain extent. If I didn't, I wouldn't be able to operate effectively in human society. As it is, I don't operate with a high efficiency. Though I am under no compulsion to be frank when I am disgusted with hypocrites, which means that I can keep silent under most conditions, I seem to radiate disgust. I betray myself in a silent language with certain inflections of stance, gesture, and facial expression; and most humans detect this. They resent it, of course, which makes it difficult to generate any warmth, any feeling of closeness or of equality, between me and most human beings.

As for frankness, I have observed that people who boast of being frank generally are so for one reason. They want to hurt others. They say they are frank because of their love for truth. But they lie to themselves and fail to deceive others with this lie.

I spoke of equality above. There is much talk of equality in human society but very little exists. Human beings have a pecking order just as animals and the subhumans of my tribe have one. Even two individuals of assumed social equality fight on a conscious or unconscious level for a subtly superior position. However, the pecking order is much less rigid in human society than among animals or in my tribe. Among animals the order is usually established in a very short time. It does change but not very often. Death and sickness are the chief operands. In my tribe, the order is somewhat more fluid, and the structure is dual. That is, the females' status is not altogether dependent upon the status of her mate. If she is exceptionally fertile, she may be accorded a higher position than her mate. But this usually results in some male trying to acquire her so he may acquire more status. This sounds contradictory in view of what I've said about the mate of the exceptionally fertile female not gaining status also. But the society of my tribe, like human society, contains a number of contradictory attitudes. If a male can take an exceptionally fertile female away from another male, by physical or verbal means, then this acquisition confers additional status on the male. A male with two females as mates is higher in the pecking order than a male with only one. A male with three females, two of which are infertile or not very productive of infants, has less status than a male with two fertile females. At the same time, his females may have a higher standing in the female pecking order than he has in the male order.

This could result in the females of a lower male having a higher status than the mates of the king. It seldom does because the king is keenly aware that the status of his females is a reflection of his own. The younger and more vigorous of the adult males begin thinking of challenging the king when this occurs. But the king knows this, and so he takes the fertile females away from the lower male. This is not usually done by an open and brutal assault upon the lower male. The king asks the females to become his mates. They have the option of rejecting him, but they seldom do. The females of my tribe are as impressed by social position as are the females of human society.

If the females should refuse the king, the king may then harass the lower male in a hundred different ways. If, for instance, the lower male feels that his particular feeding territory has been invaded by another male, he will appeal to the king to settle the case. The king, though he knows that the claimant's case is just, may decide against him. The king may treat the lower male with an obvious contempt or with open insults which go beyond that determined by the male's position in the pecking order. The rest of the tribe quickly perceive this, and in a short time the male is relegated to an even more inferior position.

The male can then fight the males who are pushing him on down. If he loses, he goes down to the very bottom of the hierarchy.

In effect, he has to fight every male above and below him, usually in one day, and even the strongest would tire halfway through this ordeal. So he's doomed to plumb the social abyss unless he challenges the king himself.

Possibly, he might win, in which case he comes out on top. The king doesn't then go to the lowest rank; the king is dead. Most fights between males end when one male confesses that he is beaten, but the battle for kingship is to the death.

Unless the lower male is unusually powerful, or the king is getting old, the lower male usually does not challenge the king. But he is frantic at losing status, and this may cause him to challenge the king. The king knows this, and he also knows that chance or the sheer desperation of the male may result in him (the king) being defeated. So, as often happens in human society, some sort of compromise is worked out. The king takes the fertile females of the lower male but gives the lower male his own infertile or less physically desirable females. The male retains his original status, since it is felt that a male who gets the king's females, even though they were rejected, gains a certain status. This gain cancels the loss of his fertile females.

The pecking order is not as complex or as fluid as that in human society, but it is complex enough that a 50,000-word book could be written about it.

When I say that the king can take or give away females, I do not mean that the females have no say in this. A male can divorce a female, or she him, with a simple declaration within the hearing of the king and the majority of the tribe. This applies even to the females of the king, though I never saw such an instance.

On the other hand, taking a female is not as simple as among the baboons, for instance. The male cannot take a mate just because he is a physical superior of another male. The female is free to accept or reject. And this is what my mother did. After adopting me, she divorced P/t, and she refused the king's advances. This offended both males. P/t could get no females to become his permanent mates, though I observed that he sometimes talked a female into lying with him when the two were out of sight of the others. This gave me an advantage over him. I would inform him that I'd spied on him. I would threaten to tell the mate of the female if P/t did not cease his persecution of me. P/t would rage, but he feared being beaten up by the cuckolded male and would leave me alone for a long time.

P/t was often beaten up, anyway. He had a bad temper and could not refrain from showing his resentment when the other males shoved him to the rear of the tribal assemblies or transgressed on his small feeding territory. Sometimes, he beat the other male, and it was only this that kept him from going to the very bottom of the order.

It was this bad temper, plus his ugliness, caused by a broken nose, that made the females reject him. Without at least one female as a permanent mate, he could get only so high in the order. This social inferiority thoroughly ruined a disposition that had never been sweet to begin with.

He blamed me for this, but, as B has shown, I didn't take his persecution passively. I gave more than I got; I was a constant torment to him with my tricks. Also, when I was about twelve, I thought of another way to force him to leave me in peace. I had observed that he was in fear when I threatened to tell the tribe about his adulteries. Then it occurred to me to threaten P/t with tales of wholly imaginary adulteries. In other words, I invented the lie.

P/t was so outraged at my first threat that I had to flee through the trees, take to the higher branches where he was too heavy to follow me. After he had cooled off, he realized that I had him in my control. And once more he ignored me, though, after a time, he forgot my threat and started to bedevil me. Then I had to threaten him again.

P/t was so outraged because lying was unknown to the tribe. Its members had many human qualities, since they were subhumans or prehumans. But they weren't human enough to have thought of lying. Or intelligent enough, perhaps. He was both angered and shocked when I first proposed my lie. I believe that he never did quite understand what I was doing. Or, if he did, he thought my threat was unnatural, a perversion. It was something monstrous.

So it was, from his viewpoint.

B has recorded that my native intelligence allowed me to invent a number of things new to the tribe. Such as the running noose, the full-nelson, swimming, etc. B did not record my invention of untruth, but this was because he did not know about it.

EXTRACTS FROM THE MEMOIRS OF "LORD GREYSTOKE"

Later on, when I taught myself to read English from the books I had found in the cabin of my true parents, I discovered that humans abhorred lying. And so, in my effort to become human, I too abhorred lying. After I became acquainted with humans, I found out that this abhorrence is only a pose, a major and indeed vital hypocrisy, of human society. But by then I had ingrained myself too deeply with this abhorrence. I never lie now except when survival demands it. I believe that most humans, excepting compulsive liars, don't lie except when their survival is threatened by the truth, but when they think of survival, they think of survival of their social image, of survival of their emotional and socioeconomic relationships, in fact, of a thousand things that will be endangered if they don't lie. Each individual has his own hierarchy of lying; some lies are permitted, others are forbidden, though if the going gets rough enough, the tabus are quickly shed.

Nor do humans seem to resent lies in the political field. There is a general feeling that all politicians are liars, that, in fact, a man can't be a politician unless he is a liar. I've never been able to understand this attitude. Politicians control the state; and so the welfare of the citizens depends upon being told the truth, both before and after the politician has been elected to office.

I've also never understood why the poor and the oppressed have endured their miserable state for so many thousands of years. They've always outnumbered the wealthy and the oppressors. So why didn't they just rise up and take over the government?

This is why I've never taken any interest in social reform, though I have in individuals who are suffering from poverty and injustice. But that is just because they happened to become personally involved with me.

This attitude has resulted in my being accused of being both an extreme rightist and an extreme leftist. Though by different people, of course. I won't try to change the system myself, since I am well off under it. But I am perfectly willing to grant that the poor and the oppressed should rise in revolution, a bloody one if need be, and take away from the rich and the oppressor.

I know from my reading of history that from time to time the masses have risen up but that usually they were slaughtered. These failures came about only because of disunity and fear among the masses. With a well-planned organization and enough willing to sacrifice themselves (after all, what did they have to lose?), the poor and the oppressed could have revolted successfully several thousand years ago and set up a new system. The male and female servants of the rich, for instance, were in a position to massacre their employers, wipe out the ruling class almost overnight.

But they did none of these things, just turned like rats and bit futilely when their state became so wretched they could no longer endure it. And they died like rats.

On the other hand, how many revolutions succeeded in their aims when they did conquer the ruling class? France got the Terror and then Napoleon I and then Napoleon III. The Russian Revolution wasn't really a revolt of the masses, and a small group got control and has retained it ever since. Are the Russians really better off than they would have been if the Czars were still in power? Are the Chinese better off under the Communists?

Some say they are; some say they aren't. For me the question is academic, since I personally do not care. All I know is that, if the masses under the Communists (or any other ideology) are being oppressed, why don't they do something about it?

D says that I don't understand this because I don't understand human psychology, or sociopoliticoeconomics. He may be right.

K'l's love for me resulted in much suffering for her. Because she refused to mate and because she nursed an alien, she went down to the bottom of the social scale. As the saying goes, she had to suck hind tit. When there was a kill and the tribe lined up for meat, she was last in line and lucky to get anything. She had to endure verbal abuse, though she was too powerful for another female to attack her. Also, the tribe had doubts about her mental stability. No sane female would refuse to mate or insist on suckling a being like me. Thus, she must be mad. This belief in her insanity made the females afraid to push her too far. Like most primitive peoples, and they were more primitive than even the Australian aborigine or Digger Indians, they were in awe of anybody who might be "possessed."

K'l was last in line at the table, but she was intelligent and industrious and so a good food provider. Though it scared her to go far from the vicinity of the tribe, she did so. And hence she foraged ahead of the others. Grubs, worms, eggs, grasshoppers, small rodents, birds, baby antelopes, dead animals, anything that was protein and didn't move fast enough to elude her became part of our diet. Most of her diet consisted of roots, nuts, fruits, and berries, of course, since she was primarily a vegetarian. Many of the roots she ate contained too much siliceous matter for me, and I rejected this from instinct, I suppose. Even when she offered me premasticated vegetable matter, I rejected it. The coarse gritty stuff would in time have worn away my teeth. I did not realize this consciously, but I knew I didn't like the stuff. So, in addition to much mother's milk, I ate many berries, nuts (after she had cracked them open), and fruit and pieces of raw meat from the creatures she caught. In the beginning I could not masticate the raw meat, but K'l chewed these up for me, and these I accepted eagerly.

So, though K'l suffered from a semiostracism, and I suffered too after I became aware of this attitude, we were far from being always unhappy.

Also, that we were alone against the others made us draw much more closely together than the normal mother and child of the tribe.

I sometimes believe in Goethe's theory of elective affinities. Certainly this is the only thing that can account for K'l's fierceness in raising me despite all the objections of the tribe and the abuse she had to take.

I was lucky that it was she and not some other female who had lost her infant the same day my parents died. If her baby had not been killed, she would not have wanted to replace it with me. And Kck would have killed me, too, after slaying my father. But, as chance would have it, she wanted me to replace her just-dead infant, and so she snatched me from the cradle and ran off with me. Never mind that I was a queer, even repulsive looking, creature from her viewpoint. She accepted me and from the moment I began suckling, she loved me. So, at least, she told me in afteryears. Even if her love for me at first sight was really an event of retrospect and not of reality, there was no doubt that she soon did come to love me.

Since she had no one else to talk to or to love, she spent all her energies, outside of food-gathering and hunting, on me. She was, for me, a castle with a host of defenders, which is why I had a tremendous sense of security despite my early years of alienation from the other members of the tribe. Her continuous talking to me also resulted in an acceleration of my intelligence. No doubt, I would have outstripped my contemporaries anyway, since a human being is more intelligent and faster talking than the prehumans of my tribe.

It was also my good fortune to have been adopted by a female who was possibly the brightest individual of her people.

DESCRIPTION OF THE N'K

B first heard of me when he was living in Chicago. But in the first novel he wrote about me, he pretended that he had learned of me while visiting London. His informant was supposed to have been an official of the British Foreign Service. This man was acquainted with my story because he had access to top secret documents in the Service's files. These supposedly included my father's diary, written in French, which recorded the events that led up to, and included part of, the day on which he was killed by Kck and I was taken from my cradle by K'l.

According to B, the official disclosed my story when he was drunk. When B scoffed at this, the official then showed him documents, though he had no right to reveal these and would have been discharged and possibly gaoled if the Service had known of his act.

The truth is that B was not in London at that time. As far as I know, he has never been in England. His informant was an American who had heard some of my story from an Englishman. Thus B got his facts third-hand. Nor had his immediate informant seen any documents. If these had been in the Foreign Service files, the Service would have known about my fraud. And it would have felt obligated to expose me.

After B's first novel came out, I realized that someone had talked about me. I knew that the original source of information had to be somebody close to me. It did not take me long to eliminate all but one. I confronted T,[14] and he confessed that he might have talked about me to an American during one of his alcoholic sprees. T was a splendid man. I liked and respected him very much, except for one

---

[14] Probably Greystoke's third cousin, a baron.

facet of his character. Now and then he succumbed to his compulsion and would disappear for days or even weeks. Poor H[15] would track him down and bring him home and dry him out. He had enough character, however, not to make a promise he might not be able to keep. He would only say that he would fight against his demon with all the strength he could muster.

As the Americans say, I chewed him out. He was very contrite and shaken up, so much so that he did not drink alcohol for three years. Nor, as far as I know, did he ever say anything of me again while drunk.

Well, he has been dead for many years now, killed while fighting Jerry. He died a hero's death, as they say, and was posthumously awarded Britain's highest medal for valor. I miss him.

B, realizing that his informant had given him the germ of a unique story, wrote a novel. Since he had few facts to begin with, most of the novel is incorrect in its details. It is also considerably romanticized. But he captured the spirit, the essence, of what really happened, and all honor to him for that.

One of the criticisms of B's story was that there were no such creatures as his language-using "great apes." Thus, his novel had to be sheer fantasy, as much modern mythology as Kipling's *The Jungle Book*.

The "great apes" had not been discovered by reputable scientists and hence could not exist.

This criticism came only twelve years after the discovery of the okapi, the existence of which had been scoffed at for years by scientists.

The pygmy elephant and hippopotamus were also supposed to be a mere fable of the natives. But more than one zoo now exhibits them.

There have also been rumors for years of a small maneless spotted lion existing in the forests of Kenya and Uganda. The existence of these is denied, but I have seen them. Whether or not any specimens will ever come to the attention of the scientists is another matter. They were never very numerous, and they may now be extinct.

The point I'm making is that scientists have been wrong. They

---

[15] T's wife, an American, and J's best woman friend.

are perfectly correct in refusing to acknowledge the existence of such creatures until proof is presented of their existence. But too many scientists, and educated laymen, have denied that they could, in fact, exist. And that is an unscientific attitude.

B's critics denied that any unknown species of ape could exist in Africa. They also scoffed at B because his apes ate meat. Chimpanzees and gorillas don't eat meat, they said. Therefore, no apes (even of the mythological variety) are carnivores. It seems to be true that gorillas are pure herbivores in their natural state. But Goodall has shown that chimpanzees in the wild state do eat meat whenever they get a chance; and it is known that baboons, which are monkeys, also eat meat.

The truth is that both B and his critics were half-right and half-wrong.

There is a species of primate which has not been discovered by the scientific community. Or there was, at least. I saw them several times during my childhood and youth, but they may be extinct now. It is this species which has given rise to tales of the Kenyan *agogwe* and the "wild men" observed in the eastern, central, and western areas of Africa. They are about four feet high and very hairy, but they walk upright. Hence, they are not apes, not in a scientific sense. Their pelvic girdles and feet are so similar to men that they would have to be classified as some species of australopithecoid, creatures halfway between ape and man. I doubt that they are the "missing link." It is more probable that they are a cousin of the creature that was in the direct line of man's ancestry.

In any event, I have seen them, though I never had any direct contact with them. They fled my tribe as quickly as they did humans.

My own people are, I believe, another species of hominid or perhaps a giant variety of the *agogwe*. They are not missing links, either, but cousins of man. They are not the great apes described by B, but they do, or did, exist; and it was among them that I was raised.

B was not given any clear description of them and so he visualized them as gorilloids. He had them using a language, which was correct. But in his novels he also attributed language use to the gorillas and monkeys. While it is true that the higher primates can communicate more effectively than the zoologists believe, they do not have a language in the human sense. They use signals, not verbal symbols.

It was lucky for me that the n'k were language users. If I'd been raised by true apes, I would have passed the mental stage beyond which language learning becomes possible. And I would have been not much better than an idiot. Authentic cases of feral humans bear me out in this. If the child has not experienced a human language before the age of five to eight (or perhaps earlier) he becomes incapable of learning language.

So, in a sense, I am not a true feral man. Those who raised me were quite capable linguistically. And their capabilities for learning other things were higher than those of any animals.

B didn't know this. After learning the truth, he was forced to continue the original description in order to be consistent. Not that he cared. He was a storyteller, not an anthropologist.

I have said that my people were possibly a giant variety of paranthropus. Giant is a relative term here, since the tallest was actually only about six feet. When I'd attained my full growth, I had three inches on the tallest, old Kck. He didn't like my looking down on him, and this was one more thing to make him hate and fear me.

But he was much stronger; and if it hadn't been for my father's knife, I would have been killed when he finally challenged me.

The n'k looked hairy, though this was because their body hair grew to a four- or five-inch length and was as coarse as a chimpanzee's. The numbers of hairs were actually less than that of humans. The breasts of both male and female were innocent of hair; both had short bushy beards and stiff head hairs not more than two inches long.

The n'k head was long and low, bread-loaf-shaped. They had very little forehead, and the supraorbital ridges of the adult male were almost as massive as a gorilla's. A bony crest, like a gorilla's though smaller, ran from the front to the back of the skull of the males. These were necessary to support the massive chewing muscles. The nose was not quite as flat and as wide-nostrilled as a gorilla's. The ears were close to the head and shaped exactly like a human's but about one-fourth larger. The jaws were prognathous, about halfway in protrusion between man's and the gorilla's. The lips were not the thin lips of the chimpanzee and the gorilla; they were as fully everted as the average Caucasian's. The teeth were large, fitted for grinding the tough siliceous roots or cracking the nuts which formed a large part of their diet. Contrary to B's description, they did not have the long canines of the gorilla. The teeth were quite hominid, the molars having five cusps in a Y pattern. A primatologist would see at a glance that they belonged to a creature nearer to man than the apes. The palate was not quite as arched as that of the human. The jaws, seen from above, formed a bow shape, unlike the U shape of ape jaws.

The head was carried further forward than that of the human. The pelvis was not as efficiently shaped for walking as the human's. The legs were shorter in proportion to the torso than the human's, and they were less straight. The feet were flat, and there was a wide separation between the big toe and the other toes. The arms were somewhat longer in proportion to the torso than those of a man. The hands were larger and thicker than a man's. The thumb was shorter and thicker in proportion. None of the tribe could come near my manual dexterity.

Their muscles are not only more massive than a human's but superior in quality. Even the smallest female is much stronger than the greatest human weightlifter. The muscles are attached to thick and dense bones. My own skeleton is denser than that of any modern man's. I attribute this to my feral life, to unceasing activity and hard exertion. As I understand it, the bones of the early caveman were also denser due to his exceedingly active life.

Their hair color varies from a dull black to a russet brown. The eyebrows are very bushy and black. Their eyes are russet brown; their skin, coffee with three spoonfuls of cream. Like most rain forest dwellers, they don't have or need many sweat glands. Their body odor differs from that of man. The English language does not contain the vocabulary items needed to describe it accurately. I can only say that to a keen nose it has elements both of the odor of *Homo sapiens* and of the gorilla with an indescribable element that is unique to them. Their anal excrement is softer but more adhesive than that of *Homo sapiens* and not nearly as offensive. This, I presume, is because their diet is largely vegetarian. Their urine, curiously enough, reminds me of civet cat urine, yet I would not mistake one for the other.

Extracts from the Memoirs of "Lord Greystoke"

Unlike the gorilla, they do not foul their own nest. When one has to defecate, he retreats to some distance from the feeding ground. This seems to have nothing to do with modesty. A number of adult males and females and children will retreat at the same time to the same place and there relieve themselves side by side while chatting away unembarrassedly. Nor do they leave the feeding area to urinate.

In going some distance from their feeding or sleeping places to defecate, however, they exhibit a fastidiousness superior to that of the Australian aborigine. The latter will defecate while among a group squatting around a fire and eating.

Their sense of smell is keener than that of *Homo sapiens* but not nearly as keen as a dog's, whose sense of smell is estimated to be a million times sharper than man's.

B has exaggerated my own olfactory powers. They are not as strong as a n'k's, though they are superior to any human I've ever met. But this is a matter of training. And after I've been in a city for a while, it becomes comparatively deadened. A good thing, too. During my first few days in a city, I become nauseated with the many offensive odors that exude from man and his artifacts.

Wind and sex among the n'k

While I was learning to read, I was startled and sometimes shocked. I discovered things that were completely contrary to what the n'k believed and, hence, what I believed.

One of these was that it was the wind that caused trees and their leaves to move. The n'k always believed just the opposite. Trees and grass were living things; and so, when they moved, they caused motion of the air.

Once I had read that the wind was the responsible agent, I saw why. I reproached myself for my stupidity. I should have noticed that if the tree caused the wind, the wind should have flowed out from the tree in all directions. That discovery made me determined that from then on I would be more observant. Nor would I believe anything that had been told me until it was proved.

I was upset again when I learned that there was a direct connection between copulation and reproduction. The n'k did not know this. They believed that rain and lightning fertilized women. The latter caused the birth of exceptionally strong or intelligent individuals.

When I made the discovery about the true origin of the wind, I hastened to tell the n'k. They would not believe me, even after I had offered them proof. In fact, I was scorned and laughed at, and several commented that I was not as bright as I was supposed to be. Indeed, I must be suffering a mental breakdown.

So, when I discovered the link between copulation and fertilization, I kept silent. The n'k did not want to be enlightened. They resented the truth as if it threatened them. In this respect, they are like most humans.

Every human society has adopted rules for sexual conduct by which its members are supposed to guide themselves. Conduct which breaks these rules is regarded as unlawful but not perverted, or unlawful and perverted. The former conduct can be broken down into two subclasses. One, that which is regarded with a certain limited tolerance. Two, that which is simply not tolerated, if the conduct becomes known to laymen and police.

My reading of the novels did not help me much in determining exactly what modes of sexual behavior were in what classifications. The *Encyclopaedia Britannica* was of some help, but it had been published in 1885 and was thus far from frank. The most I could find out from my reading was that certain undescribed sexual acts and attitudes were regarded by most people as disgusting and illegal and deserving of long sentences in gaol or even death.

My own sexual attitudes were determined by n'k society. Theirs were at the same time much more rigid and far more liberal than those of any civilized human society.

Much of what was permitted would be regarded as unnatural by Western societies of that day, but any deviation from the rules was regarded as perverted by the n'k. Or I should say would have been regarded so. I never saw or heard of any deviations while I was with the n'k.

Open masturbation among the children was permitted. In fact, if a child did not masturbate, he/she was an object of concern. There must be something wrong with him/her. This included both self- and mutual masturbation.

The males who were unable to get females as mates because of their low position in the pecking order performed self- or mutual masturbation. In their cases, however, they did so out of sight of the tribe. Not from any modesty but because they would be objects of derision from the upper class males.

Lawful copulation took place in view of the tribe. The sexual activities of the king were watched closely because any lack of vitality was regarded as a sign of weakening. When this took place, the males considered challenging the king.

Unlawful copulation, that is, adultery, occurred in the bushes, of course. The males were very jealous of their mates. If another male copulated with his mate(s), he was challenging his order in the social scale.

The females could be put into three classes. One included the majority of females, those who took advantage of every opportunity to commit adultery. The second consisted of females who would commit adultery only with males on a higher social plane than their mates. The third, a small minority, were always faithful.

On consideration, there was a fourth class which was a minority of one. This was K'l, my foster mother. During my infancy and childhood and early youth, she refused to take a mate. This was her right, but it caused her to be regarded as perverted. At the same time, it made her more desirable. The males thought that if they could talk her into mating, they would automatically rise in the order.

Of course, this mating would have to be done publicly. And I am not certain that K'l did not now and then succumb to her sexual drive while in the bushes. She must have been very discreet, however, since I had no suspicions that this was occurring. If I had, I would have been very jealous.

Now that I look back on it, I would not blame her if she had taken the opportunity to relieve her sexual tensions.

The favorite position of the n'k during copulation was with the female on her back and the male on top. Entry from the rear with the female standing but bent over, braced against a tree, was often performed. The king, Kck, preferred this.

Kissing as sexual foreplay was as common among the n'k as among humans. But kissing involved not only the lips and the breasts. The n'k kissed each other all over. Fellatio and cunnilingus and soixante-neuf were often indulged in, though these were not conducted to the point of climax. Though the n'k knew nothing of the connection between copulation and reproduction, as I have said, they thought that the male must ejaculate within the vagina.

Of course, accidents happened; but when they did, the couple were derided.

Though the lower scale males mutually masturbated or performed fellatio, they were not compulsive homosexuals. If a single male managed to get a permanent mate, he at once ceased any homosexual activities.

Anal intercourse was never performed, at least, not to my knowledge, and if anyone should know, I should. I was often in the trees or behind the bushes, observing the hidden activities of the tribe.

Incidence of sexual activity was much higher than the average in Western human society. The king was thought to be approaching senility if he did not copulate with his three or four females at least three times a day. In addition, he was on his good days liable to copulate with three or four other females in the bushes.

I believe that the males of Western human society would be capable of this frequency, too, if the social attitudes were different. In Polynesian societies, for instance, when the whites first encountered them, a male was thought senile if he did not copulate with his wife three or four times daily and, in addition, copulated with several of his sisters-in-law. This high sexual activity results, I believe, not from the physical superiority of the Polynesian male to the Western male but from the social attitude toward sex.

The only cases of impotency I saw among the n'k were very old males (forty-five years of age was the equivalent of the human eighty) and one young male, Lmp.[16] And his condition probably resulted from some physical deficiency, though I cannot prove this.

This brief sketch should indicate why I found the human attitudes toward sex ludicrous, incredible, and comicotragical. And it shows why J was so horrified about my attitudes.

But she got over it.

THE LANGUAGE OF THE N'K

The anthropologist Grover Krantz has studied the fossil skulls of early man (*Homo erectus*) and of his predecessors *Paranthropus* and *Australopithecus*. He speculates that the brain volume which divides

---

[16] This is so close to "limp" that Greystoke may be making a little joke.

man from his forerunners and cousins is 750 cc. The brain volume of modern man averages 1,400 cc. The gorilla's and *Australopithecus'* is 500 cc. *Homo erectus'* was between 750 and 1,400 cc.

In the late 30s I returned to my native area and looked for n'k skulls. I found three female and five male skulls and measured their capacity. The average for the females was 900 cc and that of the males was 1,200. I also studied the brain of an old male who had died from pneumonia shortly after I rejoined the tribe. I was especially interested in the development of the frontal lobes and of the three primary speech control areas: Broca's, Wernicke's, and the angular gyrus. I also dissected the oral cavity, the larynx, and the pharynx. I did this to compare them to man's and to analyze the anatomical and neural limitations of the n'k in regard to speech.

Krantz says that, at the end of his first year, the human baby's brain is approximately 750 cc. Within six months, the baby begins to talk. Based on this, Krantz suggests that the 750-cc volume is the threshold of the ability to use language. Krantz reconstructed the oral cavities, pharynx, and larynx of *Homo erectus.* Based on these, he concluded that the vocal apparatus of *Homo erectus* was closer to that of a newborn baby's than to an adult of *Homo sapiens.* Consequently, *Homo erectus* had a larynx that was situated higher in the throat than modern man's. This limited the size of the pharynx above it. *Homo erectus'* tongue, consequently, was almost entirely in the mouth; relatively little of it was in the throat. This meant that the tongue of *Homo erectus* could not act on the pharynx but was limited to varying the size of the mouth in producing speech sounds.

Homo erectus thus did not have a pharynx capable of producing the vowel sounds *a* (as in father), *i* (as in machine) and *u* (as in tool). He also suggested that the three brain areas I mentioned above were less developed than in modern man.

All these limitations, plus the low-slung and heavy jaws, meant that *Homo erectus* had a very limited speech repertoire and probably spoke very slowly.

It would follow from this that the less evolved *Paranthropus* and *Australopithecus* had even more limitations, that his linguistic capabilities were even less than very early man's.

The facts are that the n'k could produce one vowel sound, similar to that found in the English *the* when it precedes a consonant or that of the vowel in *cut*. This occurred in about one out of ten n'k words. It was, however, unvoiced; that is, it was produced without any vibrations taking place in the vocal bands of the larynx. Nor were the consonants which English speakers voice, *n*, *l*, and *w*, voiced by the n'k. These were accompanied by a heavy aspiration. But the n'k could control the vocal bands enough to produce a glottal stop. By closing them, they produced a consonant which is found in many human tongues, Danish, Scots English, Nahuatl, et al. This stop also occurs in standard English, but it has no significance, and most English speakers are not even aware that they produce it.

In addition, the n'k speech contains four click consonants. One of these is similar to that produced by a carriage driver when he is urging his horse to a faster speed or to that which is often spelled *tsk! tsk!*

N'k speech sounds perfectly natural to me, but J and D say that it is weird. The long strings of whispered consonants with no intervening vowels, the clicks, and the glottal stops seem unhuman to J and D. But there is at least one human group, a California Indian tribe, which uses words with whispered consonants and only an occasional vowel, also unvoiced. And the click consonants are common in the Bushman and Hottentot languages found in some Nahuatl dialects.

The brain size of the n'k child doesn't attain 750 cc until he is six years old. This is when he starts to babble, though the babbling is much slower than that of a human baby's and more restricted in the variety of sounds.

I started babbling shortly after K'l adopted me and was speaking as fluently as any adult n'k by the time I was four. This amazed the n'k and compensated in K'l's eyes for my lack of speed in physical development and my lengthy dependence on her. I was also able to talk, literally, five times as fast as the n'k.

If any linguists read this, they may wonder how I was able to voice sounds after I came into contact with humans. Theoretically, since I had had no experience in voicing speech sounds in my formative years, I should, as an adult, have been unable to reproduce them.

But I am a natural mimic. When I eavesdropped on the people of the river village, I would try to imitate the sounds of their language. At first, I had little success in vibrating my vocal bands. But I persevered. After a while I was able to imitate perfectly both the unvoiced and voiced sounds of the locals.

The n'k sounds are:

Vowel: the unvoiced vowel of English *the* or *done*, represented here by e.

Consonants: p, t, k, ', h, s, c, m, n, l, w, /, //, ///, ł.

    p is the same as in English but is always heavily aspirated, that is, followed by a puff of air.

    t is like the English t but made with the tip of the tongue higher up.

    k is that in *keen* and is always aspirated.

    ' stands for the glottal stop, the catch in the throat called by the Spanish linguists the *saltillo*, the little jump.

F misinterpreted something I said about the glottal stop in n'k and so made an error in the biography he wrote about me. F stated that the n'k regarded the ' as a vowel. He should have known better, since he has some knowledge of linguistics. What I said was that B often used a vowel in place of the glottal stop when he spelled out n'k words. In any case, the n'k had never heard of a vowel or, indeed, of anything connected with phonetics or grammar.

    h stands for the fricative *ch* sound in the German *ach* or Scots *loch*.

    s is the same as in English.

    c stands for the *ch* in *church*.

    m is the English *m* but unvoiced.

    n equals an English *n* unvoiced.

    l is an unvoiced sound halfway between the English *l* and *r*. B used either *l* or *r* in his system of spelling n'k words, I suppose for the sake of variety.

    w is like the English but totally unvoiced.

    / stands for a click consonant made by flattening the tip of the tongue against the front teeth and then quickly withdrawing it.

    // stands for a click made against the gums above the teeth.

/// stands for a palatal click.

ł stands for a click made with the side of the tongue close to the right side of the cheek.

B used b, d, g, and z respectively to represent these clicks. He also used z to represent s sometimes.

Each syllable of n'k consists of two or three consonants or combinations of consonants plus e, e plus consonant, consonant plus e plus consonant, or two consonants plus e.

Each word is a monosyllable, disyllable, or trisyllable, excluding the monosyllabic gender prefix.

The stress or accent is lighter than in English but relatively stronger on the second syllable within a word.

Tone, or pitch, is mid-level in a declarative phrase and abruptly chopped off at the end of the phrase.

Exclamatory, hortatory, interrogative, and conditional phrases use a rising pitch similar to that in English. This rising pitch is an important grammatical feature. B indicates this in his description of the difference between the phrase, "Do you surrender?" and "I surrender." The former is distinguished by the rising pitch; the latter is a flat "/// //."

Though the n'k speech is about five times as slow as human speech, it has juncture. That is, it has a difference in the speed of transition between the sounds in a word, between words, and between complete phrases. The second is twice as long as the first, and the third is twice as long as the second.

The n'k vocabulary items are few, possibly no more than five hundred. Its grammar is truly primitive and can be quickly described.

The parts of speech are:

Personal names.

Entity indicator: tnt = elephant; w'l = nest; "// = rock; c/// = sky; k' = I; 'sh = wind; mp// = mother.

Attribute indicator: ///e = red; klk = dangerous; s'l = skin; pkt = dead; wn// = beneficial, tasty, healthy; csł = angry; pks = motionless; 'et = state of possession; tk' = many.

Negator: tn// = no, not.

Action indicator: ///'m = run; /n// = kill; sps = snarl; h'h = laugh;

///tn = looking gloomy.

Temporal indicator: tw' = soon; //p// = sometime in the past; nw/// = dawn; nwk = between dawn and high noon; nl/ = high noon; nsł = between high noon and dusk; nw// = dusk; smk = night.

Locative indicator: wc = there; s's = out of sight; ksw = right; //e' = left; c// = above.

Gender indicator: b' = male; m' = female.

The entity indicator refers to anything that is considered in n'k as an object which is completely separate from other objects. It includes what we would classify as personal pronouns. The n'k is not as conscious of ego differentiation as the human is. At least, that is my impression.

Though he behaves as an individual with self-consciousness, he is not as sharply aware of his aloneness as a human is. *K'* means not only *I* but *we.* Where a human would say *we*, a n'k gestures to indicate that others are part of his *I.* Or he is part of them.

There is no word in n'k corresponding to the human *you* or *they.* The personal name is used instead when addressing an individual; and if *they* is indicated, a gesture indicates this.

Indeed, the *I* is not often used in a phrase, though its existence is implicit.

Why do I include the word for *skin* as an attribute indicator, something that humans would call a noun? This is because the skin is classified as an inherent undiscrete part that makes up the whole. It is no more separable than the color of the skin. Thus, my personal name, s'n-t'l, is made up of two attribute indicators.

The word for *mother,* mp//, is not used in the generic sense. A mother is an entity, either my mother or your mother. A n'k could not speak of many mothers. There is no word for father. A *father* is the mate of your mother, and the word used for him is b'-cpm, meaning *he-mate.*

The n'k have no general word to indicate emotion or feeling. The emotions or feelings have to be specific and refer to states invisible to the beholder. If a n'k feels sick, he says, "tn// wn//." That is, "Not healthy," or if he wishes to emphasize it, "k' tn// wn//," or "I am not healthy."

It seems strange to an English speaker to classify a verb, 'et, meaning *to possess,* as an attribute. But this word indicates a non-physical relationship, an invisible connection between the speaker and the object referred to. No physical action is implied. The relationship referred to is as unchanging as the color of one's eyes. For example, take a sentence translated as, "She is my mother." In the first place, no n'k would say *she.* He would use her personal name. If I said this in n'k, I would say "k'l wc. mp// wc. k' 'et k'l."

Literally, "K'l there. Mother there. I state-of-possession-K'l."

The indefinite plural indicators and the numerical indicators, *many, few* (more than two), and the numbers one through ten are thought of as attributes. Ten is as high as the n'k can count. Anything more is *many.*

An action indicator describes or prescribes movement. Movement includes facial expressions of internal states. To a n'k, rain is not drops falling but an entity that appears from time to time. He would not say, "It is raining." He would say, "Rain here." Or "Rain there." Or "Rain soon."

N'k is uninflected except for the gender prefix, which is always attached to the entity indicator, but to that only.

There is no tense. To indicate the past or future, a temporal indicator is used.

There are no words to indicate aspect, that is, whether the action occurred some time ago and then stopped, occurred in the past and is still operating, is now occurring but will soon stop, is now occurring but will run for a long time.

A n'k phrase seldom consists of more than three words and often only of one. Where gesticulation will suffice, a n'k prefers not to verbalize.

There are no connectives such as *and, but,* or *or.*

N'k has no passive voice, and tone indicates the difference of indicative, subjunctive, imperative, potential, conditional, and obligative modes. Actually, the same tone is used for all but the indicative. The others can be lumped together in the mood of dubiety.

The word order of the most complex phrase is locative indicator-temporal indicator-personal name or entity indicator-attribute indicator-action indicator. The negator is used just before the indicator to which it is most relevant. The attribute indicator is the only one which cannot be used as a complete phrase, though, since personal names often consist of attribute indicators, this is an exception. One n'k can utter another's name to attract his attention.

B has described me in the first novel and in a short story as teaching myself to read English. This is correct. I started off with children's picture books, which my mother (my human mother, of course) had intended to use to teach me to read. I associated the letters of the alphabet with the pictures just as B depicted me. I started with the simplest word-picture books and progressed to the less elementary books. But this was fortuitous. If I had not just happened to pick up the most basic book first, the one that my mother would have used when she started teaching me, I may not have made any progress at all.

One of the things B neglected mentioning when he described my self-education in literacy is punctuation. I had no idea, of course, that these were aids, auxiliaries, for bridging the wide gap between the spoken and the written. I thought they were words too. It took me almost two years to grasp their nature. And I pronounced them, too, giving each a syllabic value.

One of the many features of English that I had trouble with was grasping the distinction between the definite and indefinite article, between "a" or "an" and "the." N'k has neither, but then this lack is nothing special in human languages. Many neither use nor need these articles.

Inflection and conjugation, prepositions and adverbs, and the verb *to be,* caused me much trouble also. These features are totally lacking in n'k; and if I had not been both so curious and intelligent, I might never have understood their use. But I persevered, and I began to comprehend, though, truth to tell, it was not until later after I had been living among English speakers that I fully understood them.

Or I should say, among English and French speakers. After all, French was my first spoken human language.

If anybody other than myself ever reads these words, he or she will probably smile at my egotism when he reads that I call myself intelligent. But this is not egotism. I lack false humility, since I was not raised in a human society. I tell facts as I know them, and the truth is that I have an I.Q. of 197 on the Terman scale. I don't know that this means much; the various I.Q. tests are much subject to criticism. Nor would I have ever succeeded in my self-education if I had not had a tremendous drive to learn. I might not have had this if it had not been for my feeling of alienation from the tribe. I identified only partially with them, and the discovery that there were others like me in the world made me lust to know everything about them. I intended to find human beings some day and to live with them. I expected to be accepted by them, to dwell with them completely happy. Of course, this was in the early days of my self-education. When I began to read with some fluency the novels and the history books and the *Encyclopaedia Britannica* in my parents' library, I also began to understand that things would not be so simple. It would take more than just being born in a society to be accepted and to be happy.

RELIGION

When I got deep enough into the books, I despaired. Apparently, a man had to have much money (a concept I never understood from just reading about it). A man had to be on guard all the time to keep others from taking his money away. A man had to watch other men to make sure that they did not take his mate away from him. A man might not even want his mate after a while because, inevitably, he and she would be struggling for dominance in familial affairs. Or the mate would be possessed by drives over which she had no control; she might have enough money but not a high enough position in the pecking order. She might be rejected or think she was being rejected by her parents, and she could not rest until she had fulfilled their image of what a daughter should be. And so on. Of course, men were in the same unhappy situation.

Then there were religious conflicts in history and in the novels. I did not understand this at all, perhaps because the religious sense in the n'k was so rudimentary. But I did understand that the religious sense in human beings was highly developed, yet they had no idea of what was true and what wasn't true in their religions. The Christians claimed fiercely that only their religion was true, that they alone had access to divine revelation. Yet the Christians were divided among themselves, calling each other liars and wicked; and while preaching charity and love and peacefulness, they were killing and torturing each other.

Extracts from the Memoirs of "Lord Greystoke"

It all seemed simple and clear-cut to me. If you had a creation, then you had a Creator. At least, it seemed obvious to me at first. Later I went through the stage that every person of any intelligence goes through. Who created the Creator? How could the world have come out of nothingness? What existed before time began? Why were suffering, illness, and death inevitable?

If I had been presented with only one explanation of these, if, say, I had only the Bible available, I might have believed a monolithic explanation. But the books told me that there had been many differing explanations; and quite possibly, all were false.

I didn't think religious or philosophical issues were worth fighting over or even getting excited about.

I could understand why men schemed and fought for control of land and money and position in the pecking order. Survival is dependent upon these.

But, I asked myself, if man is so intelligent, why hasn't he developed a system where hypocrisy and greed and ruthlessness and oppression are not necessary?

I still ask myself this question, though I know that there isn't any answer. I also know that if there were an answer, it would be rejected by most people. Most humans are not much advanced beyond the n'k when it comes to freeing themselves from their social conditioning. Those who do so generally only seem to do so. They extricate themselves from one set of conditioning only to switch to another. And they do this because of their genetic dispositions. I am convinced that individuals are born Catholics or Methodists or Moslems or Jews, born Tories or Whigs or anarchists. Their genes predetermine them to a certain form of religion or ideology or economics. Some are never able to free themselves from their parents' religion or ideology, and this results in unhappiness for them. Others are able to do so, though their struggles make them unhappy.

As for me, my being an alien, an outsider to both the n'k and the humans, resulted in an unhappiness and confusion in my childhood and youth. But no longer. I am insular. The troubled waters of others affect me only in a physical sense. I am sometimes swept into the difficulties of others, and I have often sided with one group against the other. But the question of which side is morally right or wrong doesn't concern me.

I happen to be a British citizen because circumstances made me so. I was born of British parents, but in my early contacts with civilization I could easily have become a French citizen. Only the fact that my British parentage was established and that this meant I could gain a high position in British society without much effort determined me to be British. If I had been, say, Russian, I might have become Russian and fought for the Russians.

On the other hand, being much more rational and objective than most humans, because I was an outsider, I would have observed that the British society was relatively freer and contained more justice. The conditions of British society were appalling; but compared to those in Russian society, they were less objectionable.

At first sight, American society might seem relatively freer. But it didn't take me long after I'd been in the United States to see that it was a slave society. The whites denied this, of course, but the displaced Africans knew it was a fact. And though the whites thought they were free men and democratic, the fact that they were living in a slave society colored their every thought and action and institution and made them, in a sense, slaves to their slaves. They might not know it, but it did. There can be no truly free men where some citizens are slaves.

This applies not only to ethnic, but to economic, attitudes. The poor are, in fact, slaves, though a white person can get out of that slavery if he is vigorous and intelligent enough. Or ruthless enough.

All human societies are slave societies, some more than others.

To return to my reading.

At first, I could not distinguish between fact and fiction. I thought the novels were true stories. Then I found out that they were only exercises of the imagination. I shouldn't say only, since the concept of fiction was new to me. It was, in fact, staggering. The n'k had no fictional stories with which to entertain themselves; any tales they told were of events that had happened in reality.

After I was able to ingest this concept, I still believed that the histories and the sacred books were true. But when I came across references to the Koran and the Book of Mormon and the Christian Science books and the religions of ancient peoples, I saw at once that they couldn't all be true. Somebody was lying. In the end, I concluded that they all were. Or, if one was right, there was no way of finding out which one.

All contained some truths, though even these were distorted.

Then there were the scientists. They denied the claims of the religionists. But scientists had often been wrong and probably still were wrong in many of their conclusions. The scientists were just as prone to dogma and prejudice as the religionists.

The difference between them and the religionists was their method of searching for the truth. Actually, the religionists were no longer searching. They had found the truth, and their searches were only for rationalizations to bolster their claims. The true scientist doubted anything unless it could be proven to be fact. And he still had a mental reservation, because he knew that what seemed established today might be unseated tomorrow.

But though scientists could uncover physical truths, they were as helpless as the religionists in the supernatural or in the cosmogony and cosmology of things and spirits. Nobody could answer my youthful questions nor was anyone ever going to answer them.

Neither deliberately blind faith nor highly rationalized faith was for me. I told myself that all religions were, to be blunt, nonsense skillfully arranged to look like sense.

Human economic and political systems were not nonsense. They were machines for the operation of society. But they were all, capitalist, socialist, communist, highly inefficient, and the rationalizations for justifying them were often as transparently false as those used in religion.

That's the way it was and is and probably will be.

The admission of this does not mean that I am cynical or bitter or despairing or depressed. I am not like that "ape-man" in that story by the Czech author,[17] who killed himself because he could not endure the hypocrisy, greed, and injustice of civilization.

I accept this as the way things are, and I adjust accordingly. I had a very difficult time in my early contacts with humans because I didn't know the rules. People learn the thousand and more subtle laws of social behavior easily because they are brought up from infancy surrounded by adults who know them intimately. The children only have to imitate their examples. Even so, if they are thrust into a segment of society where the rules differ, they make mistakes. And quite often they are incapable of adjusting themselves.

---

[17] Josef Nesvadba, *The Death of an Apeman*, in *The Lost Face; Best Science Fiction From Czechoslovakia*, Taplinger Publishing Co., 1971.

I wasn't entirely innocent when I ventured into civilization, since I had read the novels and histories. But these more often confused than helped me. They gave a partially false picture and, also, the rules had changed somewhat between the time the books were written and the time I experienced society. But I learn quickly. If need be, I can pass as easily for a London dock laborer or a Yorkshire farmer as an English aristocrat. Or, for that matter, skin color and hair aside, for a Masai cattle herder or a Texas rancher.

My ear for sounds and rhythm of a language and my ability at mimicry enable me to do this. Inside of course I am still the "ape-man."

TIME HAS NO SHADOWS
In the beginning was greenness and timelessness.

The rain-forest trees with their thick canopy of vegetation binding them cast few shadows. And time cast no shadow at all.

Those who've read Hudson's *Green Mansions* know that the rain forest is not the same as the bush jungle. Large areas of the latter are often comparatively clear beneath the trees and their connecting many-leveled awnings of branch, vine, and creeper. A twilight and a hush spread through the rain forest; the trunks of the trees soar upward branchless for a hundred feet, looking like the columns of a huge badly lit temple. Most of the forest life, the birds, monkeys, civets, rodents, etc., is in the upper levels; and it is only seldom that a ground-dweller glides through the semidusk.

The n'k's territory was mainly in the rain forest, though part of it was in the bush jungle of the lower ground near the ocean or that along a nearby river.

The silence was often broken by the speech or cries of the n'k but even their language was whispering and quite appropriate for the living temple in which they dwelt.

This can be easily visualized by people who have never been to the rain forest.

But I have never met a person who could truly comprehend my sense of timelessness. On the other hand, I do not truly understand the sense of time which humans have.

I suppose that I have more of it than the n'k, since I am genetically a *Homo sapiens*. But I don't have much more.

How can I describe something for which no human languages seem to have words?

The preliterate and less technologically advanced peoples perhaps have a somewhat similar attitude. But they, too, are bound to their economics, which is considerably more complicated than that of the n'k. The latter are not even much guided by the sun, which they may not see for days or sometimes weeks except for fleeting appearances through a break in the canopy. The night pales into the semitwilight, and they may or may not rise with dawn. They eat when hungry, which is, however, most of the day. Being primarily root-grubbers, they spend much time digging up roots and stuffing their paunches, which are as big and rounded as those of the gorilla.

They have almost no ritual or ceremony except the feast under the full moon, when the entire tribe dances. If a large animal has been killed, or a member of an enemy tribe of n'k (which doesn't happen often), they eat the body as a climax to the dance. B, by the way, was correct when he said that an earthen drum is pounded by three old females while the tribe dances. I know that some critics have maintained that B got the idea for this from descriptions of chimpanzees pounding on earth or logs with sticks. But they are wrong.

I've asked the n'k why it was always three females who drum, but they didn't know. It is just the custom, they said.

If the tribe happens to be in a completely covered area where the full moon is not visible, the tribe doesn't dance. Nor does it seem to know that it's missing its monthly event.

The point is that the n'k have no sense of time except when arranging meetings, and that seldom happens. Nor does their sense of tense extend beyond today, the day after today, and a vague past. They don't even have a distinction between the rainy and dry seasons. Gabon gets abundant rain through most of the year, and there is little variation of temperatures.

The essential difference in the attitude toward time between the n'k (and hence mine) and humans is this: Humans think of time as a steady flow which can be sectioned by natural or artificial means. The natural is comprised of the sun, the moon, the stars, and the seasons. The artificial is comprised of clocks and calendars.

The n'k think of the sun, moon, and stars as living beings and wouldn't be surprised, though they would be dismayed, if the sun did not appear when it should. They just exist in the now, and the past and the near future are nearby limits to now.

That is the best I can do in trying to explain my original sense of time or lack of it. I'm sure that if some human could look through my mind and eyes, he would be lost and perhaps even scared. He would not know what he was experiencing. The closest he could come to describing it would be to compare it to a nightmare. Dreams are lost in timelessness; things are out of sequence; there is often no causality.

Of course, I became somewhat aware of the concept of time through reading the books in my parents' cabin. But I didn't truly comprehend it until I was in civilization. Even so, I never came to accept time-markers as natural. I went along with clocks because humans lived by them, and I was trying to live by their rules. But I never felt the sense of urgency that accompanies clocks and calendars.

And when I am back in the jungle, it is with relief that I sink back into my natural timelessness. I become one with the beasts and the trees, and I can laze away weeks or months with no thought beyond the now. If I were a true n'k, I would be unable to imagine beyond now.

This was the essential difference between the n'k and me. They had very little imagination, just enough to distinguish them from the beasts. This little difference is, of course, enormous, since it does make them partly human. But I had much imagination. And so I was all human.

Despite this, I am much closer to the n'k than to humans in my sense of time. Perhaps imagination is the ability to comprehend time. The greater the comprehension, the greater the imagination.

Extracts from the Memoirs of "Lord Greystoke"

Addendum

During the research for this book, a single extra page of memoirs was found among Farmer's papers. It seems likely this was part of a larger letter written by Tarzan to Farmer. But no further pages were uncovered, despite a diligent and extensive search. Knowing Lord Greystoke's frankness, it is possible that what followed the found page was unprintable (or held information potentially damaging to Tarzan and his family) and Farmer simply destroyed them. But why, then, did he keep this one page? Did it accidentally escape destruction? Or did it hold something that Farmer wished to keep a record of?

What follows is a transcript of the one page of typed paper. In the grand scheme of things, it is a paltry addition to this book, but to leave it out would seem to be a disservice. It will be up to the reader to judge the sagacity of including it here.

With relation to L

There must be many readers who have wondered why I repulsed L. After all, I had lost my memory of all my past except the earliest period. And this, my life among the great apes before I met white humans, was hazily recollected. So, since I did not remember J, nor, for that matter, my own great ape name, and since L was beautiful and passionate, why did I repulse her?

The answer is that I did not—wholly. For one thing, I was not well disposed to anyone who would attack me and tie my hands and feet and then propose to knife me through the heart. It's true that L offered to release me if I would become her mate, but I thought of myself as a great ape then and did not want to be shut up in the stone ruins of Opar. Now that I reconsider it, I would have acted intelligently if I had promised to do anything she wanted and then have escaped at the first chance.

But even in my amnesiac near-brute condition, I felt that my word, once given, was binding. I know that civilized people find this attitude puzzling and even consider it to be a form of stupidity. So much the worse for them, the assholes. To me, my word is me.

As for the statement that she loved me and wanted me to love her, it must be understood that this is a paraphrase by Burroughs. L could not say she loved me, because she spoke in the great ape language, there is no word for love in this language. Not as civilized people define the word. The word she used—kuf—indicates only passion and a desire to form a permanent relationship. There are no other overtones or undertones to the word.

And so L tried to get me to change my mind. As Burroughs says, she kissed me on the forehead, eyes, and lips. She also kissed me elsewhere.

<Page ends>

THE MAIN EVENT

AN EXCLUSIVE INTERVIEW WITH LORD GREYSTOKE

FARMER'S INTERVIEW PREPARATION

Sometimes it is better not to look behind the curtain, but Farmer's notes as he prepared for the meeting of his life hold a wonderful fascination. Although typed, with numerous handwritten additions, these pages, found in Farmer's personal files, were uncorrected, loosely ordered, and full of speculation and supposition. They are presented here to illustrate the thought processes Farmer was going through and how he chose what questions he might ask. It isn't always clear what Farmer intended by some of his comments, and only a very few corrections have been made to aid the reader. For the most part, they are presented here as typed and annotated by Farmer. Certain abbreviations have been expanded, where the meaning may not be obvious, but many have been left as is. Where deemed advantageous to the understanding of the reader, footnotes have been added by this editor.

Please be warned, the notes are very rough in parts and were obviously typed and annotated at speed. (You can sense the urgency with which Farmer was trying to get his thoughts down on paper.) Capitalization is missing. Punctuation is erratic; questions are often presented as statements (i.e., missing the question mark). Thoughts are expressed in Farmer's own shorthand. Although never intended for publication this is, nevertheless, a fascinating artifact that will send chills of joy down the spines of Farmer and Tarzan scholars alike, and provides plenty of detail for experienced and budding Tarzan scholars to pick over.

Analysing the draft papers, it appears highly likely that Farmer had these notes in front of him during the interview itself and used the pages to scribble down answers (presumably immediately after Lord Greystoke had left the room). Although not completely discernible, it appears Farmer also typed in some rough answers onto the original sheets of paper, presumably to keep as much of the knowledge together in one place until he was able to start work on the finished article, which can make discerning the timeline of when entries were made problematic.

Farmer stresses a number of times that the interview was limited to an exact fifteen minutes. We can only speculate, but that may have been a literary device used by Farmer to add some tension to the piece. Although obviously a short meeting it does appear that, like the location of the meeting itself, Farmer may have misled us slightly on the duration of the interview. After all, an experienced writer such as Farmer would have been aware that the editor of the publication where the interview was to appear, *Esquire* (dated April 1972), would likely require changes for spacing reasons and that a complete transcript of the interview was unlikely to be printed exactly as it occurred.

The reader is free to skip this article altogether, or, if preferred, to refer back to it after reading the polished article.

Problems to raise with LG

Too many lost cities

Too many doubles

Hollywood episode

Fuwalda, currents—to st. Helena? Check currents, time of year—

Why didn't the three just up and walk along the coast?

Location of birthplace

Lack of mention of T's real son except in TELover[1]

What happened to Esmeralda—last mention of her is in TEL, in fact, she's mentioned only in TOTA, TEL (midsummer 1914)—TROT? (?)—indications are that she was probably in London with Professor Porter—he's last mentioned as recovering from a serious

---

[1] *The Eternal Lover*. ERB's fantasy-adventure novel, originally serialized in *All-Story Weekly*, featuring Tarzan as a minor character.

illness, probably he and Esmeralda staying in the London Greystoke house, which I place as at the exclusive Carlton House Terrace, part of which was destroyed during the bombing, and so its possible that Porter and Esmeralda, if still living, would have been killed by bombs—Porter was born in 1839 (circa) so probably died long before WWII, especially since been ill—in what year would that be?—

Porter a southerner yet there is the flintlock of his puritan ancestor, so may have been from a puritan who came to Va instead of New England or migrated from NE to Va after failing to find the religious toleration he'd expected.

Esmeralda seems to be about 40 or so in 1909—in 1939 would be about 70—

T's strange failure to learn MBonga's people's language.

Waziri speak Swahili according to ERB, but this is unlikely—truth to tell, ERB didn't bother to get facts of language, used his Swahili reference books; but also unlikely that Waziri is really the tribal name, in which case we can't even be sure that the Waziri are bantu speakers—

Moves location of Opar around, approx. location in different books figured out by travel times from and to—would he give proper compass directions?—probably not, so even these can't be relied upon . . .

Lost adventures—ancient Spanish or Portuguese skeleton and his story? (Use in pastiche?)[2]

Recruiting of British subjects—not done by Belgium until about ten years after 1888—in building railroad

Miranda in British T and the Ant Men

---

[2] It appears that it was in his preparation for this interview that Farmer first had the idea for the book that would become *Tarzan and the Dark Heart of Time*. His first thought must have been to create a story of pure fiction and present it as a pastiche and, although not recorded, we can speculate that Farmer raised this with Lord Greystoke and gleaned enough to be able to write a previously untold Tarzan adventure.

Jane's death in magazine version of TTU

Tarzan writing his own name

Name of the ship from Dover, sailing date, passenger list

Records of Freetown Port authorities

Language among lower animals

Great apes—really aust. Robustus

The tin box and the diary

Chronology—would ERB give real date of Greystoke's trip

Means used to suppress publicity re T's discovery

What happened to Opar?

Names of mangani and M's people, etc—

Language of knights of TLOTJ

Tailed people of TTT

Lack of sickness on T's part—unhealthiness of Gabon—healthiness of equator. Closed canopy rain forest.

The beasts of Tarzan—the big island, etc.—Akut ignore—Sabrov vs Paulvitch—

Paulvitch's name peculiar—why not Pavlovitch or Pavlitch?—ERB misread it and used a fake name to conceal the real and ignorance of Russian caused Paulvitch?

Scanning of Burke should reveal Tarzan's identity if ERB told facts straight but he wouldn't, of course, otherwise it'd be too easy to track him down, because some nosey bastard is going to come along, like myself, inevitable and scan the Peerage for him—so his true story would not be told straight—and, in fact, it's highly likely that Tarzan never claimed his lordship on advice of Jane and others—that but ERB, with his Anglophilia and especial regard for the British nobility and for his readers like for romanticism, continued the peerage myth—in which case Tarzan would not be in the Peerage and you wouldn't find a space reserved for the family in the Peerage but would in the Extended Peerage. Title lapsed with death of WC unless a near relative claimed it. This is most likely to have occurred.

The saga of the knife, not included in bio

Pastiche of Tarzan story—delves into old manuscript of Spanish giant skeleton and indicates therein directions to a city much like Carcosa—in fact, that's what the Spaniard calls it—

Use in pastiche or separate story for fanzine—BB—?[3]

Interview: The Man Behind the Mask of Tarzan (Further notes)

Movies—Tree house

Sophisticated—his accent, changeable but with a very slight strangeness

McLuhan[4]

Chomsky

The mangani, australopithecus?—knuckle walkers?

Zantar, oral structure of mangani

ERB's coding, see the Australian article[5]

Albert Schweitzer[6]—trader horn, lesson: don't trust anybody, not even Albert Schweitzer—bananas

---

[3] See earlier footnote re *Tarzan and the Dark Heart of Time*. This comment seems to have written at a different time, perhaps explaining the repetition. It looks like this idea really tantalised Farmer.

[4] Presumably **Marshall McLuhan** (21 July 1911–31 December 1980), Canadian communications theorist and educator.

[5] This may be a reference to **Michael Fomenko**, known as Australia's Tarzan. Son of a Russian princess he shunned society to live rough battling crocodiles and cyclones in North Queensland.

[6] **Ludwig Philipp Albert Schweitzer** (14 January 1875–4 September 1965), referenced in more detail in the published interview.

Jane, professor porter

<u>How I found the real Tarzan</u>—a title for the interview?

ERB's descent, common, with Tarzan

Relationship with some people used as basis for fictional characters—drummonds—fairlie—arpad, Orczy—rurik, yaroslav—woden—egbert—Charles II *(*descent from Woden*)*—duke of st albans (listed in peerage but tarzan not really descended from Charles II through st albans, someone else—lots of candidates—

Arms—

How could the real tarzan be kept from being exposed? (Money, lots of it, I guess)

The real reason for tarzan's parents going to Africa—

His self-education, father's diary—cabin now gone—

Tree traveling, vine swinging

How did he escape disease?—healthy eq. rain forest but I suspect he must have some mutational resistance—

The kavuru pill, the witch doctor treatment—

La of Opar (parallels with Nina T——, She, the Lovedu, et alia)

A real Opar—the inland African sea—the lost city, why not found now?

Forest fire —must have run not swung through trees—obviously he couldn't go by himself thru trees let alone carry Jane—

Tarzan last of the real golden age heroes—some parallels with ancient mythological and legendary elements—give these—tarzan a real peer or just a baronet?

Why greystoke chosen? More of ERB's coding, Doyles, etc. the sixth duke of Holdernesse's story—shaw—starr—trader horn—leopold Bloom—the shadow—the spider—b drummond—professor challenger—don't forget shell scott—lew archer—

The three holmes, which one is Tarzan related to?—some discussion of this—Harrison-wendell Schier[7]

Limited time—perhaps wanted to see if I was sincere—tell of my trail thru burks peerage and suspicion that doyle, shaw, and ERB coding things—

Tarzan's real character, faithfully portrayed in book but badly distorted in the movies—the last tale of his adventure gives his wisdom, almost Christian character—a natural philosopher—

Something of the WWI in east Africa, von lettow-vorbeck, etc. some things seem too pat and coincidental to be true but tarzan's life has actually been dictated by an author.

The scarlet pimpernel—orczy's disclaimer—perhaps she didn't know of him—

No lions, zebras, giraffes in Gabon.

Why did ERB put Tarzan's birthplace in Portuguese Africa?—because trying to divert from real tarzan and help the Greystoke family but also knowing Tarzan was a real person didn't want to be sued?

ERB's main interest, a good story, hence most of Tarzan's adventures highly fictionalized—some all fiction, of course—

Did get involved with an olga de coude (not quite her real name) had a rotten brother and some of the episodes of the beasts of tarzan quite true—but

Big korak discrepancy, explained?

---

[7] Handwritten and not totally legible.
"Harrison" possibly refers to **Michael Harrison** (25 April 1907–13 September 1991), noted British Holmes scholar.
"Wendell" likely refers to **Oliver Wendell Holmes Sr.** (29 August 1809–7 October 1894), American physician and poet. Inspiration for the name Doyle gave his famous detective and, Farmer may be hinting, a relative.
"Schier" possibly refers to **Norma Schier** (20 September 1930–15 November 1995), writer, notably of a Sherlock Holmes pastiche in *The Anagram Detectives* (1979).

Send along transparency of arms in case they want to use with finished interview—descent—tarzan jewish origin—pemberley house—

The natural children of the british peerage—including Smithson of the Smithsonian institution—

One of those amazing coincidences: starr's article resulted in finding the truth—

But stress that tarzan unlikely the son of a duke and may be the son of a baronet, a sort of hereditary knight—founded by Charles I?

black michael-black peter?

Birth—sag. Scorpio?—

Tarzan: 6' 3", as desc., features, as in JTOT, heavy bones, built leopardish, quality of muscles and heavy bones, not massiveness built much like the young Weissmuller but his face very handsome and intelligent looking—does have the scar described by ERB on forehead and many more—no racial prejudice (ERB advanced for his time, some traces of prejudice but not many) but tarzan himself free, and not much real patriotism, though fights very well for his country, his views on conservation—

Opar presumably not as big or in good shape as ERB described—but the oparians do have their myths, and they seem to point to an origin from people who erected the earliest civilization around the great inland sea, which we know existed—tell of leys facts, surmises, etc. Harwoods and Brueckels—a tabu area for natives in that area and also hard to get to—but Tarzan did take care of it, dismantling an entire city—actually, they were presumably more like the ruins of Zimbabwe, but was a treasure of gold and jewels

Coincidence apt to occur when one is born on cusp of scorpio and sagittarius—does Tarzan believe in astrology?[8]

Question: why are chimps so neglected in the books but Tarzan pals around with a chimp in the movies—movies pay little attention to the book Tarzan, and he had much contact with the chimps of

---

[8] See "I Still Live" for the horoscope Farmer commissioned on Tarzan.

forested Gabon, but ERB never felt it necessary to put them into a story—actually, as anyone knows, chimps usually flee o people, very shy, and since Tarzan was associated with the australopithecus robustus, who ate chimps, they weren't friendly with him at first. But established communication with them later[9]—no, chimps don't have a language though recent evidence indicates they have more capabilities than man have though see Science News article[10]

/// Arthur Koestler and his article, wrong; Sprague de Camp and his vine-swinging article.

At this time, hadn't read h & b's speculations anent the food of the oparians. Couldn't ask him about that. But La (this is a truncation of her true name, by the way) just didn't get old very fast.[11]

(NOTE: He does look like the early Burton, point out illo in the book, Burton without his moustache and no slight nystagmus? —no, what the hell is that word, I have the condition. Anyway, this is what Tarzan looks like though his lips are little thinner and his eyes are dark grey. Brow of a god and jaw of a devil, distantly related.[12]

But Tarzan as influenced by two things: his tribal code and what he read in the books, which he did not understand as well as ERB made out, though much better than most people would believe. Could print sentences in English. (Objection: how could you print your own name when you'd never heard it in English, had no idea what English sounded like, and it wasn't an English word? Explanation: white skin he wrote: translation of his name from mangani, actually it's what? ERB wrote Tarzan because he didn't want to detract from the story at that particular time with an explanation.[13]

---

[9] Although impossible to tell for sure, the offsetting here does appear a little different from the surrounding text, suggesting it was added after Farmer posed the question.

[10] This appears to be a further note that Farmer added at a later time.

[11] Obviously added after the interview itself.

[12] This is not referenced in the finished interview. Presumably Farmer never got to raise this with Lord Greystoke, or the answer was withheld. Farmer has hinted at this familial link elsewhere, see "From Forne to Farmer."

[13] This appears to be Farmer speculating to himself; trying to formulate the question(s) he wants to ask.

The use of white skin as a name indicates that the mangani were not as hairy as ERB painted them, otherwise they would have named him hairless, nor were the mangani as dark as the natives otherwise why would they call them black mangani? But mangani wasn't used by the mangani, so this must be an invention of ERB's.

Anyway, what about mangani females, mbongas women, jane? Did he actually rescue her from a lioness, or, rather, leopardess? Did he actually behave so much like the knights of old were supposed to, but seldom did?

Yes, with jane, he did. In first place, anxious to please her, he wasn't any rampaging gorilla monster of the movies (sexuality of gorillas, size of penis, shyness, trader horn's story of white man who locked native girl in cage with gorilla); he didn't want to offend her, nor were mangani expected to violate females, though could kidnap and run off with others of other tribes[14]

La was the beautiful high priestess who fell in love with Tarzan and whose adventures are recounted in *The Return of Tarzan*, *Tarzan and the Jewels of Opar*, *Tarzan and the Golden Lion*, and *Tarzan the Invincible*.

[END OF NOTES]

---

[14] This appears to be speculation on Farmer's part.

AN EXCLUSIVE INTERVIEW WITH
LORD GREYSTOKE

A subgenre of biographical literature is that which claims that certain people thought to be fictional are, or were, very much living. Splendid examples of this are Blakeney's *Sir Percy Blakeney: Fact or Fiction?* (a biography of the Scarlet Pimpernel), Baring-Gould's *Sherlock Holmes of Baker Street* and *Nero Wolfe of West Thirty-Fifth Street*, Parkinson's *The Life and Times of Horatio Hornblower*, and the Flashman Papers (three volumes so far) by Fraser. In fact, some public libraries stock these in the "B" or biography section. (The Blakeney book is in the "B" section of the Peoria, Illinois, public library.)

I've written two such "lives": *Tarzan Alive* and *Doc Savage: His Apocalyptic Life*. (The former is in the biography section of the Yuma City, California, library.) I plan to write biographies of The Shadow, Allan Quatermain, Fu Manchu, d'Artagnan, Travis McGee, and a number of others. Fu Manchu, by the way, may have been based on a real-life model, a Vietnamese named Hanoi Shan whose operations in early twentieth-century France were every bit as sinister and fantastic as Rohmer's creation. I was informed of this after I'd made the statement in *Tarzan Alive* that Fu Manchu had no living counterpart.

This form of apologia is a lot of fun and much hard work. It requires as much imagination as the writing of science fiction but more discipline. Historical facts must not be ignored. Baring-Gould, in writing his Holmes biography, had an enormous amount of scholarship, articles published in *The Baker Street Journal* and other periodicals, to draw upon. But he had not only to read all these but to study them and make decisions. He found many conflicting theories, and he had to pick the one that seemed most valid. In addition, where theories or speculations were lacking, he had to generate his own. He had to explain discrepancies, which are numerous in Watson's account of Holmes' life. And, I might add, Burroughs, in his semifictional narratives of Greystoke's career, left many discrepancies for the scholar to reconcile, if he could. There are also gaps in the life of the hero which the biographer must fill in. And if the original writer has neglected the hero's genealogy, the biographer must research this.

Sometimes, a biographer makes a statement which he cannot substantiate. Thus, Baring-Gould said that Holmes was a cousin of Professor Challenger. He has been much criticized by the Sherlockian scholars for this because he presented no evidence from the Canon. Fortunately, in my *Tarzan Alive*, I was able to validate the relationship. The fact that Tarzan's mother was a Rutherford gave me the clue needed to track down the cousinhood.

The following article is part of my interview with "Lord Greystoke" and appeared in the April, 1972, issue of *Esquire* under the title of "Tarzan Lives." It was accompanied by the first authentic portrait of Greystoke, a photograph of a painting by Jean-Paul Goude. The staff of *Esquire* went to great lengths and much trouble to acquire this, for which they should be thanked. The report that Goude got the commission to do the painting because he is a relative of Admiral Paul d'Arnot of the French navy, Greystoke's closest friend, is being checked. It is said that Goude, like Holmes, is a descendant of Antoine Vernet, father of four famous French painters.

[Esquire] Editor's Note: For a number of years Mr. Farmer, who recorded the following interview, has been engaged in writing a definitive biography of the man Edgar Rice Burroughs called Tarzan of the Apes. Mr. Farmer's book, Tarzan Alive, *to be published by Doubleday in April of this year, is similar in method to Baring-Gould's* Sherlock Holmes of Baker Street *and Parkinson's* The Life and Times of Horatio Hornblower, *with the very important difference that Mr. Farmer firmly avers that "Lord Greystoke" or "Tarzan" is really alive. In fact, Mr. Farmer was able to track his subject to earth in a hotel in Libreville, Gabon, on the coast of Western Africa just above the equator, where he was granted this interview. "I met him," Mr. Farmer tells us, "in his hotel room—fittingly enough, on September 1, Edgar Rice Burroughs' birthday. He is six feet three and, I suppose, about two hundred forty pounds. I did not have the opportunity to see him in action, of course, but just from the way he moved about the room I could guess at his immense physical strength. As Burroughs said, he is much more like Apollo than Hercules; his power lies in the quality not the quantity of his*

muscles. I don't hesitate to admit that I was awed. I was concerned, of course, that after all my research I might still have been the victim of a hoax; but from the moment I knocked on the door and heard that deep, rich voice say 'Enter,' I knew I had the right man. And of course I was even more convinced when I saw him move—like a leopard, like water falling." The text of Mr. Farmer's interview follows.

TARZAN: How do you do, Mr. Farmer.

FARMER: How do you do, Your Grace.

T: If you don't mind, Mr. Farmer, I should prefer simply to be called John Clayton. I own a good many titles, both real and fictional, but John Clayton is, as it were, my real name. Though not my true *identity*, so to speak. As you apparently know.

F: Excuse me, sir—Mr. Clayton. Mr. Clayton, you told me over the phone that you would see me for fifteen minutes only, so I'd better work fast. I'll start asking questions right now, if you don't mind?

T: By all means. You don't have a tape recorder on you, do you? No? Good.

F: May I ask first, sir, why you were kind enough to grant this interview?

T: Mr. Farmer, my reasons are my own. But I will say that I appreciate the very great efforts you have gone to in researching the details of my life. It is very flattering to me, and I am not entirely immune to that. Besides, you seem to have information about my family that even I myself don't know. Your genealogical researches provoke my own curiosity, which has always been ample. I may ask you a few questions myself.

F: Of course. First, though, may I ask how it happens that you seem to speak English as you do, with more or less of an American accent? You speak as though you came from Illinois, which is my own home state. I seem to recall that on the phone you spoke—well, as I imagine dukes speak, the educated British accent.

T: I speak more or less as I am spoken *to*. You will recall that English is not my first spoken language—though it was my first *written* language—very unusual business, that—or even my first spoken *European* language. But the first English-speaking country

I visited was the United States, Wisconsin in particular, back in 1909. I was not quite twenty-one years old at the time. So when English was fairly new to me, I had rather a large dose of American. Nevertheless, in Britain I do speak British. I have a gift for mimicry, I suppose you might call it, and I conform pretty much to the dialect of my interlocutors. When I gave my first and only speech in the House of Lords I did speak as dukes speak, or at least as dukes think they speak. You seem nervous, by the way. Would you care for a drink? I believe I will join you in a small Scotch.

F: Thank you. But I'm surprised to find you a drinking man. I thought—

T: That I was an abstainer? For many years I was. In my early days among civilized people I not only saw the results of excess but, I'm afraid, committed it myself. For many years I abstained completely. However, I believe the rash impulses of youth are safely behind me now. I can be abstemious without being teetotal. After all, I am—

F: You are eighty-two years old. When this interview is published, you will be eighty-three. But I suppose as far as physical appearance is concerned, you look about thirty-five. It must be true, then, that story about the grateful witch doctor who gave you the immortality treatment—

T: That was in 1912. I was twenty-four then, so as you see I have apparently aged about ten years since. The treatment merely slows down the aging process. Burroughs exaggerated its effects slightly, as he often did. I'll be an old man by the time I'm a hundred and fifty or so.

F: I'd like to return to your physical condition. But since you bring up Burroughs, and since Burroughs is the principal source of information about your life and family—

T: You would like to discuss the accuracy of Burroughs? Go ahead.

F: In *Tarzan of the Apes*, the first Tarzan book, Burroughs says that in 1888 your mother, then pregnant, accompanied your father on a secret mission to Africa for the British government. They hired a small ship, but the crew mutinied and stranded your parents on the coast of Africa. They were left on the shores of Portuguese Angola at approximately ten degrees south latitude, or about fifteen hundred miles north of Cape Town. But it seems to me that many of the scenes in the book could not have taken place in Angola.

T: That is correct. Actually, my parents were marooned on the shore of this very country, Gabon, which was then part of French Equatorial Africa. I was born about 190 miles south of here, in what is now the Parc National du Petit Loango. Any researcher, I believe, could have deduced that from the facts. There were gorillas in my natal territory, but there are no gorillas south of the Congo, and Angola extends far to the south of the Congo. Also, it was a French cruiser that landed near the same spot years later and rescued the party of Professor Porter, including my wife-to-be Jane, but left behind Lieutenant d'Arnot, my first civilized friend. Why would a French warship be patrolling the shores of Angola, a Portuguese possession?

F: Nor are there any lions, zebras, or rhinoceroses in the Gabonese rain forests. What about the lioness whose neck Burroughs said you broke with a full nelson when she was trying to get into your parents' cabin after Jane?

T: The lioness was actually a leopard. It was about the size of a small lioness, one of the big leopards that the natives call *injogu*. I did break its neck. As you know, I had independently invented the full nelson a few months before when I fought the big mangani ape that Burroughs calls Terkoz.

F: Well, then, how do you explain the discrepancies between Burroughs and the facts?

T: Mr. Farmer, the relationship between my life and Burroughs' narration of my life is exceedingly complex. I don't choose, for various reasons, to tell you all that I know about Burroughs' methods or my own; but I can tell you a number of his motives, some of which you may have figured out for yourself. First of all, Burroughs was essentially a romancer. He was not obligated to stick to the facts, and even if I had chosen to try to compel him, litigation would have been involved, and I would have had to appear in court and submit to questioning, which I would rather not have done. I entirely appreciate the feelings of your own Mr. Howard Hughes in this regard. In fact, after Burroughs wrote *Tarzan of the Apes*, I communicated with him, and I told him he should continue to make the narratives highly romantic, even fantastic. Jane advised that, because she said that if people found out I was not a fictional character, I would never again have a moment of privacy.

In the second place, Burroughs himself was not always fully informed. He first heard of me in the winter of 1911. I had then been known to the civilized world for only perhaps two years, and the records of my existence—including my father's diary, which he kept until his death in Africa—were then in England. By the way, here are some photostats of that diary. You may examine them, but you may not take them with you. In any case, Burroughs had not been to England, much less to Africa, and had his information by word of mouth at several removes. In many cases he had to fill in gaps by sheer guesswork, some of which is accurate, some not. For the sake of verisimilitude, Burroughs pretended to be much closer to his sources than was in fact the case.

Finally, certain facts are disguised in the books because they are best left disguised. Burroughs gives directions for getting to the lost city of Opar, with its spires and domes and vaults of gold and jewels. But those directions will lead the curious nowhere. Not that it matters so much in that case, because I have long since disguised the ruins of Opar completely. You could go there today and never know you were there. But I hope you won't try.

A few of Burroughs' stories are pure fiction. In *Jungle Tales of Tarzan*, I am supposed to have shot arrows into the sky in an effort to stop an eclipse of the moon. But the story happens in 1908, and in fact there was no such eclipse visible from my part of Africa that year. Sheer fabrication.

F: I see from your father's diary that he delivered you himself, though he had nothing but some medical books to go by. You were born a few minutes after midnight of November 22, 1888. On the cusp of Sagittarius and Scorpio. Scorpio the passionate and Sagittarius the hunter.

T: I know that. I have read much about astrology, though I believe in it about as much as I do in the speeches of politicians. Still, Sagittarius, the centaur with the bow, could not be a better symbol of the half-animal, half-man that I have been. And I am a very good archer indeed. And Scorpios are supposed to be ingenious, creative, true friends, and dangerous enemies, all of which I am. We're also supposed to exude sexual power. Hmm.

F: Burroughs gives many instances of women attempting to seduce you. You are certainly not the inarticulate ape-man of the movies. What you say about being a good archer, however, reminds me of some critics who maintain you could not have accomplished this. They refer to Marshall McLuhan's thesis that only literate peoples can produce excellent marksmen.

T: I've read *The Mechanical Bride* and *Understanding Media.* McLuhan forgets the medieval English bowman, who was certainly illiterate but undoubtedly a great marksman. And the critics forget that I taught myself to read and write English. I was not illiterate, though I couldn't *speak* the language.

F: What do you think of the Tarzan movies?

T: I saw the first one in 1920, the one with Elmo Lincoln. I came very near to leaping up onto the stage and tearing the picture apart. That fake jungle, those doped-up, scraggly circus cats! Lincoln was built more like a gorilla than like me, and he wore a headband, which I have never done. All that swinging on a vine is movie invention as well, as is Cheetah the chimpanzee. Nowhere even in Burroughs will you find me swinging on vines, though it's true that he did greatly exaggerate my tree-traveling abilities. I'm too heavy to go skipping along the, ah, arboreal avenues like a monkey. And the chimpanzees would never trust me because they identified me with the great apes who brought me up. We—that is, they—used to eat chimps when they could catch them. But later on I began to find the Tarzan movies more amusing than disgusting. Jane helped me to learn to tolerate them.

F: Arthur Koestler wrote an article claiming that you couldn't have escaped being mentally retarded. He said there had been a few authentic cases of children raised by baboons or wolves and then found by humans. These were unable to master any language. Apparently, if the child doesn't experience language before a certain age, it is forever incapable of learning speech.

T: Koestler must not have bothered to read the Tarzan books. Otherwise he would have learned that the great apes *did* have a language. He should have deduced, as many have, that the great apes, or mangani, were really near-humans. Hominids, in fact. Remember what I said about the sketchy information upon which Burroughs' early books were based? He supplied missing data with imagination or even misinformation. He made up names. He put animals in the Gabonese jungles that did not belong there. He described the mangani as great apes. My father had thought they were apes, and so called them in his diary. But my father was not a zoologist or a paleontologist.

The mangani were a very rare, nearly extinct—even eighty years ago—genus of hominids, halfway between ape and man. They might have been a giant variety of Australopithecus robustus. The fossil remains of this hominid have been found by Leakey in East Africa, you know. The mangani—and I use Burroughs' word for them, since their own term is an unpronounceable jawbreaker—had crested skulls and massive jaws. They had long arms and often used their knuckles to assist them in walking, but they had manlike hips and leg bones. They could walk upright when they chose.

Burroughs later had better information about his *great apes*. However, for the sake of consistency he described them in the later novels as he had done earlier on. He slipped in the sixth book, *Jungle Tales of Tarzan*, when he said they walked upright and were manlike.

I can speak mangani fluently, of course. But can't pronounce it quite perfectly. The mangani oral structure is different from man's, and many of their speech sounds have no exact equivalent in human speech. So though I can speak English with any of several accents, I always speak mangani with a *human* accent.

F: Did the big mangani, Terkoz, really abduct Jane and try to rape her? And you killed him with your father's hunting knife?

T: Yes. And there you see, by the way, another reason why the mangani should not be classified as apes. They are capable of raping a human being, whereas a gorilla is not. I once read in the memoirs of Trader Horn about a white trader who put a male gorilla in a cage with a native girl. The gorilla did nothing but sulk in one corner while the poor girl wept in the other. Horn said he shot the white man when he found out about it. In any case, gorillas have forty-eight chromosomes, humans only forty-six, so a gorilla-human hybrid is not possible. But Burroughs knew of instances of offspring being born to a human and a mangani.

F: Albert Schweitzer maintained that Trader Horn, aside from some trifling discrepancies, was generally accurate. Did you know that Schweitzer built his house on the site of Horn's trading post?

T: Yes, at Adolinanongo, a little distance above Lambaréné on the Ogooué River. I know it well. There's a Catholic mission there, founded in 1886. That's where Lieutenant d'Arnot and I came out of the jungle on our trek to civilization.

F: Would you care to comment on how you taught yourself to read and write English? As far as I know this is a unique intellectual feat, especially since you had never heard a word of it spoken.

T: I was about ten years old when I discovered how to unlock the door to my parents' cabin, and there I found, as you have read in Burroughs, a number of books, all of them perfectly meaningless to me, of course. But one of them was a big illustrated children's alphabet book with pictures of bowmen and the like, you know, and legends like "A is for Archer, who shoots with the bow," that sort of thing. Finally it dawned on me that the writing had something to do with the picture, and I spent I don't know how long puzzling it out. When I was seventeen I could read a child's primer. I called the letters "little bugs," or the mangani equivalent rather, and I knew how they worked. One detail you may find rather amusing is this: I had to invent, and did invent, my own manner of pronouncing the English words, which had nothing to do of course with real English but was governed by the usages of mangani grammar. Mangani has two genders, indicated by the prefixes *bu* for the masculine and *mu* for the feminine. Now I supposed that the capital letters were masculine, since they were bigger, and the rest feminine. And as children will do when they know the alphabet but don't yet know how to read, I pronounced each letter separately, using arbitrary syllables taken from mangani. Does this all seem terribly complicated? For example, I pronounced *g* as *la*; *o* as *tu*; and *d* as *mo*. Now take the English word God; adding the prefixes, I pronounced it *Bulamutumumo*. The equivalent in English would be *he-g-she-o-she-d*. Now that's very cumbersome, of course, but it worked. I could read my father's books and know what I was reading.

I had no idea how to write my mangani name, but I had seen a picture of a little white boy, which in Anglo-Mangani, I suppose you might call it, is *Bumudomutumuro*, or *He-she-b-she-o-she-y*. That's what I called myself.

F: Burroughs says that when you discovered intruders had messed up the cabin, you printed a threatening note to them. You signed it with your mangani name. How could you do that if you didn't know how to write it in English?

T: I didn't. I printed a translation of my mangani name: White Skin. When Burroughs wrote *Tarzan of the Apes*, he had no record of the exact text of the note. He made up the text, and he did not care to take time out from the action to explain that I couldn't use my mangani name. Remember he was first and last a storyteller.

F: Your reading must have given you some strange ideas about the outside world. You had no proper references to give you a full comprehension of the books.

T: My ideas were no stranger than the reality. My initial encounters with human beings were extremely unpleasant. The first human being I ever saw had just murdered my foster mother. To him she was an ape, but to me she was the most beautiful and loving and lovable person in the world. The first time I saw white men, one was murdering another. I am fortunate that that didn't make me shun mankind forever. Otherwise I'd never have known human love.

F: When you matured and discovered that you were not an ape but a man, didn't you think of turning to the native tribes for companionship?

T: No. I hated them all for a long time, because I blamed them for my foster mother's death. Also, they were cannibals, and anybody not of their tribe was meat to them. And they had had unfortunate experiences with white men. In addition to that, the women coated their bodies and hair with rancid palm-nut oil. I have an unusually keen sense of smell, and consequently they repelled me. Still, if Jane hadn't come along—

F: Burroughs portrays you as free of racial prejudice.

T: Like Mark Twain, I have only one prejudice. That is against the human race.

F: Let me not pursue *that* further. Many readers have found your behavior with Jane when you were alone in the jungle incredibly chivalrous. Burroughs attributes this to heredity, but no one today would accept this explanation.

T: Remember, I read all the novels—Victorian novels, mind you—in my father's library. And I read Malory's book about King Arthur and the knights and the fair ladies. I believed in chivalry quite literally. And I was in love with Jane and did not want to offend her. Besides, the mangani have a code of ethics, you know. They are not apes. They do not copulate in public; they demand, though they do not always get, marital fidelity; they punish rape with death, if the injured party wishes it. Consider all the factors and you'll find my behavior credible enough.

F: You became chief of a local tribe which Burroughs called the Waziri. Are you aware that Robert Lewis Taylor, in his biography of W. C, Fields, says that Fields once went with Tex Rickard on a world tour? And that Fields entertained a tribe of naked Waziri? That would have been in 1906 or 1907, several years before you encountered the Waziri. Did your Waziri ever say anything about Fields?

T: I have no comment on that, I'm afraid.

F: How much of Burroughs' *Tarzan and the Lion Man* is true? It seems to me that Burroughs wrote it mainly to satirize Hollywood.

T: Yes, nearly everything in that book is fiction. But I did visit Hollywood once, though I told no one except Burroughs who I was, of course.

F: Did you actually try out for the role of Tarzan in a movie? And were you rejected because the producer said you weren't the type?

T: No, though I wouldn't be surprised if such a thing were to happen. In any case, I went there too late to try out for the Weissmuller movie *Tarzan the Ape Man*, and too early for the Buster Crabbe movie *Tarzan the Fearless*. I did meet Burroughs, secretly of course. I liked him very much. He was gentle and broad-minded and he didn't take himself or his works too seriously. He saw many things wrong in civilization, many sickening things, and he satirized them in his books, you know, but his mockery was Voltaire's, not Swift's. He was never soured or snarly. But since we are now discussing authors, let me indulge my curiosity a moment. I gather that you have been led to me by a fairly elaborate trail. Would you mind explaining to me how you first caught my scent, as it were?

F: I had long suspected that Burroughs, Arthur Conan Doyle, and George Bernard Shaw had all written stories about your family. Each, however, used more or less sophisticated systems of code names for your various relatives. If these codes could be cracked, and used as guides to the right places—*Burke's Peerage*, for instance—they would lead me right to you. And as you see, they have. The reasoning I have employed is long and complex, and I hope you'll be willing to delay a full understanding until I can send you a copy of my book, since our time today is short. Suffice it to say that I have shown you are closely related to the men who were the living prototypes of Doc Savage, Nero Wolfe, Bulldog Drummond, Sherlock Holmes, Lord Peter Wimsey, Leopold Bloom, and Richard Wentworth (also known as G-8, the Spider, and the Shadow), and a number of other notable characters in nineteenth- and twentieth-century fiction.

T: Indeed.

F: I have also found the explanation for the remarkable, almost superhuman powers exhibited by yourself and many members of your family. As you know, a monument marks the spot today where a meteorite hit Wold Newton, Yorkshire, in 1795. It just so happened that three coaches were passing by when the meteorite struck, and in them were the third Duke of Greystoke and his wife, the rich gentleman Fitzwilliam Darcy of Pemberley House and his wife Elizabeth Bennet—the heroine of *Pride and Prejudice*—Sherlock Holmes' great-grandparents, and a number of others. All the ladies were pregnant. Everybody was exposed to the radiation from the meteorite. Ionization accompanies the fall of these, you know. And the radiation must have caused favorable mutations in the party. Otherwise how do you explain the nova of genetic splendor in the descendants of these people, including yourself?

T: I will not say that I am entirely convinced. Nevertheless yours is a very probable theory. My own skeletal bones are half again as thick as normal, which might well indicate that I am a mutant. Moreover, even before I received the immortality treatment from the witch doctor, I was developing oddly, though I had no one of my own race to compare myself with at the time. I was six feet tall at eighteen years of age, and grew three more inches in the next two years. I did not have to shave until I was twenty. I have never been ill or had a toothache. So your mutation theory seems likely enough. And now, I'm afraid, our interview is over. May I have the photostats back, please?

F: My time's up? But—

T: I don't need a watch to know how many minutes have passed. Good-bye. I won't be seeing you again. May I ask you to remain in this room a few minutes and allow me to leave first? I have already checked out and shall soon be gone.

F: May I ask where you're going?

T: To arrange a seemingly fatal accident. Too many people are wondering why I look so young. One reason I gave you this interview is that I'm disappearing. Your book won't help anyone find me. But I hold you to your promise not to reveal my true identity for ten years. I'll be living incognito with Jane in various countries under various names. Occasionally I'll return to the jungle. There are still vast tracts in the rain forests of Gabon and the Ituri where the only men are a few pygmies. The rain forests may disappear someday. But I think that the worldwide pollution is going to result in a collapse of civilization and a drastic reduction of population. Perhaps the forests will be spared after all, and many of the species now threatened with extinction will come back. In any case, I intend to survive. If I don't, well, death gets us sooner or later, and I won't be able to worry about its being sooner if I'm dead. As I told you, I'll be old anyhow when I'm a hundred and fifty. Send your book to my bankers in Zurich.

Then, Mr. Farmer tells us, he left the room and was gone.

ADDENDUM

As well as Farmer's interview notes, several pages of the "complete" interview were found that do not match exactly with the final, published piece.

We know that Farmer stated that the interview was limited to a strict fifteen minutes but it seems likely Lord Greystoke was slightly less fixated on that than Farmer indicates and that the strict time limit was added for dramatic effect. Indeed, Farmer himself hints at a longer period when, in his introduction to the interview, he states: "The following article is part of my interview with 'Lord Greystoke.'"

Undoubtedly, this was a short meeting but it looks as if Farmer had a bit more information from LG to work with than made it into the finished piece. If nothing else it seems very likely that Farmer edited the interview and may even have prepared some of the finished text in anticipation of the meeting.

We know that Farmer eventually admitted that he had misled us as to the location of the interview (at Lord Greystoke's behest) and it is conceivable that, likewise, the fifteen minute rule was not as strictly enforced as portrayed in the published article.

What follows is slightly over two thousand words, expanding on an answer from the interview as recorded in *Esquire*. It is interesting to note that Farmer experimented, as evidenced in this extract, with a different format for the interview, choosing to portray it more as a conversation than in a traditional interview format.

It is followed by some unedited standalone paragraphs.

"Opar actually existed then?" I said.

"Not on as grand a scale as Burroughs said. But why should Opar be unbelievable? You have Zimbabwe and the other impressive stone cities in Rhodesia."

"What about the genetically impossible discrepancy between the Oparian male and female?"

"Is it impossible? Yerks[15] criticized Burroughs' great apes as impossible because they ate meat. And along comes Miss Goodall and her meat-eating, tool-using chimpanzees. My lion, Jad-bal-ja, was derided and along comes Elsa the lioness. Remember how people

---

[15] **Robert Mearns Yerks** (26 May 1876–3 February 1956), American psychologist and pioneer in the study both of human and primate intelligence and of the social behavior of gorillas and chimpanzees.

scoffed at stories of the gorilla before its existence was verified, or at the Okapi, which was found as late as 1900. Moreover, G. H. Bourne, the primatologist, has said there's no physiological reason why apes and humans couldn't have hybrids. Perhaps the Oparians had hybridized with the mangani, as they claimed.

[handwritten text—unreadable]

Africa is no longer the dark continent, why hasn't Opar been found?"

"It was found a number of times, but I managed to keep word of it coming out," he said. "After World War II, I dismantled it, with the help of my Waziri, and I diverted a river over it. There is still much gold in the hills around it. In the jungle, money has value only as toilet paper, and who needs toilet paper in the jungle? But I live in the jungle only now and then. So I need money. Jane can't stand the jungle very long, you know. That tree house they show in the movies with Jane doing light housework in it is absolutely ridiculous. And so, by the way, is that swinging on the vines. That's a movie invention, just as Cheetah the chimp is a movie invention."

My time was running out. I said, "There's one big point I have [to] clear up. That's the immortality pills you got from the Kavurus in *Tarzan's Quest*. And the other immortality treatment you said you got from a witch doctor whose life you saved. You told that story in *Tarzan and the Foreign Legion*."

"I haven't read that book," he said.

"It's about your experiences when you were an R.A.F. group captain attached to the U.S.A.A.F. in the Far Eastern theater. You were in an American B-24 which was shot down over Sumatra. You were supposed to have told the American fliers about the witch doctor."

"I told Burroughs about it, but no-one else," he said. "That's more of Burroughs' romanticization. ~~I'll have to read that book some time. But I never let on to those fliers, or to anybody that I was Tarzan, regardless of what Burroughs said. Nor would I let anyone know of my having such a treatment. I'd have too many people after me or after my family.~~[16]

"I did find an isolated group in Abyssinia who had a chemical preparation that slowed down the rate of aging. I had the preparation

---

[17] This redaction was made by Farmer.

analysed and synthesized, so I have a supply on hand. As for the witch doctor, yes, he did give me a complicated treatment lasting a month. And it apparently worked. But I think he and the Kavuru used the same basic ingredients, though in a different manner. The stuff isn't any 'immortality' elixir, by the way. It delays aging but not nearly as effectively as Burroughs said."

"I wouldn't believe it if I didn't have the evidence right before me," I said. You're a very lucky man indeed. You evidently had a unique inheritance, given your physical structure and seeming immunity to disease. You had a unique upbringing; at least, you're the only intelligent feral man I ever heard of. You . . ."

"I'm not feral, not raised by beasts," he said. "The Folk were near-humans. No beasts have a genuine language."

"All right," I said. "And now you have discovered, not one, but two, means for prolonging youth. And you have become, literally, and pardon the cliché, a living legend."

"You're angry, aren't you?" he said. "One of the first things I learned in civilization was not to pay much attention to *what* a man said. It's *how* he says it that's important. I watch not his mouth but his eyes and hands, especially the hands."

"It's only natural that I should be angry," I said. "Why can't I, why can't the world, be given this elixir?"

"Yes, it's only natural. But why should I give it to you, for instance? How do I know you deserve it?"

"Do you?" I said.

"Perhaps not," he said, his big gray eyes steady on me. "But I'm selfish. I want my family and my pets to survive. But a means for prolonging the majority of men's lives would be the worst thing possible. Man has progressed only because the old die and make way for the young. Medical science has allowed great numbers of people to live to a ripe old age. As a result, men, generally speaking, can't adapt fast enough to the ever-accelerating rate of change brought by his science.

"You probably are adjustable and flexible enough in your thinking but I can't start making exceptions. And I won't be living forever. The law of averages says that every day I live the odds of my having an accident or being slain get bigger. But I live each day for itself. I have an almost animal-like sense of time. Time for me is two-dimensional. To me, each thing that I see has not always been there, waiting for me to come across it. It seems to be created just before I encounter it. Do you understand? I didn't think so. You would have to have been raised as I was to grasp it. My attitude isn't quite human, or not fully human, anyway. My way of life influenced me very much, of course, but the mangani language was the biggest factor. It's a language even more weird than Shawnee or Navaho. If you've read Benjamin Lee Whorf, you know how alien, how Martian almost, those speeches are."

He paused and then said, "You have exactly two minutes left."

There were no chronometers in the room. He must have had a biological clock ticking away in his mind. Perhaps he had glanced at a watch several days ago and still knew exactly what time it was.

"How much of *Tarzan and the Lion Man* is true?" I said.

"Just about everything in it is fiction. But, I did visit Hollywood [unreadable handwritten text]."

"Did you actually try out for the role of Tarzan in a movie. And were you rejected because the producer said you weren't the type?"

He smiled and said, "No, though I wouldn't be surprised if such a thing did happen. I went there too late to try out for the Weissmuller movie, *Tarzan the Ape Man*, and too early for the Buster Crabbe movie, *Tarzan the Fearless*."

"How did you like Mr. Burroughs?"

"We met secretly and talked for an hour. I like him very much, one of the few men I thoroughly liked. Of course, I'd been secretly corresponding with him off and on for some time."

"As you know," I said, "one of the things that started me on your trail was my suspicion that Burroughs, Doyle, and Shaw had all told stories about your family. Each, however, used different names for them. Burroughs and Doyle had made up code names which, if followed in the right places, such as *Burke's Peerage*, would lead to you. In Burroughs' original draft of *Tarzan of the Apes*, he gave your family the title of Bloomstoke. Then he changed it to Greystoke, probably for esthetic reasons. But the *Bloom-* was one of the multidirectional codewords he used. I traced it through the *Peerage* and other works. I found, curiously enough, that this clue led to Leopold Bloom, the hero, or antihero, of James Joyce's *Ulysses*. Rather, to the person who was the living model for the fictional character of Bloom. Tarzan was second cousin once removed of Leopold Bloom. The wandering jewgreek of Dublin was a relative of the wandering ape-man of the rather large [unreadable] Africa. [unreadable text in the margin] I don't have time to explain how I arrived at this now, but you can read all about it in my addendum to *Tarzan Alive*. I also give evidence that you're closely related to the men who were the living prototypes of the fictional characters of Doc Savage, Nero Wolfe, Raffles, Sherlock Holmes, Professor Challenger, Lord Peter Wimsey, Bulldog Drummond, and Richard Wentworth who was the basis for G-8, the Spider, and the Shadow. And all of you are descended from the man who was the model for the Scarlet Pimpernel."

"I know about that," he said. "But what was this you mentioned over the phone about my being descended from Woden and being the last hero of ancient myth?"

"Like the Queen of England, and many others, including Burroughs himself, you're descended from Egbert, King of Wessex," I said. "Egbert had a traditional genealogy that went clear back to second century Denmark. He claimed to be the descendant of Woden, the ancient Germanic chief god, and a mortal woman.

"Like Romulus and Remus of ancient Rome, and the infant Zeus, you were raised by beasts. You were an unpromising child, like so many heroes of myth; the mangani thought you ugly and retarded. You were given three gifts which saved your life, like the children in many fairy tales throughout the world. These were your father's knife, the books, and the cartridges which Teeka exploded accidentally and saved your life. That's in the *Jungle Tales of Tarzan*. You had your animal helpers, various monkeys, various great apes, Tantor the elephant, Jad-bal-ja and other lions. You killed the wicked stepparent, though in your case it was your stepfather not your stepmother, who was wicked. You were the lost or abandoned heir to the throne or ducal title who regained his birth rights and got the beautiful maiden and the great treasure. You resisted attempts at seduction by various temptresses. You were the living embodiment of the cruel and bloody trickster of so many primitive legends when you were young. You fought wicked magicians, in your case, Mbonga's witch doctors.

[unreadable writing at foot of page]

"I could go on, but I do cover these aspects of you in detail in my book. The psychologist, Carl Jung, maintained that mankind had a collective unconscious. Similar archetypes, dream figures, exist in every man's mind, and these are what give rise to similar myths among peoples of all the world. Now, I'm somewhat of a mystic, and I believe that Nature, or the Creator, made one last hero. He was born in the late 19th century, and he emulated the lives of the Heroes of ancient myth and legend from the beginning. He did not do so consciously, of course.

"Then a writer of romances heard about him and fashioned a cycle of partly feral [unreadable handwritten text] epics about him. These were partly true. The writer was Burroughs, and the Hero was you. Burroughs has all the faults of Homer but enough of the virtues to become very popular. His Tarzan is, with Sherlock Holmes, the greatest popular character of the 20th century. Indeed Robert Ruark thought he was the greatest fictional achievement of our time. He is the Noble Savage and also the last of the Heroes. He strums good vibrations in the hearts of millions of people; he is generally scorned by literary critics in England and America but his true nature seems to be better understood by European critics.

"You, as depicted by Burroughs, are the flesh and blood incarnation of man's basic dreams of freedom, strength, cyclic adventure, and eventual victory. According to McLuhan, myth is the sudden vision of a complex process which usually extends over a long time. It's an implosion of any process. And you are the living implosion of dreams."

[unintelligible handwritten notes in the margin]

"You could have asked some questions instead of making a speech," he said. He rose and held out his hand. "I won't be seeing you again."

"May I ask where you're going?"

"To arrange a seemingly fatal accident. There are too many people wondering why I look so young. [Unintelligible handwriting] Then I'll be living incognito with Jane in various cities under various names. Occasionally, I'll return to the jungle. There are still vast tracts in the rainforests of Gabon and the Ituri where the only men are the pygmies. [Unintelligible handwriting at foot of page] The rainforests may disappear someday. But I think that the worldwide pollution is going to result in a collapse of civilization and the disappearance of the majority of humanity. Perhaps the forests will be spared, and many of the species threatened with extinction will come back. In any event, I intend to survive."

T's sexuality?—masturbated because that was expected of the mangani children, male and female: no value put on virginity, but fidelity expected in the tribe and, unfortunately, male has dominance, tho female has certain rights which can't be denied without intervention of tribe; in small preliterate tribes, the greatest force is social approval or condemnation and the worst punishment, exile from the tribe.

Tarzan's answers re his early sexuality: moral code of the mangani just as complicated and irrational as any human tribe in the amazon or new guinea, which is very complicated indeed, or among so-called civilised people. There is shame and guilt but not very much and mainly about different things than those which people get shamed about in human world.

Discrepancy of male and females in Opar much exaggerated for romantic purposes. Actually, Tarzan suspects that there was a strain of old Boskopoid[17] blood in the Oparians—what about coincidence of Opar and Ophir? asks int. Opar was derived from Ophir, since real name too unpronounceable—the Oparians didn't use mangani language, that's one of ERB's romantic fables, their own language was polysyllabic and as weird from Indo-European viewpoint as Shawnee or Navaho. Opar was name picked for convenience and association with gold and jewels, etc.

---

[18] Boskop Man was a modern human fossil of the Middle Stone Age (Late Pleistocene) discovered in 1913 in South Africa.

A Retrospective View

From ERB to PJF:
How Burroughs Inspired Farmer

Speech by Win Scott Eckert at the 2018 Dum-Dum
Morgan City, Louisiana, August 3, 2018

A fitting coda to this book is a speech Win Scott Eckert gave at the most hallowed of Burroughs gatherings, the annual Dum-Dum.

The journey Eckert takes us on is a personal one that gives us a very intimate, but also a very shared, experience of Burroughs and Farmer fandom and the areas where they not only intersect but complement each other. The love and respect he has for both of these authors are palpable in this heartfelt presentation. Along the way, Eckert gives us a thoughtful insight into many of Farmer's most iconic Tarzan-related writings, a good number of which are included in this book.

Although we have not included the images used in this presentation they can all be found (alongside many other images) at pjarmer.com and philipjosefarmer.com

Eckert mentions in his speech that Farmer never completed the fourth novel in the Secrets of the Nine series. Using a previously published extract, further unpublished prose from Farmer, and copious notes left by the Grand Master, Eckert has now completed that eagerly anticipated book. This fourth instalment is titled *The Monster on Hold*; published by Meteor House in 2021.

My name is Win Eckert. I want to thank everybody here for having me as a guest speaker. I'm very honored to speak with all of you today. For those of you who don't know me, my path

into participating in Burroughs fandom has been a very long one. I attended my first in-person event just last summer at the ECOF in Dallas. This is my second in-person event, and I'm having a great time.

I got into Burroughs at a very young age. I read my first Burroughs book when I was eight years old when the movie tie-in version of *At the Earth's Core* came out. This was the Ace edition. I then immediately devoured the rest of the Pellucidar books. And, of course, just like everybody else who probably have very similar stories, I graduated onto the Martian series and the Tarzan books, and so on.

By the time I was hitting early adolescence, and after college in the 1980s, I really wasn't looking for any kind of in-person fandom. In the '90s I was doing other things, post college. So, my path to in-person fandom with Burroughs came through Philip José Farmer. I'd discovered Farmer's writings at much the same time as I'd discovered Burroughs, so I was reading them in parallel.

In the late '90s, I started a fan website for Farmer's Wold Newton Family, and from there graduated to in-person visits to Farmer's house in the mid-2000s. This led to putting on annual FarmerCons with several other fans, initially at Phil's house while he was still alive. They would have taken place between 2005 and 2009. In 2010, we held a FarmerCon in Seattle in conjunction with the Locus Awards, and we subsequently hooked up with PulpFest, which is an annual convention focusing on all things pulp era related, and we've been riding their coattails ever since.

So that's my path. And that's why I'm here with you all today.

The premise of what I wanted to talk about is something I've seen a lot of in Farmer discussion groups in pulp fandom. Many times these discussions have overemphasized the "controversies." These also occur in the Burroughs and Doc Savage fandoms. I'd like to bring another perspective because I think Phil was a great, great fan, not just a professional writer who got Hugo awards and the Grand Master Award, but who was also truly interested in, and engaged in, the fandom aspect. Certainly, I want to discuss some of his professional works that were inspired by Burroughs, but I think he was always thinking about this throughout his whole career, and so I'd like to give an overview of how Phil was a fan, and that this is much more important than the so-called controversies.

Here is a quote from a little piece Phil did as an introduction in a fanzine: "I fell under E. R. Burroughs' spell at the age of nine . . ." ("A Fimbulwinter Introduction"). This was about the same age that I got into Burroughs, and probably very close to the age many, many of us here did.

Most of you are probably already aware of this but Philip José Farmer received several prestigious awards over his professional career:

- 1953 Hugo Award for the Most Promising New Talent, primarily for "The Lovers"
- 1968 Hugo Award for the novella "Riders of the Purple Wage"
- 1972 Hugo Award for the Riverworld novel *To Your Scattered Bodies Go*, the first in what is probably his best-known series of books
- Damon Knight Memorial Grand Master Award (awarded by the Science Fiction Writers of America), 2001

He is also well known for the World of Tiers series, which we'll talk about a little bit more, and the Wold Newton Family biographies.

But he never gave up being a fan. So, we have his piece "The Golden Age and the Brass" (*Burroughs Bulletin*, #12, 1956), in which Farmer discusses his early reading and his mythological heroes who were all left in the dust when he discovered Edgar Rice Burroughs. This was Phil's Golden Age. He discusses discovering Burroughs, his love of Burroughs, and also laments that his son, also named Philip, was much more interested in comic books than in reading Burroughs. So, it's interesting that even moving on from 1956 to 2018, we're still having that same conversation, right? How do we get the next generation involved? Phil was actually quite disappointed, he wanted his son to read the Burroughs books and not just the four-color funnies.

Phil Farmer the Fan was also Phil Farmer the Satirist. "The Jungle Rot Kid on the Nod" has a really interesting backstory. The premise is, what if William Burroughs had written the Tarzan novels instead of Edgar Rice Burroughs? Phil is having a lot of fun here. It first appeared in a small publication called *Broadside*, Vol. 4. No. 2, 1968, and we've just recently reprinted it in Meteor House's *The*

Philip José Farmer Centennial Collection. It's been reprinted in some other publications as well, and obviously, it's not really a straight-forward read, but he does capture that late '60s William S. Burroughs style very well.

So, again, Farmer the Fan. He was awarded the Golden Lion by the Burroughs Bibliophiles at the 1970 Dum-Dum in Detroit. In the same year, he mentioned, and then put out the next year, '71, his essay "The Arms of Tarzan." This is the Greystoke coat of arms that he constructed in painstaking detail. Every element was deeply thought out. Phil did the outline design, and Bjo Trimble—who many of you, if you're a *Star Trek* fan, will have probably heard of as the author of the original *Star Trek Concordance* that was self-published in 1969 and then updated in 1976 from Ballantine Books—did the actual artwork.

Interestingly, in this article Farmer also does a little bit of his speculative stuff; he proposes that the Outlaw of Torn was actually the same person as John Carter and that he was also Tarzan's ancestor from several hundred years back. This first appeared in *Burroughs Bulletin* #22, 1971.

The 1970s were prolific for Phil in terms of a lot of these types of fan articles.

"A Reply to 'The Red Herring.'" In this one, Farmer is going back and forth with other experts about the great controversy concerning Tarzan's true birth date, and what Korak's age is, and all of the theories to try to explain some of those discontinuities in the original Burroughs books. Phil also refers to his biography of Tarzan which, then, was coming out in April, referring to it by his original title of *The Private Life of Tarzan*. (*Erbania* #28, December 1971.)

"The Lord Mountford Mystery." Phil wrote a speculative article, just a very short piece. But again, very interestingly connecting the two Lord Mountfords, one who appeared in H. Rider Haggard's 1917 Allan Quatermain novel *Finished,* and the other one who appeared in *Tarzan the Magnificent.* Farmer speculates that the parents of ERB's Lord Mountford appear in *Finished.* (*ERB-dom* #65, December 1972.)

And then of course we have "Tarzan Lives," maybe better known by now as "An Exclusive Interview with Lord Greystoke," appearing in

Esquire magazine in 1972. This is where Farmer actually interviewed John Clayton. The interview allegedly took place in Gabon, but as he revealed in 1989 when he gave his "I Still Live" speech, the interview really took place in Chicago. (The speech was Farmer's 1989 keynote address at the dinner commemorating the 75th anniversary of the publication of *Tarzan of the Apes*; the dinner was put on by the Normal Beans Chapter of the Burroughs Bibliophiles and was held at the Adventurers Club in Chicago on October 21, 1989.) This also appeared in *The Book of Philip José Farmer*, 1973.

Then we have another article, "The Great Korak-Time Discrepancy," which has more theories around how to reconcile the dates and the information given in the books regarding Korak's age. (*ERB-dom* #57, April 1972.)

Many of these appeared in my first published book, *Myths for the Modern Age: Philip José Farmer's Wold Newton Universe*, which came out in 2005.

"From ERB to Ygg." Farmer traces Edgar Rice Burroughs' genealogy all the way back to the Norse god Ygg. That was interesting to try to reproduce in my book because it's a very long, vertical family tree. (*Erbivore*, August 1973.)

"Extracts from the Memoirs of 'Lord Greystoke.'" After Farmer interviewed Lord Greystoke, Greystoke sent him selections from his memoirs for publication. (*Mother Was a Lovely Beast*, 1974.)

"The Feral Human in Mythology and Fiction." Phil explored the possibility of human babies being raised by animals and the probable outcome of such unusual parentage. (*Mother Was a Lovely Beast*, 1974.) Phil was interested in how Tarzan could be real. How could this have really happened? He did a lot of work around Tarzan's development of language. Phil was an anthropologist and he was a linguist, and so he took this stuff seriously. He was really into proving that this could all happen. There were all the naysayers out there, saying, "Well, it's a wonderful fantasy story for film . . ." No, absolutely not, this was real, very real, to him.

"A Language for Opar." Phil, the scholar and linguist, played with his favorite material, Tarzan. (*ERB-dom* #75, 1974.)

Jump to the '80s. Phil was asked to write an overview of Burroughs' early career. This resulted in "Edgar Rice Burroughs," a short essay discussing ERB and his most important character, Tarzan. (*20th Century Fiction*, 1985.)

Next, here's a piece that was printed for the first time in *Pearls from Peoria*, which came out in 2006. It came from Phil's personal files, so *Pearls* did have some previously unpublished material. This piece is called "The Purple Distance." It was originally slated as a foreword to a Fokker D-LXIX edition of *The Love Song of Hiawatha*; Phil found many things about Longfellow's poem that are of interest to Edgar Rice Burroughs fans.

In "Hayy ibn Yaqzan by Abu ibn Tufayl: An Arabic Mowgli," (which I'm sure I haven't pronounced correctly), Phil again talked about one of his favorite topics: humans raised by animals. This first appeared in *Journal of the Fantastic in the Arts*, Vol. 3, No. 3, 1994; and was also reprinted in Meteor House's *The Best of Farmerphile*.

I already mentioned the 1989 "I Still Live" speech, so the next item is a documentary film called *Moi, Tarzan*. This was a 1996 French documentary, in which Farmer was filmed at his home, speaking of how he met the real Tarzan. A French documentary filmmaker made it and interviewed George McWhorter in addition to Phil. If you haven't seen this you can do an internet search for the title "Moi, Tarzan" and it will take you to a French website where you can pay to watch the documentary online for a three-day window. Phil discusses how Tarzan is real and he is very deadpan and serious about it. He gets asked over and over, "You really believe it?" And Phil responds, "Well, yeah, of course, of course I believe it. How could I not believe it? I met Tarzan." And he just plays it so straight, it's amazing. It's not very expensive, so I highly recommend checking that out.

Again, I want to bring forth aspects of Phil that don't necessarily get discussed a lot, Phil the Fan.

I wish I'd been at his 80th birthday party in 1998 when a man dressed as an ape showed up and rang the doorbell.

Next, let's discuss a brief overview of Phil's works that were either clearly related or clearly inspired by Burroughs, or maybe not so clearly. So, going in chronological order, *Cache from Outer Space*. When I read it, I certainly thought it was an unofficial, secret sequel to *The Red Hawk*, taking place hundreds of years further on.

But, to be fair, I had not read Burroughs' Moon trilogy immediately before I read *Cache*, so there could have been contradictions.

My friend Chris Carey said he just reread it and while it's certainly an homage in that it takes place in the same type of post-apocalyptic world that *The Red Hawk* would be in, there are some differences, so it's maybe not literally a sequel. But, certainly, we could say, it was inspired by Burroughs' third Moon book. Phil did some of the same things that Burroughs did in terms of names in *The Red Hawk*, particularly how names and language changed over hundreds of years, and how Phil's main character from Phoenix has an adventure going from Arizona to the east coast—again in the far distant future.

The World of Tiers is, in my opinion, Farmer's best series. By the time we get to the third book, *A Private Cosmos*, he reintroduces a lesser character from the first book that he sticks with for the rest of the series: Kickaha, or Paul Janus Finnegan. And Kickaha is very much that same type of Burroughsian hero who gets taken from Earth and dumped in this other world and has all of these amazing adventures. It also follows the Burroughs romance pattern, but over the course of several books, rather than resolving the situation in one book. Kickaha actually has a relationship with one of the gods, one of the Lords who created these artificial worlds, and at first she's very hostile toward him because he's a puny human. That's an interesting storyline to follow and clearly inspired by the types and patterns of stories that Burroughs told.

I will say one other thing: Phil was notorious for not finishing his series or for leaving things undone with a lot of loose ends. This series is one that he finished, so it's got a nice capstone and a wrap-up—although, in true Farmerian fashion, he did so with a twist.

All right, the controversial stuff.

A Feast Unknown, Lord of the Trees, and *The Mad Goblin.* In particular *A Feast Unknown.* It's probably no secret to anybody here that this was very controversial when it came out in 1969. But I think something that's missed is that Phil was a joker and a provocateur, and he meant to provoke that reaction. He intended to elicit that reaction and he succeeded.

Lord Grandrith and Doc Caliban are clear analogs for Lord Greystoke and Doc Savage, and when he was writing these books, the late 1960s, it's probable that his approach was that these characters actually were *the* Tarzan and *the* Doc Savage. There are a lot of characteristics making the inspiration clear. But by the fourth, unpublished, book, *The Monster on Hold*, of which there exist several chapters introduced by Phil at the 1983 World Fantasy Convention, it seems that Phil was saying that Doc Savage and Doc Caliban were alternate universe versions of each other, with Caliban's adventures taking place in a parallel world. And I know that there continue to be different viewpoints about that among Farmerian fan scholars, which is great. I'm just pointing out that I believe this was Phil's direction by 1983, the time of the as-yet unpublished fourth book in the series.

In any event, to me, and maybe it's magnified by being online, it's unfortunate that it sometimes feels as if *A Feast Unknown* is the only thing being discussed in terms of Phil's Burroughs fandom and his Burroughsian inspirations. And again, that could just be the negative magnification of social media, but he has done so much more for fandom and as a fan. Some people call it porn. Some people don't. But in any event, it was controversial, provocative, and I think it distracts from all of the other aspects we're discussing today, it reduces the discussion of Phil and Burroughs to just that one book.

Lord of the Trees and *The Mad Goblin* were sequels. These were not controversial in that Phil just wrote them straight without a lot of the aspects that upset people in the first novel. They are inter-twining novels in that they take place at the same time and they tell the continuing story of Lord Grandrith's and Doc Caliban's battle against the Nine, who are the secret rulers of the world.

Lord Tyger is an excellent novel. If you want one standalone novel, if you haven't read Farmer, this is a very well written book. It's about an experiment that a multimillionaire conducts to create a real Tarzan. So, an orphan is dumped in the jungle and the millionaire basically plays God to try to figure out how to create a real-life Tarzan. Joe Lansdale did an introduction for the most recent edition from Titan Books.

Now we come to *Tarzan Alive*. I think what's interesting about Phil is that he didn't get stuck in one interpretation. He loved to play games, he loved to undertake mental exercises, to say, "Well, I approached it from this alternate universe Lord Grandrith, but now I want to play a different game. I want to play the game that Tarzan was a real person and I'm going to write his biography." And he wrote it based on a template created by another writer, named William S. Baring-Gould, who had written *Sherlock Holmes of Baker Street* and then *Nero Wolfe of West 35th Street*.

So, Phil was following in a tradition of writing biographies of these characters, written straight as if they were real people, as if they really lived. He went back and reviewed Tarzan's life, filled in holes that were not covered by Burroughs, and wrote it from a real-world perspective. This was a game to him, and yet it was also not *just* a game to him. It's a real-world perspective and therefore real-world physics apply. And so, *Tarzan and the Ant Men*, maybe part of that was fictionalized. *Tarzan at the Earth's Core*, well, we in the real world know that there's not a hollow Earth, so that was probably made up.

But then he gave himself an out.

And he said, "But if it did happen [*Tarzan at the Earth's Core*], then here in Tarzan's chronology is *when* it happened."

He could never really let go of it.

So, when people read these books, and they say, "Well, I don't like it because he said *Tarzan at the Earth's Core* was fictional," they're missing the point of who Phil was and what he was doing. He was just playing the game with himself and with everybody. And like I said, he would change the rules of the game from book to book because that's what he enjoyed. He was challenging himself, constantly.

The latest edition of *Tarzan Alive* came out from Bison Books in 2006, and it's still in print. This also has Phil's favorite cover for the book. This is the cover that he had always wanted to have. The image accompanied the 1972 *Esquire* interview "Tarzan Lives," otherwise known as "An Exclusive Interview with Lord Greystoke." I mentioned that one earlier.

This is a very, very different take on a Tarzan cover. But this would be Tarzan as he appeared when Phil interviewed him. The cover painting is by a gentleman named Jean-Paul Goude. And the story goes that the model for the cover was the janitor at the *Esquire* offices.

All right, as many of you may know, *Tarzan Alive* also spawned this other mythology called the Wold Newton Family, where Tarzan and many other fictional characters in this vast genealogy are tied together by a celestial event, which is the falling of the Wold Newton meteorite in Yorkshire, on December 13, 1795.

I won't spend any more time on it right now, we can talk about it later if you want, because that's my thing and I could go on forever, and it's how I got deeply into the fandom. You can tell how dedicated I am because in 2009 a group of us went to the spot where the meteorite fell. There's a monument there that was erected four years after it fell. It was put up in 1799. It's out in the middle of a field. That was an amazing trip. Just like Burroughs fandom, where Burroughs fans go to different spots and locations, we're doing that with Farmer as well. Obviously, if we're going to be in the UK, we couldn't help but go up to visit Greystoke in Cumbria.

Also in the Wold Newton cycle of books, Phil wrote *The Adventure of the Peerless Peer*, featuring Lord Greystoke and Sherlock Holmes. This was a 1974 limited hardcover, and, subsequently, it came out in paperback in 1976. And then, admittedly, Phil began to have maybe an up-and-down relationship with the Edgar Rice Burroughs folks. We're really happy that it's so good now, but it's been decades and there have been some ups and downs. This book was not very happily received, and it was withdrawn. Phil rewrote it as a Mowgli crossover, writing out Lord Greystoke, and then in 2008, he received permission to bring it back into print as the original version.

While this was not a licensed, work-for-hire Tarzan book, he did get approval to bring it back out; it came out from Subterranean Press, in a collection called *Venus on the Half-Shell and Others*. Titan Books reprinted it three years later as a standalone as part of their Further Adventures of Sherlock Holmes series.

Next, we have the Khokarsa series, otherwise known as the Ancient Opar series: *Hadon of Ancient Opar*, *Flight to Opar*, and *The Song of Kwasin* (written with Christopher Paul Carey). The latter book came out in 2012, in an omnibus edition of all three novels, from Subterranean Press, and so finally finished the trilogy that we'd been waiting so long for.

But what's a little bit unknown, perhaps, is that the series really started with the science fiction novel *Time's Last Gift*, where this mysterious immortal from our future, I think 2070, goes on a time travel expedition 14,000 years into the past. When it's time for the expedition members to leave and to go back to their time, this man, who, again, is an immortal, decides to stay. He's much happier in the past with native peoples and jungle creatures. He lives forward through the centuries because he's immortal. It's probably also not well known that *Allan and the Ice Gods* by H. Rider Haggard is also an inspiration for this series. So, the series was in fact inspired by both Burroughs' and Haggard's works.

I love time travel stories, so that was the reason that, when I was a kid, I picked up *Time's Last Gift*. Of course, it was by Farmer, and at that time I knew of Farmer only through his Doc Savage biography. I didn't figure out for years who the main character was supposed to be. So, he pulled one over on me for a long time. The main character is a jungle lord under an assumed name. To be fair, I was only ten years old. Later on, I mean with several more years of reading under my belt, I read it again and figured it out.

Still on the Ancient Opar series, the second book, *Flight to Opar*: the latest edition was put out by Meteor House. We found additional text that had been edited out of the original publication. Chris Carey is a name well known to a lot of you here. He has continued the Ancient Opar series with Meteor House, again with the kind permission of Edgar Rice Burroughs, Inc. And so, with *Flight to Opar*, Chris Carey took on the Herculean task of smoothly editing in the text; we call this a "restored edition." And then we put out our own standalone edition of the third book, *The Song of Kwasin*.

Chris, while he was working on the manuscript for the third book, had access to a lot of notes about Phil's intended storyline, and he had many conversations with Phil himself. There were also a lot of notes about the proper pronunciations of the Khokarsan language.

I think Phil originally thought this was going to be a ten or twelve book series, but by the time he was working on the third one, that idea fell through. There may have been some thought that it could be wrapped up in the third book. But he also left notes behind on where he would have taken the series after wrapping up the first cycle. So, if you think of this as the first cycle, the first three books, then books number four and five by Chris are definitely based on notes and thoughts from Farmer. They're just not made up out of whole cloth. These are titled *Hadon, King of Opar*, and *Blood of Ancient Opar*. Chris also wrote a prequel called *Exiles of Kho*.

All right, in 1999, Phil realized his lifelong dream. You know, he was born in 1918. This was quite a journey for him in his life, to realize his lifelong ambition to finally write an authorized Tarzan novel. It originally came out as *The Dark Heart of Time*, as a mass-market paperback from Del Rey. I'm not sure anybody was that happy with the positioning or the marketing of the book. If you look at the cover, the name Tarzan is not very prominent, it doesn't jump out at you. And while it's great that Phil's name is prominent, I think we all thought it was a lost opportunity to sell it to both Farmer and Tarzan fans.

So, working with the Burroughs folks over the past year, we—Meteor House—have been able to bring out a new edition, for the first time in hardcover. And I think it really did deserve a hardcover treatment. We've retitled it *Tarzan and the Dark Heart of Time*, which was honestly Phil's preferred title. That's the title he wanted. The manuscript was originally titled *Tarzan's Greatest Secret*, and then it was *The Dark Heart of Time*. And Phil had said, "I wanted to call it *Tarzan and the Dark Heart of Time*," but the response was no, just *The Dark Heart of Time*.

I feel like we've been able to go back, and even though Phil is no longer with us, we've been able to do it the way he would have wanted. We've been working very hard over the past couple of months and put a lot of energy into it. And I just want to really thank the Burroughs folks because they let us do everything that we wanted to do, from the dagger logo to the scroll logo, they even let us put the ERB doodad symbol on the spine, and so I think, I hope, Phil would be very proud.

It's my hope that my discussion here today will help a few Burroughs fans who may have had misconceptions about Phil, who may have prejudged him, to recognize my main point—the point being, Phil *loved* Tarzan, *loved* Burroughs. He was their greatest fan.

Thank you.

ABOUT THE AUTHORS

Philip José Farmer was born on January 26, 1918 in North Terre Haute, Indiana. He grew up in Peoria, Illinois where he spent much of his childhood reading everything from the Bible and books on mythology to the classics by Baum, Carroll, Cervantes, Defoe, Dickens, Homer, London, Swift, and Twain to popular works by Burroughs, Doyle, Haggard, Verne, and Wells.

He sold his first story, a mainstream tale titled "O'Brien and Obrenov," to *Adventure* in 1946 before he decided to try his hand at science fiction. His next published story, "The Lovers," appeared in the August 1952 issue of *Startling Stories*, and is noted for breaking the taboo on sex in science fiction, as well as for earning Farmer a Hugo Award for "Most Promising New Talent."

Married and with two children, he soon quit his job to become a full-time writer, but after selling several more stories to the science fiction pulps, his career hit a stumbling block when he "won" the Shasta Prize Novel Contest. The grand prize was four thousand dollars (a lot of money in 1953), but he never received his winnings. Instead, the publisher asked Farmer for rewrites while the prize money was invested in another book, which bombed. By the time the truth came out, Farmer had lost his house and was forced to take up full time employment.

Farmer left Peoria with his family in 1956 and moved around the country working as a technical writer for the space-defense industry, eventually ending up in Beverly Hills, California in 1965. All the while he continued to write and sell science fiction short stories and novels, launching his popular World of Tiers series and even winning a second Hugo Award for the novella "Riders of the Purple Wage." Then, just before the moon landing in 1969, he was laid off from his technical writing job, so he decided to write fiction full time once again. This time it stuck.

In 1970, Farmer moved back to Peoria with his family and again his career began to take off, this time with a third Hugo Award win, for *To Your Scattered Bodies Go*, the opening novel in his bestselling Riverworld series. For the next few years Farmer sought inspiration from the popular literature he so loved, writing novels such as *The Mad Goblin* (a Doc Savage pastiche), *Lord of the Trees* and *Lord Tyger* (both Tarzan pastiches), *The Wind Whales of Ishmael* (a science fiction sequel to *Moby Dick*), *The Other Log of Phileas Fogg* (the "true" story behind Jules Verne's *Around the World in Eighty Days*), and *Venus on the Half-Shell* (written as if by Kilgore Trout, a character from the works of Kurt Vonnegut). He also wrote two "biographies" during this period: *Tarzan Alive: A Definitive Biography of Lord Greystoke* and *Doc Savage: His Apocalyptic Life*.

The next two decades saw the publication of the Dayworld trilogy, as well as further installments in the Riverworld and World of Tiers series. Farmer also fulfilled his lifelong ambition to write an Oz novel, and authorized Doc Savage and Tarzan novels, with the publication of *A Barnstormer in Oz, Escape from Loki*, and *Tarzan and the Dark Heart of Time*. Late in his career, Farmer tried his hand at a different genre with *Nothing Burns in Hell*, a detective novel set in his hometown of Peoria.

After Farmer retired from writing in 1999, new collections such as *Pearls from Peoria* and *Venus on the Half-Shell and Others* continued to appear, as did new collaborative works such as *The Evil in Pemberley House* (with Win Scott Eckert), *The Song of Kwasin* (with Christopher Paul Carey), and *Dayworld: A Hole in Wednesday* (with Danny Adams).

Farmer passed on February 25, 2009, but his fan base is as ardent as ever, still gathering at annual FarmerCons.

Henry G. Franke III is the editor of The Burroughs Bibliophiles, the nonprofit literary society dedicated to advancing the works and life of Edgar Rice Burroughs. The Bibliophiles has published the *Burroughs Bulletin* since 1947—the only fan organization and fanzine approved by Burroughs himself. Henry has been a past editor of the Edgar Rice Burroughs Amateur Press Association (ERBapa) and the North American Jules Verne Society (NAJVS). He was the contributing editor for and author of the Introductions to IDW's four-volume archive set reprinting Russ Manning's Tarzan newspaper comic strips, as well as other comic strip archive editions published by IDW and Titan Books.

Christopher Paul Carey is the coauthor with Philip José Farmer of *The Song of Kwasin*, and the author of *Exiles of Kho*; *Hadon, King of Opar*; and *Blood of Ancient Opar*, all works set in Farmer's Khokarsa series. He is the author of *Swords Against the Moon Men*, an authorized sequel to Edgar Rice Burroughs' classic science fantasy novel *The Moon Maid*, as well as the forthcoming ERB Universe novel *Victory Harben: The Fires of Halos*. He has scripted several comic books set in Burroughs' worlds, including *Carson of Venus: The Flames Beyond*, *Pellucidar: Across Savage Seas*, and *Pathfinder Worldscape: Dejah Thoris*. His short fiction may be found in various anthologies. He is Director of Publishing at Edgar Rice Burroughs, Inc., the corporation founded by Burroughs in 1923, and he has edited more than 60 novels, anthologies, and collections for a variety of publishers. He lives in Southern California.

Win Scott Eckert is a novelist, editor, essayist, and writer of short fiction. He is steeped in the works of famed science fiction writer Philip José Farmer, particularly Farmer's shared universe literary-crossover Wold Newton cycle and the Lord Grandrith/Doc Caliban series. He is also the authorized legacy author of Farmer's Patricia Wildman series (*The Evil in Pemberley House*, *The Scarlet Jaguar*). His latest releases are an authorized Avenger book from Moonstone Books, *Hunt the Avenger* (2019) about the 1940s pulp hero, and an authorized novel in the new Edgar Rice Burroughs Universe series, *Tarzan: Battle for Pellucidar* (2020). Find him online at www.winscotteckert.com and @woldnewton (Twitter).

METEOR HOUSE TITLES

THE WORLDS OF PHILIP JOSÉ FARMER
Anthology Series edited by Michael Croteau
Volume 1: Protean Dimensions
Volume 2: Of Dust and Soul
Volume 3: Portraits of a Trickster
Volume 4: Voyages to Strange Days

The Man Who Met Tarzan by Philip José Farmer
A Rough Knight for the Queen by Philip José Farmer
The Best of Farmerphile edited by Michael Croteau
The Philip José Farmer Centennial Collection edited by Michael Croteau
Greatheart Silver and Other Pulp Heroes by Philip José Farmer
Up from the Bottomless Pit by Philip José Farmer

SECRETS OF THE NINE SERIES
The Monster on Hold by Win Scott Eckert
It's Always Darkest by Frank Schildiner

WOLD NEWTON SERIES
Doc Savage: His Apocalyptic Life by Philip José Farmer
Tarzan and the Dark Heart of Time by Philip José Farmer

THE KHOKARSA SERIES
Exiles of Kho by Christopher Paul Carey
Flight to Opar (Restored Edition) by Philip José Farmer
The Song of Kwasin by Philip José Farmer and Christopher Paul Carey
Hadon, King of Opar by Christopher Paul Carey
Blood of Ancient Opar by Christopher Paul Carey

THE PAT WILDMAN SERIES
The Evil in Pemberley House by Philip José Farmer and Win Scott Eckert
The Scarlet Jaguar by Win Scott Eckert

THE PHILEAS FOGG SERIES
Phileas Fogg and the War of Shadows by Josh Reynolds
Phileas Fogg and the Heart of Osra by Josh Reynolds

THE TWO HAWKS SERIES
Man of War by Heidi Ruby Miller

THE DAYWORLD SERIES
Dayworld: A Hole in Wednesday by Philip José Farmer and Danny Adams

SCIENCE FICTION ADVENTURE
The Abnormalities of Stringent Strange by Rhys Hughes
Airship Hunters by Jim Beard and Duane Spurlock

REFERENCE - CROSSOVERS
Crossovers Expanded, Volume 1 by Sean Lee Levin
Crossovers Expanded, Volume 2 by Sean Lee Levin

CHAPBOOKS
Being an Account of the Delay at Green River, Wyoming, of Phileas Fogg, World Traveler, or, The Masked Man Meets an English Gentleman
by Win Scott Eckert
The Adventure of the Fallen Stone: Being the First Part of the Account of The Dynamics of a Meteor by John H. Watson, M.D.
edited by Win Scott Eckert
Watch Your Back, Mr. Minamoto by Frank Schildiner